Destiny of Angels

Eric Myers

Destiny of Angels

This book is a work of fiction. Names, characters, places and incidents are products of the author's imagination and are not to be construed as real. Any resemblance to actual events, locales, organizations, or persons living or dead, is entirely coincidental.

COPYRIGHT

Destiny of Angels

Criminal copyright infringement, including infringement

without monetary gain, is investigated by the FBI and is

punishable by up to five years in federal prison and a fine of

$250,000.

Except for the original story material written by the author,

all songs, song titles, and lyrics mentioned in the novel Destiny of

Angels are the exclusive property of the respective artists,

songwriters, and copyright holders

Trient Press
3375 S Rainbow Blvd
#81710, SMB 13135
Las Vegas,NV 89180

Ordering Information:
Quantity sales. Special discounts are available on

quantity purchases by corporations, associations, and others.

For details, contact the publisher at the address above.

Orders by U.S. trade bookstores and wholesalers.

Please contact Trient Press: Tel: (775) 996-3844; or visit

www.trientpress.com.

Printed in the United States of America

Eric Myers

Publisher's Cataloging-in-

Publication data

Myers, Eric

A title of a book : Destiny of Angels
ISBN Hard Cover: 978-1-953975-65-2
Paperback: 978-1-953975-63-8
E-book: 978-1-953975-64-5

Dedication

It took a small army to create this work. To all of them: editors, graphic designers, publishers, collaborators, research librarians, motivators, and all those who offered honest feedback, I am profoundly grateful. This work contains a little bit of each of you. Its success is your success. Thank you. To each of you I owe a lot.

There is one person to whom I owe everything: My Dearest Daphne. Sweetheart, you gave my so much in little ways. The cup of coffee brought to me at 2am. The endless suggestions and ideas. The patience to go about life as I write, "just a few more pages." And your steadfast belief in me are all things I will forever be thank for.

I love you, Kitten. Thanks for being my wife.

PROLOGUE

On the second floor, above the clamor of palace staff bustling about the kitchen, were the barracks. There, off-duty guards often stayed up until sunrise and filled the night with inside jokes, friendly jibes, and stories of battles fought.

Here in this large room, lit only by a sliver of moonlight through a dusty window, one guard sat on his narrow bed and thought about his life. His loneliness intensified by what he knew the dawn would bring.

The palace guard felt a stupor creeping over him. The gnawing ache in his stomach had passed; his headache had faded. If he closed his eyes, memories of happier times kept him company. But he could not escape the stench. Smoke from the pyres, driven by a desert breeze, crept around corners of the palace, and lurked in the dark streets of Peyrvi. His body would be tossed on those pyres soon.

Death was a part of a guard's existence. All guards had, since the first day of training, accepted their lives were of little value. They belonged to Frederick, the Pontix of New Hope.

In the busy kitchen lies and truth about Frederick were exchanged like livestock by servants who had never seen his face and who would have fainted—justifiably so—at the thought of being summoned to Frederick's office.

Guards died. But it had been twelve years since the last foreign campaign, so guards no longer died in battle. Still, guards' lives were often cut short. With a flick of his hand or a nod of his head, Frederick would identify a guard—or an occasional citizen—who displeased him. There would be yet another body for the pyre. The "Sweeps" were kept busy burying the charred remains.

This guard's unpardonable action was not that he left his post to venture into a secured area. What would bring his death was that he saw something no one should ever see. Something that Pontix Frederick claimed had been destroyed.

This guard had seen the *One True Book*. He read about the angels.

It was not guilt that compelled him to confess his deed to a fellow guard. It was to see the expression his comrade had upon learning the *One True Book* had not been destroyed during one of their excursions.

"You will die for this." said his friend, his voice low so to not carry past their circle of moonlight.

"I know."

"Why? Why did you do it? I mean, was it worth it?"

"You tell me. How does it feel to know the truth?"

His friend nodded. "Thank you for telling me. But... I have to report you now."

The guard did not reply. After a moment he extended his hand and his friend, eyes blurred, held the guard's hand in farewell. His friend had gone to make the report. It would not be long now.

They came for him.

As the guard was escorted across the courtyard to Frederick's office, he thought it strange that this is how his life would end. He survived seventeen battles and countless skirmishes and participated in the obliteration of entire cultures. A guard judged his life by how strong the enemy was who finally defeated him. Frederick claimed divine power. Mere wishes of the Pontix became law. His verdicts were never overturned. His authority was absolute. It took a Pontix to end the guard's life. There could be no stronger foe.

The guard was dropped before the door of the office, and his escorts took a position on either side.

He stood slowly, steeled himself with a slow breath and rapped on the door.

"Yes."

8

The guard entered the office for the first time in his career. It was a small room, understated yet elegant, with rich red carpeting and bare walls. In the center, two high-backed chairs faced each other with a small table between. A fire burned in a hearth on the opposite wall. Even with the heat from the fire the room felt cold. The only decorative object, a rather hideous-looking creature, black with red eyes and horned wings, sat on the mantle.

This was the closest the guard had ever been to the Pontix. Frederick's presence was intense, his two dark eyes like cave entrances. Inside the cave, a beast lay waiting. Frederick's silver hair had a reddish aura from the light of the fire. He glowed like the *One True Book*. But a menace, though, and not true power, emanated from him.

"My Pontix, I humbly present myself." The guard bowed and remained there.

"Sit down."

"Yes, Your Eminence." The guard sat in the chair opposite Frederick.

Frederick looked at the guard like a chess player contemplating his next move. "You are not worthy to address me with that title."

"Nor are you worthy to wear it." the guard said. With considerable effort he held his composure.

"You have seen the Book?" Frederick said, ignoring the insult. The guard noticed a flicker of rage in Frederick's eyes. The beast could be hurt. A bit of the guard's confidence was restored.

"Yes, I have, Your Eminence."

"It is very secure. How did you manage that?"

"I left my post and ran down the stairs."

"And?"

"Something happened to me."

"No attempt to lie. Good. You understand that deception is pointless. I watched you go down there."

"What?" All confidence bled out.

It took a second for the guard to recognize Frederick's laughter, because it was unlike any the guard had ever heard.

"You give yourself too much credit." said Frederick. "Yes, you worm, I set up the whole thing."

"Why? Why allow me to see something we tried so hard to destroy?"

"One far more powerful than you questioned my motives. I did not answer to him either." Frederick pressed a button on his armrest. The guard's heart lurched.

The escorts entered the room.

The guard stood slowly. The inevitable was more disturbing than he thought it would be. He was still a guard. He would face his end with dignity. He walked to the doorway and turned to face his executioner. The escorts waited for Frederick's order.

Frederick held the guard's stare and asked. "When you saw the Book, what happened?"

"I felt power, real power. I learned about the angels, and not your twisted versions." The guard motioned towards the creature on the mantle. "They are nothing like that. What you teach is a lie. And I know about the Four. They are real. I learned the truth."

Frederick smiled. "I see. How nice for you." He nodded to the escorts.

A rapid twist of the condemned man's head was all it took to turn him into a lifeless heap. The escorts waited for Frederick's next order.

"Report to your Captain. All guards assigned to the inner door are to be removed from their duties. So is the Captain. Carry out all executions immediately."

"We serve with our lives, Master." The escorts saluted and dragged away the guard by his wrists.

Frederick stared into the fire to collect his thoughts. He ignored more than a few screams from guards abruptly awakened and killed.

The Pontix of New Hope stood slowly and headed to his chambers to prepare for bed.

CHAPTER ONE
Drace

He felt a drop on his face. Drace L'Adam was lifted momentarily from his thoughts. Breath came in a long, shuddering inhale as he looked over the city of Peyrvi. A semblance of hope briefly surfaced—a drop could mean that rain was approaching. Might it also bring lightning? It could strike the tree he leaned against and answer his prayer quickly.

It was not a raindrop, but a tear.

He wandered the streets of Peyrvi before coming to this spot on the hill. For how long? Hours, Days? A Lifetime?

It was sunset now, only a few hours since his beloved departed. He sat once again at their favorite location, this time alone.

In the distance, next to the palace, the Sweeps were preparing another funeral pyre. Drace wondered briefly who would be on that pyre. Jen would never see another stunning desert sunset. She would never witness another of Frederick's pyres either. Small comfort, that.

Drace could see the Merchant Academe. The view reminded him of his less-than-scholarly activities as a student. Tossing dice with friends was a way to distract him from the monotony of philosophy and business strategies.

He called to mind a memory of leaving their apartment in a hurry.

"Where are you off to, Sweetie?"

"Off for a little gaming with the guys, Jen."

They argued briefly. He finally stopped the disagreement by making a case that playing a game of chance was his way of honoring the more playful of the Angels. She rolled her eyes, and that was the end of it.

Troy was the Angel with whom Drace most identified. The angel was depicted as intellectual, clever, and crafty. He was thought of as playful to the point of whimsy and saw the importance of all manner of mental stimulation. Troy would certainly approve of an occasional dice game.

Tonight, Drace would distract himself with a different sort of game, one none of the Angels would approve of.

Jen was gone. That truth pummeled him until he ached.

His thoughts went back to that final visit with the woman he adored.

"Sir, can you answer a few questions, please?" Drace said as he chased the physician down the hallway.

Reluctantly the man in the long white coat faced Drace. Worry was etched on both of their faces.

"I wanted to ask you about my girlfriend, Jen. She is still in a coma. Have the tests come back?"

"Yes, well." The doctor shuffled his feet and focused his attention on the charts in his hands. Clearly, he wanted to be anywhere but there.

Drace sensed his reticence and tried to control his panic. He asked, "Some results have to be back by now, right? What's going on? Why is she still out? What about the child?"

After a long pause and a heavy sigh, the doctor resigned to the fact the conversation he had been avoiding for hours was going to happen. "Why don't we go in here? We can talk in private." He motioned to an empty patient room.

Drace allowed himself to be led by the arm. It was not a good sign. He was no longer so anxious to hear what the doctor had to say.

"Mr. L'Adam. Jen is still very sick. The labs showed highly elevated levels of ..."

"Sorry... in simple terms, please? What did you find?"

The man looked Drace in the eye. "Her body is no longer fighting to keep her alive. Her system is shutting down. She's dying, Drace."

Drace's mind numbed as it raced through the millions of questions to find one that would bring the answer he needed. If he asked the right question would he get a better answer? "What about the child?"

"I am sorry. There is nothing we can do. The fetus is too.... Well. I am truly sorry."

"That can't be right. What about an operation... like a transplant? Maybe more transfusions? Are you giving up? Come on, let's do something!"

"Mr. L'Adam..." Drace hated being addressed so formally, with such finality. "We have done all we can. This was an especially difficult case.

"Can nothing else be done? Nothing at all?"

"Well, there is always prayer."

"Yes, there is always prayer. But is there any hope?"

Silence. Drace had his answer. This cannot be happening, he thought. He searched for something to say.

"Again, I am very sorry." the physician said. "You should be with her now. You do not have much time left."

Drace wanted to shut down himself as he went to her room.

"Jen? Can you hear me?"

There was raspy breathing as a reply.

"If you can hear me, Love, squeeze my hand."

Just her breathing. Confirmation she was still alive, at least.

"It's okay, Jen. It's okay. I am right here."

Her breathing was getting weaker. It was time. A few more breaths and she would no longer be there. Drace could tell the very moment she left.

He held her hand a little longer. There was still love. There would always be love. But in the end, there was no prayer... and no hope.

In the end the doctors were useless. Typical. Drace thought. They try to look important. They dress in long robes and speak in medical jargon. Treated special wherever they go.

In the end, they are inadequate. If there is an afterlife, perhaps people who give false hope should suffer the most.

Drace wondered if anyone could pray to God and whether it would help deal with this kind of loss

The simple truth remained that humanity still did not understand why life was the way it was. Why do some individuals suffer a painful ending to a short life while others linger on to become shadows of their former selves? Why do good deeds often go unnoticed and hurtful behaviors get rewarded? Why do so many outcomes in a person's life seem to come down to mere chance? Would it matter at all if he ended his life today?

These questions drove Drace back to their favorite location.

Where else could he go? He could go back home to Selvine in the North Ward, live there and start a mercantile, marry someone his father chose, socialize with friends and grow old. He might one day be thought of as a success in his own right. The idea made him smile, for a moment.

He could travel east to the Great Ocean to sit on the shores at Helmshorn and watch fishermen bring home their haul. It would be a life of writing and solitude and slowly restoring his wounded soul.

He might go further west where New Hope became a strange and different land. Huge forests towered over the city of Ariasni that blended into the surroundings. He would be independent and self-sustaining and all the more lonely for it.

Drace's was a privileged lineage, with wealth and superior education. Yet the world had no place for him. No matter where he went, memories of Jen would haunt him.

Drace first came to Peyrvi for the beauty and solace it offered. The magnificence of nature surrounded Peyrvi but was never taken for granted. It was compensation to the 14,000 or so residents who endured the uninhabitable heat of midday. Each evening they would come out of their underground homes and enjoy another sunset.

It was on this hill he met his Jen. They came here often to watch the day surrender to the night. Tonight, amber hues melted distant mountaintops and sent out their color to streak the violet sky.

Not a single cloud was in sight. No lightning then to take Drace away quickly.

"There's never going to be an easy answer for anything." he said, as that agonizing truth twisted his soul.

His voice silenced the crickets droning in the background. He wiped away his tear, picked up the pencil nub and began his letter:

June 13, 12th Year of Frederick
My Darling Jen,
You are gone. I cannot begin to understand life without you. I loved you as I loved myself and the entire world will suffer with you no longer here.

With you gone, I return to my unfeeling world. I want to leave it all right now, but I do not think of this as merely suicide. I seek far more than just an end to my life.

What does my life mean anyway? What does any of this mean?

How can what I am doing be wrong? That would imply there is a God who will judge my actions. If there is a God, then why did he take my family? Where was God when I was in our empty bed as tortuous whispers had me dancing on the edge? No more dancing, just one last step.

Your Ace

Drace put his pencil down and felt drained as the last of his life's love poured onto the page. To find your heart's desire is a rare gift. To lose it is the ultimate tragedy. Drace's life was now emptiness in a world full of idiocy.

He sat with bony knees tucked under his chin and thought about the townspeople who came out to share the sunset. Would they find his suicide shocking? People die down there every day. He thought. Why should they care about one more death?

"Because you are a Divine Child." said a voice. It resonated in Drace's head and briefly brushed aside his ponderous thoughts.

"Are you really back?" Drace asked.

His old companion had returned. Drace had new images in his mind. There were reflections and memories of far better times, serene times when the world was pure, ambitious times in the classroom earning praise from his instructors, expressive times when his family gathered for his birthdays, and harmonious times when people did not yet fear each other.

These are no longer ideal times.

Toxins and fallout destroyed Drace's chance for a family. With so many fathers lost in combat, though, how could anyone have a true family?   These days more families gathered around funeral pyres than dinner tables.

Drace's desire to achieve had long been buried under a mountain of cynicism. Drace was despised for his family's wealth, his political name, and because of unwanted attention from Frederick.

Drace's final exam at the Merchant Academe was proctored by Frederick himself, in his grey suit and ceremonial gown. Rather than a mundane affair, it was an elaborate ceremony with his parents, David and Abigail L'Adam, bribery and corruption part of the process. How could it be otherwise?

Drace was the pride of his parents, who felt that their strained marriage now had some purpose. To have a child must be a sign their union was meant to be. All manner of privilege and favor was afforded Drace, further making him a despicable outcast.

Wealthy families were blamed for The Great Cataclysm. "Blame the rich." An entire world's history was vulgarly summarized in that one sentence.

In a flash, the Great Cataclysm changed humanity irrevocably and cruelly. Entire cities were blinked out of existence by those acting in the name of justice. Survivors felt justified in avenging their lost civilizations and let loose their own barrage of armies and technological terrors. Every society acting justly. All but one was eradicated.

His was the last country standing. The idiocy created by billions of indignant and vengeful inhabitants left little more than the 14,000,000 scattered across all New Hope.

Frederick claimed their survival was because they believed in themselves and not some non-existent God. In fact, it was allegiance to a deity that led to the destruction in the first place. Nationalist identity and religious conflict contributed to societies downfall.

In truth, it was through barbarity and cruelty New Hope remained, certainly not through self-sufficiency.

As a child, Drace's inner voice offered hope, inspiration, and companionship. Now its appearance was a reminder of how much worse his life had become.

Drace paused briefly and thought about the unpredictable ways in which one's destiny would unfold. Drace remembered being at her bedside as she struggled to stay awake. He thought again of her delicate face slowly drained of life. He thought of his final goodbye.

"Maybe Frederick's was right about one thing. Perhaps there is no one out there who will help us. I am sick of doing it all myself. Tired of being the only one who can decide the events in my life. This cannot continue. If you really are out there, God. Can't you do something, anything? Please...?"

The Sweeps lit the pyre and the flames grew. Maybe they will toss my body on there, too he thought. Drace twisted the top off his flask and brought it to his lips quickly before the foul smell could deter him. The only life available to him now was a life of bitter memories. He would rather see what happened to him after death. Maybe God would sympathize with his pain and allow him one more moment with Jen. It would be better than a life without her. He downed the entire homemade concoction in one gulp. And regurgitated it a few minutes later.

CHAPTER TWO
Buscillo

It was sunset, yet the heat was still uncomfortable. Fans entered the stadium, made their obligatory bow to the statue of Raiki and searched for one of the remaining marble seats.

There was another capacity crowd this evening. It always amazed Buscillo these competitions drew so many. A chance to see their reigning Champion, Buscillo Lane, compete in Peyrvi was a rare event.

"A moist towel, sir?" Today's assigned assistant asked.

"Not yet."

"Another huge crowd, sir."

How old was this kid? Buscillo wondered. Fifteen? Sixteen at the most? Could he—or could anyone else—comprehend how important these competitions were for Buscillo?

He understood why these events were always sold out. In a society were law and order were strictly, unmercifully enforced, Huge crowds came to express in public feelings best kept private. Their bow before the Angel of Wrath was not devotion, of course. In strict accordance with the policies of Frederick, there were no longer any public forms of worship. Vengeance and retribution found natural expression in heated competition. Bowing before Raiki was the only safe place to express those desires.

Those who knew the joy of vanquishing their opponent respected Raiki and all she represented. The inscription on her statue summed it best, *"In my eye the prize, in my mind the goal ... destroy their heart for the Victory."*

Buscillo believed his success was simply a matter of effort. Bowing before a statue was pointless superstition.

Statues were merely plunder from cultures made extinct by Frederick and his armies.

How could honoring an icon from a vanquished culture help anyone? It didn't help the fallen society it, did it?

"It's time, kid." said Buscillo. He took the towel this time and wiped the sweat from his brow, then reached into a gold-plated bowl to dust his hands with resin.

The assistant backed away from Buscillo.

Buscillo declared war against the mediocrity of his existence at an early age. He was not an especially large person with sinewy muscles. Beady eyes, thinning hair, and what his mother called "skinny chicken lips" completely ruled out any hope of distinguishing himself through appearance.

Buscillo did not set himself apart by being an Educator at a Sports Academe, either. After all, he wasn't an Educator at any of the Academes for Scholars or even at a respectable Artists or Merchants Academe.

Buscillo did not want to be celebrated because of a job title, anyway. Such a detail was irrelevant.

Frederick often proclaimed that Buscillo's victories showed New Hope what humanity once was, and what it could be again.

At each award ceremony, as Buscillo was handed yet another trophy, Frederick whispered to him, "They are counting on you. Show them what this really means." Frederick attributed Buscillo's success to being from New Hope. Buscillo wanted Fredrick to give him more credit.

He was Buscillo Lane, the reigning archery champion for nearly fifteen years. His string of victories began before the Great Cataclysm. Buscillo had been Champion even longer than Frederick had been Pontix.

Most of society, and thus most of his competitors, perished during the Cataclysm. Yet, this did not diminish Buscillo's reign in any way. No sportsman ever came close to Buscillo's record.

The Pavilion was the only place Buscillo ever wanted success. Here was where he experienced the satisfaction of victory. He filled stadiums with fans. Some people talked disdainfully about Buscillo's string of victories, saying anyone with proper training could do the same.

Still, thousands came to chant his name. Nothing else in his life offered such fulfillment.

To win this competition was not his goal. Buscillo had to own it. It was his heart's desire to grab the victory and proclaim to the world, "Here is your redeemer." The words were dramatic, but wouldn't the Angel of Wrath have destroyed him if his heart were not true?

In the arena he truly was a being of mythical dimension wayward heroes tried to defeat. They all came to dethrone the reigning king. No one in fifteen years lived up to the challenge. They became another ritual offering at his altar.

Today's sacrificial lamb had the audacity to treat this competition as a mere family outing. By their clothing and blond hair, the competitor and his family were from the North Ward. They were probably one of the privileged of Selvine where enormous wealth still rested in the hands of a few dynasties. This man lived in a home—not an assigned dorm—and would have been trained by a private tutor.

To these North Warders, this competition was simply one of the sights to take in on a trip to Peyrvi. How dare they not take this event seriously. Shouldn't the lamb be frightened as it is led to the altar?

After all, the fair-haired man was competing with a legend. Buscillo's victories were the only real glory this society could claim. Each trophy was meant to show New Hope even in Frederick's wretched society there was nobility.

Life was a circus. The arena was Buscillo's chance to be center ring. To the ringmaster, Frederick, Buscillo was merely a sideshow magician performing simple tricks. Buscillo, though, did not use boxes with trap doors or hide cards up his sleeve. Buscillo's victories were not illusion.

Publically, Frederick lavished Buscillo with great rewards. Coveted things like an above ground residence and an enormous salary were proof to New Hope Buscillo was highly valued. Even some of the priceless statues from Frederick's palace were gifted to Buscillo.

In private, Frederick made it clear to Buscillo much was expected.

Buscillo was bought, paid for and now wholly owned by Frederick. His life was purchased at an exorbitant price, but Buscillo was owned just the same.

Buscillo was a symbol to all New Hope, but he was not his own man. The world wanted him to win. Frederick expected him to win. It was for his own self-worth Buscillo needed to win.

Each competition, Buscillo yearned to show the world he was more than Frederick's pawn. The size of the event didn't matter. Buscillo was who he was. No failure would be tolerated.

The blond man demonstrated competence and, going into the final round, was tied with Buscillo.

On this last round, the fair-haired opponent went first. The man kissed his wife and daughter and walked to the line for his final three shots. His wife broke the tension by shouting, in her endearing North Ward accent, "You can do it, Sweetie."

Such disrespect. Would anyone approach the Champion and give him a sweet nuzzle on the neck? Would one kiss Pontix Frederick on the forehead? Would one begin a contest without bowing to Raiki? It was time to put this man in his place.

The opponent's first arrow was true. Buscillo controlled his reaction with a deep breath. The crowd, however, showed their appreciation for a marvelous, dead center shot. The first mark of the final round was fifty points.

The North Ward challenger was poised for his second shot. This time his daughter cheered him on. "Come on, Daddy! Win this one for me!"

When I was her age, I was winning my own contests. Buscillo thought. The second arrow nestled within a few finger widths from the first, another effortless fifty points.

"Damn, this guy is good." the Champion said, loud enough to be heard.

"Thank you." said the blond man. "Means a lot coming from you."

"You still have one more, Hotshot." Buscillo said, more aggressively than he wanted. "This cannot continue." Buscillo thought.

The challenger graciously ignored the petty comment and proceeded with his final shot. He pulled the bowstring and every person present felt the tension. Wife and daughter held hands. The crowd held their breath.

Buscillo saw the imperfection. "One of the feathers is slightly off. Why doesn't he stop?" Buscillo fought the urge to shout a warning. The arrow did not find its home with the others. The imperfection was enough to deny a bullseye. There was a moan of disappointment from the crowd. Life truly is a circus.

That's what you get for not taking this seriously.

Wife and daughter began to console the blond-haired man. He shrugged off a sympathy hug and said, "It's not over yet. He's good, Sweetheart, but have faith."

"It's going to take more than faith." said Buscillo as he walked to his place at the shooting line; center ring.

"What's going on? Why is my audience leaving?"

"There is a pyre just after sunset, sir." his assistant said. "Everyone is ordered to attend."

"It's almost over. Can't they wait a few more minutes?"

"It's a good idea to arrive early for these things, Sir."

"Indeed."

Buscillo thought about the unpredictable ways in which one's destiny would unfold.

As Buscillo drew his bow for the first shot he heard an all too familiar voice in his head. "So, do you think you are good enough?"

Thoughts of his mother always came to him at this moment. Buscillo despised her harsh and demanding comments. He hated how she drove him mercilessly but knew somehow it was a critical part of his success.

"So, Buscillo. Are you good enough?" The voice asked. It was not his mother, though. This voice was gentle. It was encouraging, loving even.

"I am." he replied, but without the defiant tone used with his mother.

"Are you good enough?" The tender voice asked again.

"Yes, I am. At least, I pray to God I am." Buscillo said, allowing that tenderness to caress his spirit.

CHAPTER THREE
Marina

Marina Scerpio was jarred from her daydream when the Educator entered the classroom. Marina turned from watching the sunset through the window and prepared for another lecture on language fundamentals. As a writer hell bent on transforming the world with her ideas. what possible use did she have for a class in basic grammar, especially in this classroom full of uninspired cretins? This sunset would likely be the only source of inspiration this evening.

Her class greeted the older gentleman, "Hello, Educator Levons."

How many times has this man heard that greeting, Marina wondered? Five thousand, ten? Yet, it always catches him off guard.

"Oh. Yes… well now. Thank you, class. Hello, to all of you."

Marina took one last look out her window. She saw the Sweeps preparing another pyre at the Palace. Great, she thought, another night of stench.

"Hey, Marina, nice outfit." An elegantly dressed girl arrived late and was forced to sit next to the class outcast. Some believed Marina dressing like a Sweep meant she was more likely to spread diseases. Though it was certainly not true, people tried not to sit next to her.

"Thanks." Marina said. "Where did you get that lovely blouse? Did one of your customers buy that for you?"

A hate-filled look was the only reply. The class found the remark hysterically funny. Oh, how Marina despised these people. Truly this sunset would be the only thing worth her time this evening.

This cannot continue, Marina thought.

Marina simply did not fit in. It would be easy to blame it on being an olive-skinned immigrant from the Western Ward.

Marina saw herself as much more than a token minority from the less developed region of New Hope. She had outstanding marks in Fundamentals school, and the highest score possible on the Academe entrance exam. Yet, few had as many difficulties fitting in as she.

As a child, Marina shrieked anytime someone picked her up. That was merely the beginning. Now her screams were directed at all the people who rejected her. They were aimed at each person who avoided her because of her race, her culture, or her choice of dress. Anyone who rejected Marina felt her wrath.

After twenty years of this self-imposed exile, Marina applied to the Peyrvi Academe of Scholars to become a Scribe; the fancy New Hope term for writer.

Her application to the Academe of Scholars in Peyrvi involved a petition to immigrate, a housing allocation, residency affidavits, and a psychological profile. There were quite a few bureaucrats who were suspicious of her background. Many were concerned being from a conquered region may give her divided loyalties. Marina's views may have undesired effects on the other students. They blamed most of her "odd behavior" on this notion.

Her parents were recognized as Educators of considerable merit. They cashed in all their favors to petition Frederick himself. The Pontix granted an audience and met the Scerpio family. Both parents, and a nervous seventeen-year-old, stood before Frederick as he casually reviewed the top few forms in Marina's file.

"Marina Scerpio ..." he said to no one in particular. "From the Western Ward, though originally from Senika Bay."

"Yes, Mr. Pontix." Marina said, unsure of the correct form of address. His looked directly at her and she feared she might faint.

"Marina, I have my eye on you. As a youth from a conquered land you are a symbol for New Hope. You represent our vision for a peaceful world, a place where all people can coexist. I will offer you every opportunity to prove yourself. Request granted. You will enroll at the Peyrvi Academe of Scholars under full scholarship. Courses to begin this coming term."

Frederick left the room. Marina and her family were left to absorb his words. An aide escorted them through the grand foyer. Marina was too stunned to appreciate the magnificent art around her.

Outside Marina allowed herself to react. She stood in the middle of the street and screamed. Her mother grabbed Marina's arm and urged silence. The smile on her mom's face betrayed her true feelings. All three shocked at the blessing so casually bestowed upon them. There were still mountains of paperwork to plow through, but Marina was going to attend the most prestigious Academe of the entire system. The Pontix himself said so.

Fellow students didn't accepted her. All things finally said Marina knew it didn't matter. To be rejected still hurt, though. Marina was used to that sort of pain. Impetuous artists had to deal with those emotions every few hours or so.

She channeled that hurt into her writing. To her it was all about wanting to express to the world. This is really me. That one thing was all she ever wished for. Her heart's desire was to one day hear someone say, "I see who you are, and I understand."

"Okay, young people. The Educator said. "We are going to do something different today."

Marina groaned at the thought of yet another silly exercise.

Trite or not she would not let a classroom assignment get her down.

She thought about the unpredictable ways in which one's destiny would unfold.

Her inner voice came as a whisper, "It is time, Dear One."

CHAPTER FOUR
Val

Valessa's treasure box, hidden away in her attic, was more than just a place to store mementos. It was her way of feeling alive.

At her job, it was about making a tired routine erotic enough to bring in tips. With her hellion son, her whole mission was to minimize the damage as he went through yet another rebellious phase. At home, it was about maintaining the image of a responsible mom. Here in the attic of her humble home, all those burdens were put aside. In her box, tucked in neatly with drawings and old jewelry, were memories of a better life.

She wanted to brush off her son's problems as growing pains. In her heart, she knew his hurts went deeper. Blaming the alcoholic father who abandoned them was a convenient excuse. It was the one she used in those rare letters to her mother back home in the East Ward city of Helmshorn.

The part about her son being ashamed of his mother's job Val chose not to mention.

She was expelled from the Academe of Artists in her apprentice year and took a job as a dancer. She promised her son she would only perform long enough to finance her education at a different Academe.

Once Val graduated and became a doctor, she would be able to support herself with a proper job. She could become a physician in a respectable clinic. She did help people feel better, at least. The small theater in which she worked was a place where people came to escape and enjoy some small pleasure. Okay, that one was a stretch. People did go there to feel something other than misery for a time, and that mattered somehow.

Val found herself in possession of a secret. She wanted to tell everyone, especially those who looked down on her, the real reason she was asked to leave the Academe. It was not prejudice towards her career but something far more sinister.

No one would ever hear the truth, although it was not so outrageous a story. Once, a palace guard requested she accept the honor of a private meeting with Frederick.

In the anteroom to Frederick's personal chambers, she waited. Frederick wanted her to relax in opulence, perhaps even grow fond of such surroundings. Val did love the silk pillows on the couch. The gold tea set was ostentatious, yet elegant. She did not recognize the art displayed but assumed they were priceless treasures from an extinct society.

Once inside his chambers, Frederick was polite but direct. He moved quickly and gracefully, like a wolf cutting off his prey, and sat to one side of a couch built for two. The position of his arm suggested that she was to sit next to him. Behind him were thick, satin curtains parted to allow an expansive view of Peyrvi. This room was obviously not an official meeting chamber with its warm fireplace, thick rugs, and four-post bed.

Val sat next to him, afraid not to. She sat upright, poised to move quickly if necessary.

"Relax, Child. I am not going to hurt you. Quite the opposite. Are you comfortable? Would you like something to eat, some fruit perhaps?" he said, indicating a bowl of apples on a table.

His voice was smooth and controlled though disturbing because of the effort she knew it took to sound that way. His face was relaxed and gentle. This was a man comfortable with giving commands. Grey hair suggested a man of some years. His face was angular and sharp yet youthfully unlined despite the grey.

She was asked to be a dancer in Frederick's court. Knowing that the term "dancer" was a euphemism for concubine, she refused. She declined the offer politely, of course, stating maternal obligations. Frederick was not easily deterred, nor was his offer easy to refuse. A button on the armrest was pushed. Curtains opened fully. A sweep of Frederick's hand added emphasis to, "All of this is mine, and I share generously with those I am fond of."

The luxury was undeniable. Never had she seen such opulence. Likely, she never would again. It was easy to imagine all of it hers. She pictured sitting at this couch with an adorable dog lying by the hearth. Frederick smiled, and her dream shattered. A wolf had taken the dog's place in front of the fire.

Everyone knew of Frederick's appetite for beautiful girls. No one could deny Val's beauty. She could have done well in the personal service of her Pontix.

Val declined him again. He grew tired of asking. Another button was pushed, and a bell sounded. Two servants appeared at the entrance.

"Miss Nemah is finished here. Please show her home."

She fumbled an apology and knew that dire consequences shall certainly fall upon her. Guards escorted her, walking two steps behind, the entire way home.

It was an extraordinary tale, but Val told no one. Not such a shocking story, really. Most people would believe it. Matters could only get worse, though, if Val told others how she denied the Pontix. Better people think bad behavior or poor decisions put her in these circumstances.

People understood Val was a bit "different" and she allowed that lie to remain. Let that be the reason why the chancellor dropped her from the Academe. One as headstrong and proud as Val does not think about the consequence of a noble act.

Having the entire town believe the lie was not as hard as she expected. People took to the story Val was kicked out of the Academe because she was a non-conformist. Losing her spot at the Academe was the difficult part.

Someone from Frederick's administration approached a faculty member at an Academe graduation reception. Frederick had given another of his speeches full of flowery words and trite niceties. Words like 'hope' and 'change' were thrown about to signal to the crowd that this speech was purely ceremonial. After the rhetoric, the crowd clapped politely as they headed to the buffet for sweet ribs and spiced potatoes.

It was a time for mingling and maneuvering. The administrator approached the faculty and said, "Valessa Nemah... you know her, yes? Isn't it a pity her outlandish behavior forced you to dismiss her from the Academe? Such a shame when a promising student sabotages their future like that, don't you think?"

The faculty member stammered a bit. His face brightened as understanding came. "Ah yes, it is truly a shame. She is a bit reckless, is she not? No way to predict what poor behavior she is capable of."

"Yes. You have a good memory for details I see. You will make an excellent chancellor one day. Perhaps one day very soon."

"We serve with our lives."

"Indeed."

The faculty member was promoted to Chancellor later that week, the day after Val was asked to leave the Academe. A violation of the Academe's moral code was the explanation given.

Over time, various stories circulated explaining Val's dismissal. Recently, Val overheard one housewife say Val tried to seduce an Educator and took off her clothing in his office. As punishment, Val was forced to work as an exotic dancer.

The lies were outrageous. Still, they were better than the truth. Val chose this career. It would be easier for her pride if she had been forced into this line of work. Val was desperate, and the money was good.

She was outdoors, at least. Her home on the surface was one of the enticements Frederick offered. It would have been petty to withdraw his gift. For months, though, she feared guards would wake her at night and express their leader's frustration.

In this ward, any outdoor property was a true luxury. She spent many hours looking out this window, watching her son play. That was, of course, when playing outside held his interest. Peyrvi's lurid underground now held sway.

This view and her box of treasures kept her mind off her problems.

The small, jewel-encrusted box was brought out of its resting place in an antique trunk and gently placed on her lap with a free hand. In her other hand was her cup of desert nettles tea. She adjusted in her rocking chair and took a few deep breaths before the ritual began. After a few sniffles in the dusty air, she slowly opened the box.

On top of her stash of trinkets and treasures was a photo of her and her father. Both were smiling. A happy moment from childhood captured on film was priceless. Even more precious was her mother sobered enough to take the photo.

Her father returned from a combat excursion in Senika Bay full of hope and promise of a better life. Her mom stopped drinking, a true miracle.

Senika Bay was terribly isolated from New Hope. The Administration spin was the Information Task Force searched the territory, located survivors, and established an outpost. Everyone understood what happened to those survivors.

In the privacy of their homes, friends and family pieced together the whole tragic story. Val's father rarely spoke about his tour. When he did, the details were hard to accept.

Words were not needed. Her father's silence told her more about how horrible things were than any gossip. Not much was ever said; though her father did mention once one culture encountered had a religion that advocated wife beating. That helped justify some of the brutality inflicted.

No details were offered about the excursions. Val knew the ITF traveled quickly and were armed with technology Frederick promised was banned.

The only thing Val knew was a priority for these missions was to destroy all churches. Every other building was assimilated by Frederick's forces.

Churches were systematically eliminated. It was an odd thing, really. What value was a church with no worshippers? Certainly, none of the occupying forces would utilize the buildings for religious purposes. Yet, the edict from Frederick was followed rigorously.

Religion was not able to prevent the Great Cataclysm nor was it able to deal effectively with the social unrest that followed. Religious concepts were held to blame for social problems.

The belief humanity must suffer in life and only earn their reward when they die frustrated many. The insistence by religions that people must shun material prosperity as an expression of piety was not well received either. These teachings only fed the people's anger towards the wealthy.

People were hurting. They were not getting answers they could accept. Hurt and anger needed a target. Religion and the wealthy were natural scapegoats.

The only religious teachings allowed were about Frederick's Angels.

The end for all survivors in Senika Bay was quick. It was also cruel and inhumane, but at least it was quick. Thus, another religious culture was eliminated.

Val's mother stopped drinking when her father shipped out. They all feared her father would not return. Val's mom knew she would not be strong enough to survive such a loss as a drunk. Once Sergeant Nemah settled back in New Hope, her mother abandoned all restraint and downed liquor by the case.

When her father was away, Val's mother would sometimes talk with invisible friends who came out of her memories to console her. Val allowed her those friendships, no matter how it hurt to watch. It was a small consolation for a woman whose life had crumbled around her.

Her Dad returned from duty but never truly came home. He was never able to reconnect with his family. Val desperately needed to believe her father's compliments, but his words always seemed shallow and empty. Val didn't push him to talk about what happened overseas. He needed a break from those memories. Val's father returned with his health, a large bonus check and a renewed appreciation for his family. He had every reason to be happy. Val could see, though, how miserable he was.

Again, she felt the sadness that had been a silent family member for as long as they had been a family. Sadness was present at every outing and gathering. Sadness was there at every holiday and momentous occasion. Sadness was her escort to every event.

"Gosh, I really was beautiful then." Val said with a sigh. She examined her body to reassure herself she still had something to look at. She tossed her head to watch her long red curls bounce. She still had long legs well shaped from years of dancing. She checked to confirm her breasts were still firm and stomach was still flat and was satisfied with what she saw. Despite her positive evaluations, Val never felt as pretty as she did when that photo was created. "You were the only one who could make me feel like that, Abba."

"You are still beautiful, child."

Val's companion had been visiting her since childhood, yet she was always surprised when he spoke.

"Are you there?" Val asked. Visits from her voice had decreased over the years. What used to be long conversations were now brief, one-sided comments. The voice's remarks were meant to be reassuring. Brief comments did not justify the longing felt when her Voice disappeared yet again. Val hoped her friend might stay awhile this evening.

Dreaded feelings of loneliness crept over her again. The voice was her only means to combat feeling utterly alone in. Her sadness plunged deeper into pain. This could not continue.

It took a few moments for her to recover from the malaise. The attic was filthy with exposed beams full of cobwebs and the first signs of dry rot. Her little corner was kept orderly, and her tiny window was always clean. She felt comforted here, safe. This was her sanctuary.

Her position at the window gave her a view of the vegetation behind her house. They were not real woods like the ones back in Helmshorn, but the rocky nature path through thickets of cactus and Jaspers had a certain charm of its own.

Now, at sunset, was the best time to enjoy the view. There was another pyre being built at the palace. It was a shame tonight's sunset would be spoiled by smoke.

Her little boy no longer played around the house. The empty backyard was yet another reminder she was alone.

Long ago, Val gave up on making friends. Val was not comfortable hanging out with the other girls at the Theatre. They did not understand why she attempted to claim a normal life by owning a home. Val never told a soul how the home had been gifted to her by the Pontix. Val would have to explain she refused the Pontix. Not a safe topic for discussion.

Safer, she thought her coworkers think she spent beyond her means.

Other women in Peyrvi were not easy to talk to either. They did not approve of how she made her money.

There were no love interests. Her career interfered with that, as well. Men either had a problem with her choice of vocation or, if they did accept her line of work, it was because they had lecherous ideas of dating a stripper. It was hard to find a decent man who was comfortable with her profession. It was her heart's desire to one day live in a place where she knew she belonged.

Valessa placed her cup of tea on the window ledge as two violent sneezes attacked her. Peyrvi had been her home for several years now, but she never adjusted to its dry air.

Once, in Helmshorn, she hid in an attic to avoid her son's father and his primal urges. An attic had always been her sanctuary. Before, her sneezes were stifled to avoid giving her away. Now they were allowed with a certain amount of satisfaction.

She thought about the unpredictable ways in which one's destiny would unfold. Sneezing brought her into the present moment. The box took her into the past and her precious son made her worried for the future. She wiped her nose on her sleeve as she heard, "It is time."

CHAPTER FIVE
Frederick

It was dawn, a wretched time of day, when light overtook darkness. From his balcony, Frederick looked toward the sunrise that marked the beginning of a scheme several centuries in the making. A man running errands in the street looked up and was shocked to see the Pontix exposed. After many attempts on his life, Frederick usually remained indoors.

Frederick did not give the man's wave a thought, his mind on too many details to consider such a trivial gesture. One waving man with a confused look was hardly the adulation he deserved. Gone were the days when throngs rejoiced in the genius who brought them out of the ashes and created a new society.

The man saw Frederick's appearance as a favorable omen and made the sign of blessing out of habit. He scurried away and admonished himself for making the sign in front of Frederick. Any other time Frederick would have the man executed.

Ringing bells above his palace, a holdover from lost cultures, marked the precise moment when darkness surrendered. Not so long ago, bells announced more than the time of day. They proclaimed a time to worship, a funeral, or a victory in battle.

Those bells were destroyed. The solitary ring diminished into nothingness as the last of the darkness clawed at the horizon. "It is time." Frederick whispered. "At long last, it is time."

Frederick reentered his palace. He walked through his chambers to a door opened to the hallway. Frederick asked the posted guard, "Kto vas?'

The guard snapped to attention and responded to the ritual challenge, "Vas."

The guard fell in step with the man he swore to protect with his life. Frederick wore his ceremonial uniform with burnished breastplate and bright red cape.

With somber expression but alert eyes, the guard escorted his master towards the central staircase. Polished boots sharply struck marble flooring; their cadence reverberated throughout the palace.

As the Pontix approached the top of the stairs, a second guard snapped to attention. Frederick looked him in the eye as he asked in a language not spoken in centuries, "Kto vas?" Thousands of years ago a king would ask his knights, "Who do you serve?" His loyal knights answered, "You!"

Countless cultures were destroyed since then. This was one of the few traditions Fredrick allowed.

"Vas." The guard answered, and he too took up an escort position.

Frederick arrived at the bottom of the staircase with two guards in step behind him. He continued across the foyer and past the grandest works of art in the world.

The collection of treasures was once his obsession. Each piece a headstone that marked a civilization Frederick killed.

The priceless objects merely background as their collector made his way toward a large door.

Two guards at the door came to life as their master approached. They took their position with the others. All four guards—it had to be four—stood in formation behind Frederick. He walked to the door.

"It is time." he whispered as he opened the door and entered. It was quickly shut and locked behind him.

Frederick headed deeper underground than the lowest levels of Peyrvi.

At the bottom of the stairs, in a room carved out of earth and lit by a single candle, was the most prized item in all of history. It contained the greatest story ever written, the story of humanity. In the *One True Book*, created when Shadow first separated from Light, were God's words to his people.

To individuals, their life appears to have no more impact on history than the leaf does on the wind. Like the leaf, each individual gets caught in currents and tossed about without purpose or direction.

Yet, every leaf does have purpose and direction.

The details of that purpose were recorded in the *One True Book*, the plan for humanity was revealed.

Frederick denied humanity such knowledge. The *One True Book* and its wisdom was never revealed to the people. Frail humans tumbled through their lives driven by a wind they could not direct. Frederick, not frail and certainly not a mere human, took possession of that Book. He controlled the events that directed humanity. He was the wind.

Frederick entered the tiny room and sat at a wooden table, worn smooth from years of use. For the last time, he opened the *Book* that contained True wisdom.

When did the fall of humanity begin? He wondered. What was the precise moment? Glorious and spectacular moments stood out. The first murder, the first betrayal, the first war; these were all significant. When was the point of no return? When was it too late for hope?

At any point, humanity could have stopped the endless cycle of violence, revenge, and more violence. Early in history there was a chance for reconciliation and renewal. People had the opportunity to heal relationships and redeem lives. "They never had a chance after that, though," he said. "It was pretty easy after that."

With each generation, truth blurred and reasons for ancient animosities were woven into their cultural fabric. Civilizations went to war because they knew nothing else.

The precise beginning was hard to determine. The moment it all ended was obvious. Century after century leaders declared war in response to one thing. The world did not end with a bang but a whisper.

Frederick opened the *One True Book,* as he had countless times before. Something different would happen tonight. No more would he have to suffer through the pabulum and placating nonsense of the *Book.* Those words sought to redeem humanity.

It was immensely satisfying to use the Book's own words against humans. By twisting the teachings, Frederick made his whispers sound reasonable.

Many world leaders rose to power on merit. They possessed some great quality which helped them reach the top. Yet, each had an insecurity to be exploited. Many leaders did not require a reason to take their country into war. Often a passable excuse was all the justification needed. Frederick whispered to each leader exactly what they wanted to hear.

The last one was fun, he thought. Wow was he gullible. The ultimate destruction of humanity came about because of the color of a man's skin.

People who felt inferior were a natural target for Frederick's whispers. People who harbored anger and resentment were easy prey.

Day after day, Frederick whispered the same message. "If you destroy their country from the inside, they will have to admit they were wrong."

"They think their country is mighty, don't they? What if it was destroyed by their own hand?"

Seeds were planted early. "You have been held down. The entire country is against your race. Destroy them. Then the world will know they were wrong. Their concept of freedom is flawed if your race is not free. An economy based on achievement and merit is misguided if your race does not have the same opportunities. It only rewards *their* achievements and *their* merits. You can show this to the world."

The road to leadership was begun. Doors to higher and higher levels were opened. Each day the man rose in power, and each night he was whispered to.

"Prove your country wrong. They were wrong about their religion. They were wrong to put their faith in a god. They were wrong to judge you. Show them your race is valuable by destroying this country. Show the world how wrong they are. It is not *your* country; it is their country. Destroy it. Redeem your race."

After decades of whispers, the angry man was finally able to act on his hatred. It was by his hand the entire world was nearly destroyed. A single button was pushed, and the world was obliterated. It all started with a whisper.

The Great Cataclysm was the spectacular climax. Now for the dénouement. It is time for the fate of humanity to be decided. Frederick, The Whisperer, will claim his victory.

Frederick sought to thwart *The One True Book* at every opportunity. Light was deflected and Darkness grew in strength. It would be contained no longer.

"Only those Four stand between me and victory. This cannot continue. It happens now."

In that moment, time was distorted. The very fabric of the universe was torn. Darkness was unleashed in an explosion. A wave of Darkness swept through the Palace, across Peyrvi and beyond. Every living creature was its target. Something had indeed happened.

CHAPTER SIX
Old Man

Drace focused as well as he could in his intoxicated state. Memories rose to the surface, but making sense was difficult. He remembered being on the mountain and drinking his barbiturate cocktail. After that...?

How did he get here? Why hadn't he died? Why was his tongue so dry? His stomach felt like it was filled with rancid worms, trying to eat their way upwards. Drace bent over and forced the vile buggers out. A foul mixture of pills, alcohol and stomach contents splattered on the ground. A whiff of the concoction brought a few more memories.

He drank the infusion then passed out. Someone called his name, and Drace woke to find the source of that voice.

Obviously, the concoction was not enough to kill him, only force him to wander in this home-brewed haze searching for who called him.

Gee, what luck. He must have searched for some time. It was dark, and he was at least a forty-minute walk from where his journey took this unexpected fork. He was nearly back in Peyrvi.

"Who called me? What time is it? Why am I not dead?" Answers were still out of reach.

Wait, who is that? There was an elderly gentleman ahead. Odd someone was out at this hour, whatever hour it was. Even more curious were the man's clothing. He was dressed in the manner of a person from Astica. Why would a refugee be foolish enough to wear that in public?

Night guards obviously had not seen the gentleman. If they had, the man would be inside the palace answering questions. Drace too, for that matter, could face a guard's scrutiny He had not thought of that.

Drace fumbled in his pocket to produce a handful of ID cards. What card would he need? There was one for every situation. He had verification of graduation from the Merchants Academe, his business license, his Peyrvi residency card and some others he was told he, "must carry at all times." He wondered if he should find out what those other documents were for. One day maybe - certainly not now. If asked for documents, he was prepared.

The gentleman stood on the corner of Vista and Heritage as if waiting for the light to change. His only movement was the slight swinging of his cane. Adobe walls complimented his colorful attire.

The man's identity eluded Drace. Walking in a straight line eluded him.

With more curiosity than caution Drace approached the dapper gentleman.

"It's a nice time for it." The elder spoke with a slight hint of Astican accent.

Drace had not expected such a voice. It was melodic but raspy, like gravel in a silk bag. The Old Man spun the cane in his fingers.

"You must have a story to tell." The man said. The he pointed with his cane towards a park bench.

Drace stood with his mouth open.

The Old Man walked to the bench and sat. Drace was struck by the man's comforting presence. There was a disturbing sense the elder had, in that moment, sized up Drace entirely. Drace was now known to him and would be familiar should the two ever meet again. The Old Man patted the seat next to him and said, "I have all night to listen." He addressed Drace as if coaxing a kitten out of a tree.

Drace laughed uneasily and did not move. For several moments, the elderly man waited. The man's gentle face put

Drace at ease, but he still did not move. When Drace sorted his thoughts he said, "you must be joking."

"No." The man said with a voice Drace felt in his chest. "I don't have to be. Why don't you sit, and we can talk awhile?"

"That's pretty forward" Drace said, I like it when people are forward. Well, I like it when women are forward, at least." Stuck for something to say, Drace held out his hand and said, "Hi, name's Ace."

The Old Man accepted the handshake with a warm grip. "And I am Starik. You have questions, don't you?" Drace allowed the man to guide him to the bench.

"Who are you?"

The Old Man had deeply worn lines on his face that moved easily into a smile. His eyes were radiant and looked directly at Drace.

He said, "That would take some explaining. We will get to that when it is time."

"Is there a better time than now?" Drace wondered.

A laugh erupted more experienced than heard. "Oh, Drace, you have a wonderful wit."

"You read my thoughts? And how do you know my real name?"

"I know everything there is to know about you. You are special, and I have been keeping an eye on you."

"What is going on here?" Drace leaned away from the Old Man but resisted the urge to run. "Am I dead? Am I a ghost?" Drace pondered a moment. *Not likely. Ghosts do not vomit.*

"No, My Son, you are not dead and not a ghost. It is more involved than that."

"I'm listening." Drace said. Again, a peaceful presence calmed him.

"For example." the Old Man continued. "I know your pain, and I know how you dealt with that pain."

Drace was alarmed. "You mean you –"

"Yes, Drace, I know what you tried to do."

"Excuse me. Is this some sort of Fredricken joke?" Drace did not know how the man could know personal things and read thoughts.

Drace did know that he did not have to listen to the man judge him.

"I have heard enough." He stood quickly and immediately felt dizzy. He grabbed the back of the bench and held out his other arm for balance.

The Old Man steadied Drace with his cane and said, "Drace, I understand why you did that. You attempted to divert your destiny because you had a difficult time saying goodbye."

The man was charming. He had sharp clothes and a cool voice. But Drace was not into any psychological crap. "Have a nice evening Mister... By my soul, I cannot remember your name. Good night, Sir." Drace walked, or rather staggered, into the night.

The gentleman remained calm as the young man stormed into the night. He re-crossed his legs and examined the carvings on his cane.

In a thunderous voice, the man said, "Your name is Drace L'Adam, but you prefer to be called 'Ace' as you do not like the name your father gave you. Your last relationship was with a girl you loved though sometimes you did not give her much attention. You were aware of your failings in that area, at least, and made up for it at the end. Now Jen has died, and you are caught up in the role of martyr.

He continued softly. "This points to the two issues in your life. You carry the burden of a demanding father and search for the nurturing you did not receive from your mother."

Drace leaned against a building at the edge of the light from the streetlamp. "Not bad, Old Man, but anyone could guess that. That is not so impressive, you know."

"True. A deeper explanation is you are emotionally vulnerable to people who cannot give the nurturing a sensitive soul like you needs."

"What? You know about that too?"

"Yes, Drace, you were born an artist, but your father labeled you a freak. A person who grows up with such an issue requires a lot of love and attention."

"Born an artist?" *What in the world is this strange, strange man talking about?*

"There is more, of course. Shall I go on?"

"Yes, please go on." *This guy is whacked out of his Fredricken skull but is rather entertaining.*

Starik flashed a disarming smile and continued. "You feel unattached to society. You fantasize about living the life of a travelling salesman, an explorer or maybe even a hermit. You do not feel connected to this world in any meaningful way. Now you struggle to find a role for yourself. Half of you wants to conform to convention for the security it offers while the other half wishes to remain fiercely independent. This is the essence of your true self."

"By my soul, you are sure out there."

"Yes, Drace, by your soul." He winked. "I will give you some time for this to make sense. By the way, it is 9:25."

The Old Man crossed his legs again. "You need time to sort this out. A nice walk will help. Not too long though. You have to be somewhere at dawn."

Drace stared at the man. "Well, I don't know what to say." He truly did not. At sunset, Drace wanted to end it all. A few blurry hours later, some dashing maniac explains the reason for Drace's suicidal attempt was because Drace wanted to be a hermit. His thoughts wandered off in search of explanations which made more sense.

Rather than leave he paced. Where was he to go? Here was where Drace needed answers. How did this guy know so much?

Drace considered himself an articulate and decently educated man. When circumstances were more positive, Drace's family provided a host of tutors. Finances were not the issue. It was a matter of propriety. Spending lavishly while others struggled was not something the L'Adam family did.

Drace was invited to the Peyrvi Academe for Scholars. Shocking his family, he chose instead to attend the Merchants Academe. This distanced him even further from his father who accused Drace of not taking life seriously.

Drace never gave his father a reason for rejecting a golden opportunity. It was not lack of intellectual ability that kept Drace from the Academe of Scholars. Drace considered himself gifted in a few unique ways. The Merchants Academe offered the best opportunity for him to maximize those gifts.

Drace never explained to Jen his academic choices. In truth, the decision had a lot to do with Drace's opinion Frederick's government was far eviler and more corrupt than people realized. People made jokes in private about how awful things were. They even took to using Frederick's name as a curse word. Drace did not see much humor in the situation.

There was more to this administration than a ridiculous bureaucracy. That was what people were meant to see. What was hidden from view was something much more sinister. Frederick's reforms hurt those it professed to help. The entire system was corrupt, and Drace's father was part of the corruption. Drace wanted to separate himself from his tainted heritage.

Drace's success came through hard work. No one gave him credit for that accomplishment. Drace L'Adam of Selvine was the eldest son in the most powerful family in New Hope. People assumed Drace's success was purchased not earned.

Drace tried in vain to convince people he chose his own path. Drace's birthright was his burden. Most everyone saw it as an unfair advantage.

Frederick added to that perception. Whenever Frederick spoke in public, he highlighted certain individuals as examples of what life in New Hope could be. These people were presented as symbols for the nation. Drace was often one of those mentioned.

People saw photos of Drace standing next to their leader. They saw their Pontix with his arm around him and took that to mean that he was born into a life of privilege.

Drace had a talent for business. He could always get the best rate from manufacturers and the best price out of consumers. He was even able to negotiate better government bribes.

This was the first time in Drace's life where he could not find some advantage using his communication skills. Perhaps if he were a bit more sober, he might be able to put his thoughts to words and ask the right questions. "You say that I am in this situation because of my destiny? So, pain is my destiny? Forget your Fredricken destiny, Mister."

Drace took off again.

The Old Man returned his attention to his cane and said, "One ... Two ... Three ... Four ..." On 'Five', the Old Man pointed in Drace's direction as the young man spoke.

Drace stood again at the edge of the light. "You know, your philosophy has a hole in it. If pain is my destiny, that means life is cruel. If life is cruel, then why would I want to follow your plan?" If the Old Man was correct, then Drace was sorry he didn't end his life.

The Old Man stood and offered a smile that filled Drace with warmth.

Starik walked towards the young man and said, "You believed lies whispered to you. Drace, your suicide attempt was not part of your destiny. Neither was the pain. You suffered because you avoided your destiny. Your destiny is bigger than a lost relationship or a suicide attempt." Starik took a step closer and said, "I have said enough for now."

The Old Man held out his arms to offer an embrace.

"You must be joking. Oh right, you do not have to be. Look mister, if you think I am going to hug you then I know you are out of your mind."

The Old Man stood there with his arms open and a warm smile on his kind and gentle face.

"Seriously, I am not going to hug you." Drace felt tears welling. A hug would be very nice. Drace's defenses fell, and the tears came. There were years of stoical silence Drace wanted to make up for.

Starik held Drace through the worst of the tears and said, "There is still much to explain. First, there is something I would like you to have."

Drace pulled back from the Old Man and asked, "What is it?"

"There will be plenty of time for questions later. Remember what the *One True Book* says. 'The solution to everyone's problem is inside of them.' I offer you something that is a part of your destiny. Will you accept?"

"If it's part of my destiny, do I have a choice?" Drace asked.

"You're learning. Let me ask you this way. Do you feel unique things are happening right now?"

Drace resisted the urge to give a smartass answer. After such a loving embrace, sarcasm was not appropriate. Drace nodded his affirmation.

"Indeed, there are." Starik said. "Do you understand these events or feel prepared to handle them?"

"Not at all."

"I want to give you something that will help things make sense. Then at sunrise, you must take this back to the mountain. You will find answers there. Do not be anxious today. Tomorrow will be anxious enough."

The Old Man took an ornament off the cane's handle. On it was stamped an image of two men standing side-by-side. Drace recognized the symbol of duality. It represented that all people have two natures. There was a chain attached that was stored in the cane's hollow center.

The Old Man said, "Take this to the mountain at sunrise. You will find your answers. Do you accept?"

"Oh, why not?" Drace answered.

Starik laughed. "I do love your sense of humor Drace. Remember your instructions. Go to the mountain at dawn."

"What am I supposed to do until then?"

"Well, there is a competition at the Sports Academe about to resume. I think you will find it interesting."

"Huh?" What an odd answer, Drace thought. "Yeah, I am not that big a sports fan. Maybe I'll just go for a walk."

"You can choose any path you wish. The destination is still the same."

Drace wandered into the night to sort out those cryptic words.

CHAPTER SEVEN
Defeat

Legs square and apart, chest thrust, a distant look in his eyes gave an air of confidence. His indifference to the applause bordered on arrogance.

His eyes were fixed on the target, four colored, concentric circles one hundred feet away. His mind was on form and function.

"It is time." he said, and the ritual began again. After a few hours delay watching several guards burn on Frederick's pyres Buscillo was ready to put an end to this contest.

The first arrow did not touch the sides, as it was pulled from its place in the quiver. In one arcing motion, he notched it the powerful bow. He inhaled slowly as he extended both his arms fully over his head.

He exhaled even slower as his arms spread, and the bow was lowered into position. The motion fluid despite the amount of strength required. Only the trembling of stringy muscles in his forearm indicated the amount of exertion. Twitching muscles were pushed out of awareness.

Breath held, ready to be released in a final explosion of focused energy. Awareness drawn even further inward. The noise of the crowd and details of his surroundings were pushed out, leaving only a few sensations. Those were methodically eliminated from consciousness; pounding heartbeat, pulsing in his neck, and pain growing in his fingertips were each systematically disconnected.

Now there was only the bow, the target and the one thing that truly mattered. Quickly, and with as much determination as a living thing, a sensation came into his awareness. It offered itself, a gift beyond measure. The more the arrow was properly aligned to the center of the target the stronger the sensation.

A perfect path to the target was found.

The shot, as if on a guide wire, would fly along the path and could only strike the exact center of the target.

The tension behind his fingertips grew. Those sensations too were disconnected. Buscillo's focus intensified and so did the sensation. The whip was ready to crack. The release of the arrow seemed was a graceful and loving experience for the man at the center of that focused energy.

A sting was felt on his wrist as the string returned to its resting place. The arrow glided down the path to kiss the target.

Indistinguishable noises from the crowd broke past the barrier and smacked his consciousness. Attention was adamantly refocused to shut it out. There would be time after his victory to enjoy the applause.

The second shot was notched and ready to fly with the same ritual as the first. Posture and breathing led to the mystical part that he tried not to think about. It was just there and something he always accepted. He was afraid too much thinking would somehow kill his gift and key to so many victories. A wall of trophies was created from this thing of wonder, and he would never give that up because of intellectual curiosity. Let the philosophers seek meaning in such things. He had opponents to defeat.

The second arrow nestled close enough to the first for the feathers to touch. More applause. This time he allowed himself a brief smile of satisfaction before committing himself to the final shot. Inhale and purposeful exhale as the bow came into place once again. A strange wave of energy washed over him. The sensation wavered briefly then vanished. His will was refocused, yet something was terribly wrong. Where was the path?

There was a surge of panic, and a renewed struggle to regain his composure. He cursed himself for allowing the applause to distract him. Another steady exhale helped him disconnect sensory input as he concentrated on filling the void with purpose. Still no path. Perhaps training alone could grab the victory? Dare he make the shot without that confirmation?

Who is the champion! The voice screamed in his head.

"I am!"

He tried to shut off his voice and was furious that he felt the need to do so. How could he have such inner conflict now? What was happening? He considered bringing his arms down and trying again after regaining his composure. No, he could never admit to the crowd that he was not in control. He had to make the shot, and it had to be soon before his arms gave out. His inner voice spoke a line from The Lesson of Raiki. *"...destroy their heart for the Victory."* Then it screamed, "Let go*!*"

He let the arrow fly along with the last bits of mental control. Random images assaulted him as the arrow headed for the target. Pictures of his mother watching him with her arms folded in front of her, a stern look of judgment on her pinched face. There was another image there; a different one than the one that has haunted him for years. He saw an image of his rival's daughter. Before the arrow struck, he knew that she would have her champion.

The King of the Sport is dead. The finality of the loss was shattering.

He hated himself for such a pathetic loss. After so many years as reigning champion, to lose in such a way shocked him. Yet the image of that shining young face smiling up to her father somehow softened the blow.

He knew the final outcome and did not bother to look at the target once the arrow struck home. The reaction of the remaining crowd confirmed his defeat. Before the crowds or his competitor approached, he gathered his things and headed towards the Academe grounds. He stopped briefly to offer a lukewarm handshake to the new champion. Without any introductions, he simply grabbed the man's hand and said, "Nice match." Then he resumed his brisk walk to the housing section.

The sandy-haired man ran after him shouting, "Wait a minute, please."

Buscillo picked up his pace hoping to reach his home before having to meet this man.

"Come on, wait up."

The former Champion slowed to a walk but didn't look back. He struggled to find some composure and mutter to himself, "Okay, God, now what?" Not sure why he said that but hoped in earnest that his thrown together prayer might help.

"Wow, I never expected to meet you!" said the man as he caught up. "Certainly not like this." He matched pace with the ex-champion. "My name is Steyvan, Steyvan Shields. I just want to say what an honor it is to meet you in person." Steyvan stopped and stood with his hand extended.

Buscillo stopped too, shifted his gear to his left side and walked a few steps to accept the handshake. This time he allowed himself to give a firm and friendly one.

"It is a real pleasure, sir." The man continued. "This really means a lot to me."

"Thanks." Buscillo muttered. He allowed his hand to be pumped furiously and struggled for something to say. His face, despite heroic efforts to hide his feelings, flashed between dread and hurt.

"Look." Buscillo finally said. "I am not trying to be rude or anything, but I just don't know what to say in this situation." He paused then added. "Congratulations. Enjoy the moment."

He began towards the shelter of his domicile again but paused to add, "You deserve it." Buscillo never quite conquered the awkward silences that can come at times like these. He did allow himself to make eye contact for the first time as he offered, "That's a nice family you've got." Then headed home again

"Please, wait." said the new champion.

Buscillo muttered. "By My Soul, what now?" He paused for some time and slowly exhaled before turning to face the man squarely. His face was a mottled patchwork of emotions. "Yes?"

"Well, I am not really sure what to say either. I am usually a straightforward kind of guy. Not good with words. I think you can appreciate that." he said with a wink.

Buscillo smiled at that and allowed himself a moment to relax as the man continued to speak. He liked the man. He could not admit that right now, of course. He was bound by some warrior code he invented to maintain stern indignation and an air of pride. If he had his choice, he wouldn't even be talking to the man who denied him his victory. But at least the man was a friendly sort, so Buscillo was willing to indulge the new champion allow him his few words.

"Anyway." Steyvan continued." I wanted to give you something. Like I said, I haven't prepared anything to say. I just felt you should have this." He reached into his pocket. "My father gave this to me when I was a young boy. It was after my first contest. I had lost and felt dejected." He took an item out of his pocket and held it tightly in his hands. "My father took me for a long walk, and I will never forget what told me. He said, 'Son, there are many ways to be a champion.'" Then he gave me this.

The man opened his hand and held it out for Buscillo to see. "I never really understood what my father meant until today. I thought he gave me something, so I would not feel so bad. I keep it with me though whenever I compete. I thought it was for luck, but today you showed me that it means much more. You are right. I have a great family. I would have been a winner even if you had wiped the field with me. I am glad that didn't happen, of course." Steyvan added with a laugh. "I think you understand what I am saying."

"Yeah." Buscillo said softly. "I think I do."

"So, I can't really explain why, but I want you to have this." He held a medallion for Buscillo to see. It was a silver triangle with the image of a lion, an ancient sign of faith and courage, stamped on it. It hung point down from a faded red ribbon.

"I really don't ..." Buscillo slowly exhaled. "I mean ..." He faltered wondering where the words flew off to. "I ... really ...appreciate this." he managed.

Laughter came out of Steyvan. Not that it could be helped. "By my soul, I never knew anyone who had so much trouble saying thank you before. Shoot, what would you do if I offered you a ride home?"

Buscillo was silent. He looked rather helpless until finally his face relaxed into a smile.

Without any ceremony, Steyvan placed the ribbon around Buscillo's neck and said, "In many situations, the best answer is to have no questions."

Buscillo looked at the medallion and considered those rarely spoken words from *The One True Book*.

"See? It looks good on you."

CHAPTER EIGHT
The Victim

Whenever Educator Levons entered Marina's classroom, she always had to suppress a laugh. The man had fuzzy gray hair pushed away from a forehead littered with age spots. His bushy hair was somewhat held in place with monstrously thick glasses. Several strands of hair waved in the air with the frequent jerks of his head as if the Educator were constantly seeing something out of the corner of his eye that he could never quite find.

He always entered carrying books stacked precariously high. The Educator had to bend his head sideways to see. Tuffs of hair poked out as if helping the aging character to feel his way towards his desk. His desk was a clutter of ungraded papers and half-eaten sandwiches. The splintered desktop was also home to a human skull and a bejeweled dagger the Educator explained were from his thespian days.

"Okay, young people. We are going to do something different today." he said as he placed the stack on the desk.

Marina always smiled at his rather quaint use of the term, 'young people'. The stack of books toppled over with another jerk of the head, and Marina tried even harder to stifle her laughter. The other students did not refrain. The frazzled Old Man clapped wildly to get the student's attention.

"Let's get serious now, people. We have a lot to do today. I want you to clear off your desks."

Those words brought the group of freshmen back to business. One of them whined, "Are we having a test, Abba? We can't have a surprise test. That's not fair."

Marina grimaced at how easily the student was intimidated by something academic. This was supposed to be a place of serious scholarship. Many students were here through influence, though, and not merit. Marina reassured herself that she could get a decent education despite such classmates.

"Come on, young people, let's go." The harried man said as he picked up the scattered books. "No, this is not a test. I have an idea for something new. A test now would be okay, right? You have all studied, haven't you?"

He asked in earnest, and again Marina felt disheartened about her educational opportunities. She also felt sympathy for the beleaguered man.

Educator Levons pulled his glasses down and looked out over the class. "Well, I don't see much cooperation here. Come on, people. Clear your desks. We are going to all participate in a group project. Let's combine our creative talents and write a short story today. All of us are doing this together, and I expect every one of you to participate, even you shy ones."

He paused for a moment and then added, "Okay, Marina?"

Marina felt foolish for having warm feelings for this idiot of an Educator. He wanted a response from her, did he? No problem.

Educator Levons turned his back to the group, busy putting things under their desks.

Marina had to be satisfied with glaring at the back of the Educator's head. She was crushed, and her life's energy drained from her. Was he suggesting she was not up to the task? She was an outcast or a misfit or whatever anyone wanted to call her. But no one could question her artistic talent. She considered a prayer to the Angel of Creativity. Perhaps Teya could help? Frederick's religion had nothing to offer a girl struggling with her identity. To whoever might be listening, "Okay, God, now what?"

The Educator said. "First, we need a setting. I want you to suggest places for our story to unfold. Come, come." He clapped again. "I want you to use your imaginations and come up with a place to begin our adventure."

"A Western Ward brothel." a student blurted out.

"God help me." Marina thought. She shifted her glare from the Educator to the wealthy brat. Marina watched in disgust as he exchanged congratulations with his classmates. She rolled her eyes and shifted her attention back to the Educator.

"Okay fine, brothel. Remember a writer never edits until the end." The word 'brothel' went on the board under 'setting'. The Educator continued, "What are some other possibilities?"

The student confirmed the class's ideas would be accepted. Other students felt more comfortable about sharing. A few of the students seemed interested in the project. The frumpy man frantically wrote down ideas as they flew at him.

"A foreign battlefield", "Frederick's palace", "Ancient Helios", and "The execution pyres" were some of the students' inspirations.

Each comment was acknowledged with a positive stroke from the stringy-haired Yudish man they affectionately called Abba, a term for father. For those who never had a father, a man who dedicated his life to teaching youth was held in high regard.

Yudish scholars have a centuries-old tradition of pursuing intellectual understanding. Marina wondered if the tales of that culture were true. Did the Yudish religion really split over a dispute over the spelling of one word in the ancient texts? How far then must Abba feel from that tradition? Tremendous Intellectual prowess was no longer focused on religious mysteries. One of their descendants now struggled to motivate arrogant students.

"Good." The Educator would say with each student's contribution. "Great idea. That's very original. Yes, I like that one. Okay, I have eleven ideas on the list. We need one more, Marina." Abba kept his back to the girl.

No urging from a frustrated Educator was needed. Marina said, "At the bedside of a man dying from Blood Poison."

"Good, Dear One." Marina's inner voice said.

Marina froze. It had been years since Marina last heard that voice. Why had the voice returned?

"Keep going, child. This is the chance you wanted." her voice filled her head.

Marina's classmates waited in silence and stared at her.

The Educator wondered what this pressure would do to his favorite pupil. The suddenly bold young woman continued.

"The man got the disease from his wife. She has already died and left him alone. He lies in bed in a totally white room. White gown, white walls, white sheets contrast the red lesions that cover his body. Because of his medications and pain, he fades in and out of consciousness. It has been days since his last rational thought. One of the caregivers put her child's drawing in the room to add some color. It is the only thing in the room that isn't cold, clinical and a reminder of his imminent death.

"Well done, child." Her voice said.

"Well, those are certainly descriptive words, Marina." the Educator said. "Marina gave us quite an interesting place to start. Where shall we go from here? What about our character now? Let's look at him. What is he like? Where does he come from? These are details we can add to make our story believable."

Abba's tired, gray eyes looked out over the classroom and saw frozen faces. He may regret this decision, but he knew from experience that these students would not be the least bit responsive. He looked at Marina and chose his words carefully, "Okay dear, why don't you tell us a little more about this man?"

"This is it, Precious. Remember to speak with your heart, not with your anger."

Marina in her black clothing and heavy eyeliner said to the lavishly dressed class, "I see I have your attention. But why do you look at me now? Are you interested in me or are you too afraid to talk about things like blood poison, loneliness, or death?" Marina paused to watch some students squirm as her words hit home. Now was her chance. Marina's years of yearning to fit in and the tormenting frustration of never reaching that goal could finally be expressed.

"I think it is because you are afraid. Do you know why I say that? I see your fear every day. That's right. When I walk down the hall and you avoid me, that's fear. When I enter a room and you stop talking, that's fear. When I sit alone in a crowded dining hall, that too is fear. You are all afraid."

More of the students shifted in their seats, but Marina would not let up. She carried this pain for many years. She would gain their understanding or forever drive them away. Either way she could finally stop the struggle to find her identity.

Marina continued, "You hate my appearance? Come on, you really hate my words, don't you? That's why you make me an outsider. You look at my clothes and conclude I do not belong. It has nothing to do with what I wear. I am an outsider because I talk about things that terrify you."

"Careful, Dear One, don't lose them."

"Is it I you are afraid of?" Marina said. "Is it? No, of course not."

She took off her black shirt and sat before them in her bra.

"I am the same as you."

"Is it because I am from a foreign land? By my soul, people. Couldn't you recognize fredricken propaganda? My birthplace has nothing to do with it. Deep down you all know that. It is because I am not afraid of life. Look at you. A few words about death and you all became comatose. No, it is not my clothing or nationality that scares you. I make you look at life in a way your parents should have taught you." It was an unfair attack. They all knew that Marina was the only one who had a both parents still living. Marina regained her composure. She still had the class's attention.

"Do you know what the worst part is?" Marina's voice cracked. "I want to be friends with you. I like you." The tears flowed. Marina added, "I don't like how you treat me, but I like all of you."

For several moments, the only sound was Marina's sobbing. Abba moved to a seat next to her with a tissue ready. Marina looked at the Educator and said, "The only reason I wanted to be a Scribe was to say what I just said. If you don't mind, I would like it if someone else spoke for a while."

Abba gently brushed her cheek and returned to the front. Marina dressed and looked out the window as the class muddled on. It seemed fitting that there was a huge pyre in the palace courtyard. No wonder everyone was too traumatized to talk about death. They see it every day.

Marina shrugged her shoulders when the class gave the story a happy ending but said nothing more.

The students filed out at the end of class while Marina stayed seated. Marina wasn't avoiding the students, which she was sure they would all think. Rather, she stayed to talk with her beloved instructor.

"I am sorry about what happened." Marina said as the Educator cleaned the blackboard.

Abba faced the young woman. Marina scanned his face for any indication of emotion and was relieved to see warmth and respect.

The Educator sat next to Marina again.

Abba took her hands in his and said, "I don't think you are really so sorry. That has been inside you a long time, hasn't it?"

The girl nodded.

"You know, Marina. You have the makings of a good Scribe. The world needs writers who have the soul of an artist and the mind of a scholar. You will be a great Scribe. Not for the way you express, but because you realized there are things that need expressing. Anyone with that awareness is an artist. The medium does not matter. Do not get sidetracked by thinking that it does. The important thing was for you to learn that you have something to say. You understand what I am saying, don't you."

Marina nodded again and continued to look deeply into the man's eyes.

He continued, "I have something I think you should have, Dear." With shaky hands he took a large brooch out of his coat pocket and pinned it on her chest. It was a highly polished triangle with worn lines of an eagle stamped on it.

She studied it as the man explained, "I was your age when one of my tutors gave this to me. You know, I was much like you. I thought my work was pretty important and that everyone else was an idiot."

Marina blushed but kept her silence. She wanted to offer a smile, but it was not in her.

"My work was flawless, at least that's what I thought. One day when some students criticized my paper, I tore into them. The paper was on the positive effects of illusion weed on creativity. Turned out the other students were right, of course. No artist worth anything should destroy his gift by using substances. I was furious, though. My Educator sat me down and cooled me off with these simple words, 'what other people think of me is none of my business.' Then she gave me this pin. You know, Dear One, you accused the students of conforming. If you worry about what they think, you conform too. Keep your independence, rise above the common. Let this medallion guide you to your uniqueness."

"Abba, I don't know what to say."

"Yes, you do, Dear." He whispered as he looked into her eyes.

"Yes, you do." said her voice.

CHAPTER NINE
Loneliness

Val waved her hand a few times to find string hanging from the bulb and pulled. The bulb swung on the end of a long, frayed wire. Shadows now danced around her. All was silent in the attic except the creaking of her rocking chair. In her lap nestled her cup of tea. All was set as she waited for tonight's sunset.

The sun seemed to scorch the land as it reached the horizon. The landscape set ablaze as fingers of light reached upwards to gradually succumb to the chill of the night.

Little in Val's life offered warmth. Her radiance, too, was being consumed by the dark.

Valessa said to herself, "This cannot continue."

Before Val placed her box back in the trunk, she took out her father's medallion. She needed something of his close to her heart right now. With care, she hung the chain around her neck, positioning the triangle stamped with an ox between pert breasts.

"So, what do I do now, Father? Just keep moving, I guess."

With the medallion warming her chest, she steeled herself for another night of work.

CHAPTER TEN
The Whisperer

This was not the first time Drace wandered these streets in a state of intoxication. This time, however, there would be no one waiting at home with hot coffee. There was nothing at home now.

Drace saw an old political poster on a wall. A picture of Frederick standing in front of the New Hope flag. It read, "Change through Hope."

Drace was not interested in any propaganda that tried to sugar coat the wickedness of Frederick's bureaucracy. The evil of Frederick's administration was not the bribery and political manipulations. It was the utter contempt shown to the people that drove such behavior. Bureaucracy was not merely ineffective; it was oppressive and cruel.

Well, Drace thought. I got change all right, not so sure if I have hope.

Was running errands for an eccentric Old Man the change he wanted, though?

What right did a crazy old man have to send Drace anywhere? Sunrise would be here soon. Drace had trouble focusing on his watch. But he had a sense that sunrise would be soon.

It occurred to Drace again that Guards might see him. If a person gave a guard valid reason for being above ground, they were usually let go. Drace had no valid reason.

Drace imagined that encounter. "Well, Sir. I am running an errand for an oddly dressed stranger who explained my destiny. You see, it all started at sunset with my suicide attempt." Drace laughed. Yeah, it would be best to avoid any Guards.

No sleep would come tonight. Most nights Drace lay awake and struggled to hold on to his soul. He wanted to fly off in search of a land where women did not act in such a cruel way by going to the hospital to die.

The crisp night air helped his thinking. Drace followed that thought for a moment. Lower ambient temperature increased the percentage of oxygen to nitrogen, thus giving his brain more nutrients. It was good to figure out some things, even if they didn't make a difference.

Drace stuck to back streets and alleyways. Drace wanted to avoid guards with their harsh demeanor etched in rough, unfinished features.

Guards in Frederick's administration were handpicked. Those without an Academe certificate were assigned a trade job. The position of guard was sought after by many.

Even in Frederick's perfect society, there was still a need for garbage collectors, sewage workers, and sweeps. No one especially wanted to be a sweep, the people who disposed of remains after a pyre. The name came from an archaic profession, chimney sweep. For a worker covered in soot and ash, the term made sense.

Guards were willing to make moral compromises to obtain a job in the palace. Those with the fiercest personalities or roughest looks were sought after. The Guard Captain was given bonuses for each candidate that was accepted as an Apprentice Guard. Frederick himself reviewed each candidate and rejected those he found unsuitable. Drace knew a butcher who was asked to be a candidate. He was a beast of a man yet was rejected for not being intimidating enough.

Guards seemed to possess secret knowledge, which they kept hidden from mere mortals behind austere scowls. No one questioned the legitimacy of their contemptuous looks.

Drace passed by a store window. On display was the same dress he bought for Jen.

Memories crashed into Drace. Images of the dress in Jen's closet tormented him.

More stomach contents were forced out. Drace grabbed his amulet to stop it from swaying. Holding it made him feel better.

Being caught wandering was bad enough. Puking in public would be even more difficult to explain. It was a short stagger to an alley. Drace collapsed against the wall. Broken shipping crates blocked the view from the street.

He was a bit more secluded but felt far from secure. Drace said, "To whatever God can hear me. Please help me."

"Is that really so necessary, 'Drace?"

"By my soul!" Drace said. "Are you following me you fredricken' psycho? I will run your errand, Old Man. Do you have to mess with my head too?" He looked around. "Where are you anyway?"

"Drace." The voice was calm and steady. "I am simply saying your prayer is not necessary. Who will hear it?"

"Look, you told me a bunch of nonsense, gave me some weird medallion, and wanted me to return to where I tried to kill myself. Now you say I shouldn't pray? You are something else, Old Man. You want me to go to the mountain at sunrise? Fine, I'll go. Can't you leave me alone until then?"

"You will go." The voice came from everywhere. "It is your destiny to be there. I am not who you think I am, though. I wanted to introduce myself before we began."

"What? What do you mean?" Drace banged his head as he stood and stumbled into the wall. "Who are you? Where are you?"

"Drace, don't be silly. You can't see me yet." The voice was calm and competent, a teacher patiently explaining a fact to a student.

"Why not? By my Soul, what is going on?"

"Mr. L'Adam, certainly you don't expect me to answer your questions, do you?" The voice chuckled.

Drace shook his head at the implication behind that answer. Clearly Drace was at the mercy of a superior force.

Drace continued to look for the source of the voice and backed towards the street. "Well", Drace said. "Can you at least tell me your name? By God's Light, who are you?" Drace regretted using that epithet. Invoking God might not be a wise move. *Forget about Frederick's edict.* Right now, Drace didn't care if he upset Frederick. He was concerned about upsetting the one speaking.

"Oops, sorry. No offense."

Again, Drace heard warm laughter. Could this person, or whatever, have a sense of humor?

" No offense taken, Ace. I am called many vile things, Father of Fear, Lord of Shadows. You cannot offend me with a trite invocation. Actually, By God's Light is a remarkably interesting way to say it." Direct words were softened with a kind voice. One could even say they were spoken with compassion.

"Light on My Soul!" Drace walked faster towards the street. "This can't be happening. It's the pills. It must be. I am high, that's all. It's all in my mind."

"Why do you say that, Drace?"

"Oh, come on! Are you saying that I am talking to the Whisperer? Give me a break! I must have lost my sanity. There is no such thing, right? It is just mythology. There is no real Whisperer. Those are stories used to make children behave."

"Do people who lost their sanity understand they are insane? No Drace, all of this is real. More real, in fact, than what you believe life to be."

"Well now." said Drace, "that is a clever argument. You know, with a mind like that you could really make something of yourself."

"You have tremendous potential with words as well." said the voice. "That was a sharp comment, especially considering your circumstances. You have a gift, Drace. You already have a notion of that. Sunrise will begin the formal competition. I merely wanted to introduce myself. You will forgive me for making you uncomfortable." It was not a request.

"Uncomfortable? Are you serious? Uncomfortable is not being able to sleep at night. Uncomfortable is spending the night in a hospital dealing with doctors. This is far from uncomfortable, Sir. You talk about some competition that will no doubt destroy everything I understand about life and you call this merely uncomfortable?"

There was a cold gust of wind that carried with it feelings of death. It chilled Drace to the core and reminded him of how vulnerable he was. Surely whatever penance he deserved for the suicide attempt did not demand this.

"I am the Whisperer, Drace."

"How do I know for sure? How do you know my real name? I must be crazy."

"Drace, at sunset you tried to kill yourself. Who do you think gave you that idea?"

"You did? How?"

"Don't be dense. You know how. I whispered it."

I remember hearing, "This cannot continue. That was you? No, that can't be true."

"Drace, you were chosen for a contest. There is a reason why. You will need wisdom to face this challenge. Wisdom that can only come from this God you prayed to. I do not think you have that wisdom. I do not think God will grant it. You will give in to your true nature. This contest will end with you trembling before me. You do not have wisdom, Drace, only your pathetic sarcasm."

"I'm being judged?"

"You can say that. You are on trial, and I am the prosecuting attorney. I will prove, once and for all God is a sham. Wisdom does not connect a person with God. It only shows how far away God really is. What has wisdom given humanity? Nothing but an endless variety of religions. There are churches full of people saying those outside are immoral. And people on the outside feel those who practice a religion are intolerant. This cannot continue. When the final verdict is read, I will be proven right."

Drace's thoughts were disconnected. Memories of a happier time rushed in to help reconnect. Again, Drace saw Jen in her dress. It was an effort to focus on something comforting, but it only managed to overwhelm him.

Memories recent and of years past blended. Physical motion gave his mind somewhere to focus. Lost in the confusion, Drace concentrated on walking down the street.

Drace asked, "Why are you here? What do you want?"

"I just to see my opponent, that's all."

"I don't understand what that means. Are you mad at me or something? What did I ever do to you? This isn't fair!"

"Drace, stop whining. You are not going to get the answers up front. I have my own reasons for entering the contest. I will tell you this. The protection offered by the Light will end and the Time of Shadow will begin. You have an important role to play in this.

"A curse to the Wise Man, a joke to the Fool; when the Four are gone, then Darkness will rule." Drace recalled a children's rhyme. He couldn't remember all the verses, but that one always haunted him

"Ah yes." the voice sounded amused. "It is ironic, don't you think? The fall of humanity foretold by a children's song.

Drace remembered:

Come all children and gather around,

Come hear the tale of Four spirits unbound.
Blood for ink on faded pages,
Teaches all the wisdom of ages.
The One who Whispers unleashes his plan,
His ultimate design the end of Man.
Lies are spread and countries destroyed,
Countless souls lost to the void.
The time of the Four is close at hand,
Darkness unleashed to kill once again.
They meet at sunrise high on a hill,
The Four who are left to resist his will.
A curse to the wise man, a joke to the fool,
If the Four are all gone, then darkness will rule.

There was a long pause Drace found extremely unnerving.

The Voice continued, "This is not a children's game though. It has been a long time coming. The Reign of Frederick is the final stage. To reach the final throes of this prolonged death has required more than you can ever understand. I have looked forward to this competition for millennia, but not with someone so weak. You must stand up for yourself." Even spoken with its usual politeness there was no mistaking the imperial tone.

Drace felt chill as he listened. The words drove home his reality. *The Old Man is right. Something important is happening.* Drace felt like a puppet with his strings pulled by forces he did not understand. *Destiny does not ask our permission.*

Drace ran. There might be an encounter with a Guard, but that was preferable to squaring off with the Lord of Shadows.

A surge of adrenaline helped him run full out towards the edge of town. After a few minutes, he stopped to catch his breath.

He did not see anyone, or anything following him. On the wall was another political poster with a meaningless cliché. This sign said, "Dare to Hope."

"Hope for what?" he cried.

"By the way, Drace." came the voice, "did I mention that you can't hide from me? I thought that might interest you. Well, gotta go now. See you soon."

Drace L'Adam sat on the curb. He buried his face in his hands and said, "Why me?"

A few moments later he heard the reply. "Who else, Drace?"

Drace looked up at the Old Man and saw his warm smile again. It almost put Drace at ease. Almost.

"Drace. It has to be you." The Old Man said as he sat next to him. "You are the most qualified."

Drace looked hard at the Old Man and allowed the words to touch him. He had questions but wasn't sure he wanted the answers. He just listened to the Old Man's soothing voice.

"Drace, there are a lot of people who offer something to humanity. Soldiers, Healers, Artists, *and* even statesmen." he said as he motioned toward the poster behind him.

Drace allowed himself a smile. Humor, Drace knew from experience, had tremendous potential to relieve stress. Yet never had Drace seen it so skillfully applied or with such insightful timing.

The Old Man said, "The ones who are best suited to represent humanity are the ones who can use their gifts to express Truth. All people can communicate to some degree or another. You, however, are a Statesman. You were selected because yours is a soul completely in balance. You are not wholly corrupted by wicked deeds. Neither are you righteous and pure. You are exactly in the middle. It is why you communicate so effectively. You understand humanity's dark nature and can talk about it with compassion."

"That's great." There was a long silence. Then Drace said, "Sorry about that smart-ass crack. It's a pretty old habit, I guess. What's this stuff about being balanced? I know I am not exactly good, but am I really so bad?"

"Most of your life you've tried to be a decent person. Following Frederick's religion did not help you in that regard. You are a good person, though, despite what you have learned. Your suicide attempt brought things into balance. All life is sacred, Drace. Trying to take your life altered your soul. You are now in perfect balance. I think a part of you knew that. For this challenge, you had to put yourself in balance."

"I am not even going to pretend I understood any of that. You think I subconsciously tainted my soul, so I could prepare for a competition I knew nothing about? And you think I'm a Statesman? I'm a smart ass, sir. A charming smartass, perhaps, but still a smartass. You have the wrong guy."

"Really?" Starik said. "How do you explain this? *With you gone, I return to my unfeeling world. I want to leave it all right now, but I do not think of this as merely suicide. I seek far more than just an end to my life.*"

It was a violation of the highest order. Drace's words were meant for only his Jen. This old guy may be some sort of supernatural being. But that, in no way, entitled him to such intimate knowledge.

"You see, Drace. You do have a way with words. In fact, your gift was used so effectively, it almost cost you your life. You were in pain and went to that spot to sort it out. You were ready to believe your own words and came close to killing yourself."

"Listen here, Old Man. You have no right."

"Drace, look at me. You have something to do. Go to the mountain at sunrise. Don't wander around this time. You tend to get into trouble when you wander." Starik winked.

Drace took in his words like a starved animal desperate for food.

"One more thing." Starik said. "Remember that you can't get rid of me, either."

Drace soaked in the kindness found in the eyes of the man that was a curious blend of fussy old codger and innocent youngster. Starik was simultaneously free spirited and clearly set in his ways.

Dawn would appear soon. Drace had to decide what he would do then. How could Drace avoid doing what was asked?

In the larger view of things, what did any of this matter when compared to saying goodbye to the sunshine of his life? Drace took a deep breath and considered that notion. How did being chosen by a kindly Old Man for a simple task measure against the loss of true love and a purpose in life? In the end, it didn't matter. Even after running this errand, Drace would still be alone in this world. These bizarre events proved to be an effective distraction. His Jen was gone, and that was still very real for him.

It became obvious to Drace that sometimes you don't make a decision in life. Rather you realize the decision has been living inside of you waiting for its chance to be born. The world has harsh rules and cruel outcomes. Perhaps Drace's decision was merely a way to distract him from this bitter reality? Drace didn't understand everything in life, but he knew a few things. Life is cruel, and we are all here to suffer.

There might be a place where Angels lived—at least Drace hoped there was—and understanding could be found. If Drace were ever to go there, would he be accepted when this decision was considered? If the serenity he felt was any indication, then the answer was yes.

Drace stood and steeled himself with a deep breath. The Old Man stood with him. Nothing left to say really. Drace embraced the Old Man and walked off leaving the Old Man standing in the circle of light from the streetlamp.

Starik watched Drace disappear into the last bit of the night. He twirled the cane in his finger and whistled as if expecting a train to arrive at the platform or an encounter with an old acquaintance.

"So, everything is finally in motion then." Said the Whisperer.

"It's a nice time for it." Starik said.

For several moments, there was only Starik's whistling and the steady spin of his cane.

"Is that all you have to say? Centuries of masterful planning have reached their culmination, and all you have to say is, 'nice time for it'?' Old Man, I will not be goaded so easily."

Starik said, "That was clever how you reduced the population so drastically."

"Thank you, sir. But that really was a matter of physics."

"Of course. But there was more to it than science. First you weakened their spirit through endless wars. Then you exterminated religion, families, and a sense of community so they had no chance to rebuild their soul. That was truly evil."

"Again, sir, I thank you." The voice sounded genuinely pleased. "Listen well, Starik. If you think what I have done so far is evil, then prepare yourself. There are just the Four to deal with now. You have only seen the beginning of my plans."

Starik still spun his cane. "I allowed it all. You would not be here unless I did. You will be wise to remember that, Whisperer."

"You could have stopped me at any time, Old Man."

"I guide through love. I do not control them."

"Yes, I manipulated them. That is how I will win."

Starik continued spinning and said, "There are still the Angels."

"Ah yes, the Angels. I have big plans for them, too. Remember, Old Man, I do not have to follow any rules. They still do."

"Of course, Whisperer. You have been impressive thus far."

"Thank you." said the Whisperer. "I would not have expected your praise."

"Not praise exactly. Just appreciation for how well you are playing your part."

"I see. You manipulate too, Old Man. What about how you handed out those medallions like candy? Not exactly following the letter of the law, are you?

"I answered their prayers. That is an important distinction. They asked for help, and I gave it. That most certainly is proper."

"They prayed? Okay, I will give you the first one for the Statesman. 'God, please save me' is a prayer. But you bent the rules when you reached out to the other three."

"They prayed too."

"That is a stretch."

"All Four addressed me directly and asked, 'what now.' That is all I need. Just recognition on their part there is something greater than themselves they surrendered to."

"Fine, they have their medallions. They still must figure out how to use them. They may never make it past that step."

"Of course, they will. It is their destiny. We agreed to that."

"Then they must develop their gifts. No doubt you will have your Angels help them."

"The Angels have a destiny to fulfill, too. They will not cheat, merely play their part. What you do is cheating, pure and simple."

"Nothing I do is pure, Old Man, nor simple."

"You go too far, Whisperer. I allow their pain as a way to lead them to me. You force them to live in their pain. You give them empty promises of hope and change, all for your own power and ego. They will find their way to me. They all will. You cannot hold what is not yours."

"We shall see, Old Man. Things are underway. It is all finally happening. You and those Angels better be ready."

Frederick, the Pontix of New Hope, the Whisperer, made his way back to his palace.

"Well. It's a nice time for it."

CHAPTER ELEVEN
Dawn

It was nearly sunrise when Val rode the elevator from the entertainment level and emerged on the surface street. Shadow pulled a curtain of light from the horizon like the opening of one of her performances. Would the new day, she wondered, be as uninspired as her routine?

Tips from four performances tonight would cover a week of expenses. Val considered them performances and not stripping. That distinction helped a bit. She earned her income dancing on stage and not on someone's lap. That was something at least.

Cool wind cleared the stench of the club from her nose. It also loosened her gelled hair. She preferred her hair be loose and flowing. Her clients did not. There were other ways to express her individuality. Tonight, along with feathers and a sheer leotard, she wore her father's medallion.

She loved sunrise. It reminded her of fishing trips with her father. They would wake before dawn and watch the sunrise from their tiny fishing boat.

Thoughts of her father filled her head as she walked past the turn for her street. It was several moments before she realized the oversight. She wondered about Delvid at home alone. Her little angel would not be awake for a few hours. She could fuss over him later. Right now, a glorious sunrise beckoned. She continued towards the mountain.

Val worried about Delvid's future, although her son was not a person the future needed. He would have to find his own way through that. Still, Delvid was her only legacy.

Commanders and politicians can change the course of history. Scholars and Healers can open new avenues of thinking. Artists have their legacy of beauty. What about a dancer? What do they leave behind when the music is over? Her son was all she had.

That was something to consider later. A glorious sunrise lured her towards the summit.

Hiking the gravel path in heals and short skirt was not easy. She considered disrobing down to her leotard. Despite what her career might suggest, she was not so flamboyant. Some modesty was better than none.

At the summit, she took in the view and her heart raced. Even in heels the hike did not require much exertion. Dancing kept her in excellent shape. Her heart now beat faster for a different reason.

She entered a world far from belligerent children, wicked mothers, and horny customers. Her steps were measured and graceful as she walked to her favorite spot. She sat with her back against a small tree and her problems reduced to nothing.

The tree welcomed her as an old friend. Here was peace. She could allow herself to be comfortable for a time.

She saw her home below and again wondered about her son. What would he eat when he awoke?

A cascade of warm colors, as the sun crept over the horizon, soothed her mind. All would be fine.

Red, yellow, and orange light brought life to the plain brown earth. Overhead an eagle made lazy circles searching for a field mouse breakfast.

Such bliss was not to last. At the foot of the trail, Val saw a lone figure set on interrupting her precious meditation.

From her gate, Val knew the intruder was female. There was something oddly familiar about her. Val saw the eagle overhead. In ancient times, an eagle signaled impending crisis. Val thought the warning unnecessary.

CHAPTER TWELVE
Up the Mountain

Marina relied on a set of automatic responses to get through life's mundane tasks. Things like eating, sleeping, or avoiding people received little thought. This allowed her to concentrate on brooding as all good artists should.

This morning was different. She stopped her melancholic musing to focus on an important question. Why she was wandering some nature trail at the crack of dawn?

It started last night. Restless nights were not unusual. Usually, though, a warm bath, or herbal tea, or maybe a few minutes of yoga induced sleep. Troubling questions would not be soothed so easily.

Why had Marina's voice returned after such a long absence? Why did her voice encourage such outrageous behavior? What about that remark about Marina knowing what to say? Marina felt entitled to answers.

Marina was adept at sorting out other people's weirdness and idiocy. Sorting out her own peculiarities was more challenging.

Dreams, whether cursed or welcomed, came eventually to everyone. Most of the images evoked disappeared at dawn or, as in Marina's case, were chased away by getting out of bed in the middle of the night.

What about feelings that lingered long after she awoke? How will she make those go away?

Some people think dreams are nothing more than mental chatter. Marina thought they offered helpful insights. Dreams also showed her a world of fascinating possibilities. A world she longed to visit.

One dream came she could not remember upon waking. Yet her pounding chest and sweat-soaked shirt were signs this dream was not of a world she wanted to visit.

Marina dressed from the pile of yesterday's clothing and headed to the patio. The crisp night air might help her relax. A flickering candle was her only light as she paced. Flying insects continually got too close to the flame and perished.

A glimmer caught her eye. On her chest was the medallion, still where her Educator pinned it. In the candlelight, the medallion looked from another world. Marina knew with disgusting certainty the thing was not from a dream world. Even more distasteful was the certainty it was now a part of her life.

It was beautiful. She examined the details again. The image was an eagle in flight. In its talons were lightning bolts. It was oddly heavy for a brooch. That and its triangular shape suggested it once hung on a chain. Beyond such obvious observations, Marina had no idea of its purpose.

First-year Academe courses only provided enough knowledge to frustrate her. A filigree border suggested it was created during the Middle Era. Whereas the reverse image stamped into it was a much older technique. No doubt the pin soldered on the back was recently added. In the life of this medallion, there were many stages. To say the thing had a life felt appropriate. It seemed warm and alive as Marina held it.

"You are truly beautiful, but what in the world are you?"

"Dear One, you know more than you think."

"Goodness." Marina said. Waves of peace washed over her body. "Where in the world have you been?"

"Thank you, Dear One for calling me Goodness. You used to use an unflattering name. I like this one much better. To answer your question, I have not been anywhere in this world."

"Oh, yeah." Marina said, "I used to say, 'Holy Cow' when you showed up. I never knew you didn't like it. Why didn't you say anything?"

"No need to make a fuss. You were only six years old, after all. But "Goodness' is much better, thank you. So, do you want to tell me why you are on the porch?"

"Hmmm, do you suppose it's because I hear voices? Or maybe I am worried about the public scene I made? That might do it too, don't you think?"

"Marina Scerpio." The voice was strong yet soothing. *"I understand how you feel. Please, look at this with more strength. Being dramatic is not appropriate."*

"Yeah, I know." Marina said, "but you are pretty dramatic yourself. Was it necessary to come to me like that today? Talk about making an entrance. Nice little bit of drama wouldn't you say?"

"Oh Marina, I missed you. I almost forgot how charming you are, in your own special way, of course. It's a pity I can't stay longer."

"What? Oh no, you can't leave. You just got here. Please don't go. I have so many questions. Stay and talk, please?" There was no reply. Marina still felt the peaceful presence.

Marina asked every question that came to her. "Why did you come back? Where is it that you go? Were you always close by? Why did you decide to visit me yesterday? What's this medallion thing? Did you have anything to do with that? Is there a reason it has an eagle?" Marina's voice trailed off as she waited for an answer, any answer.

"I'm sorry, Dear One. I can't do that. You must find those answers for yourself. I've done everything I can for now."

"Damn, I knew you were going to say that. All right, can you at least give me a hint? I mean that's not against the rules is it?"

"You are dramatic, but you are also very endearing. It is wonderful how you wish to know about things that are out of the ordinary. We should embrace the unknown even if it

makes us afraid. The One True Book says that 'to avoid the unknown is to avoid life.'"

"What? Are you kidding me? What in the world does that mean? How do you know about the *One True Book*? First everyone tells me the book doesn't even exist. Now you quote it to me. No riddles, please? Can't you give me a one answer? How about one hint?"

Okay, one hint. Think back, Dear One. What is your first memory of eagles?"

With that Marina sensed the presence leave. She felt like a child again, confused, and uncertain and paced the porch. The rhythm of her feet on the planks soothed her.

As night wore on Marina settled on the porch swing. Hours passed as she got lost in her thoughts. As dawn approached, she did not have any more answers, but the last of Marina's nightmare was gone. Things seemed brighter now. Thinking about the brooch as she held it soothed her. If it weren't such a crazy notion, she would swear the thing glowed on its own. Of course, it was just a trick of the moonlight.

She was grateful for the peace she felt. It often seemed she was not born to know any full measure of peace or security.

"So that's it? You come and then take off like that?" She offered a quick prayer in case anyone might be listening, "Please, help me understand."

Worry and excitement creased her forehead. Marina said, "My first memory of eagles? What does that mean? You come out of the blue, give me a riddle then leave. Fine. I'm not a little girl anymore. I don't need you to solve my problems. My first memory of eagles was on those silver coins we used to use."

She considered that a moment. "No, that's not it, is it?" The idea struck her so suddenly she had to catch her breath. "Oh, that memory. Wow, I hadn't thought of that in years."

Eric Myers

As a child, she used to lie on her back and watch eagles soar overhead. When she lived in the Western Ward, her family would picnic on a mountain that overlooked their capital, Ariasni. After spending time with her family, she would head to her favorite spot. She watched eagles until forced to go home by parents who didn't understand. To her, flying would be the ultimate escape. She yearned to rise above the world. She fantasized soaring off whenever times were stressful. Things that seemed enormous on the ground were tiny and insignificant from up high. That was what she most craved, the ability to make her problems tiny and insignificant.

Peyrvi had a mountain. Marina looked towards it as first rays of sunrise lit it from behind. She often saw eagles flying over that mountain.

"This is crazy!" she thought. Then she shrugged her shoulders and headed out.

CHAPTER THIRTEEN
An Upper Vale Red

Frederick's gift, a statue of the Warrior Angel, stood in the entranceway of Buscillo Lane's home. It was an onyx effigy with a hateful expression, pointed wings, and a severed head in one of its hands. After each victory, Buscillo offered another trophy to the idol. Strained shelves held Buscillo's spoils of war. There would be no sacrifice at the altar tonight.

Avoiding eye contact with the icon, Buscillo headed for his living room. He selected a bottle of Upper Vale Red from his wine rack and then made his way to the couch. He piled himself in its plush cushions like a stack of dirty laundry.

Frederick allocated significant resources to making Buscillo's home a showpiece. Priceless artwork and celebrity status were not the only things given to Buscillo. Above-ground homes were only allotted to those who truly distinguished themselves in New Hope. At the presentation ceremony, Frederick said Buscillo's career was a source of pride for all citizens. Was it so terrible part of his home was marred by an ugly statue? Buscillo knew the answer but pretended it didn't matter.

The home was designed to impress friends and intimidate associates. It was pointless, though, as he had few of either. The wine rack was well-stocked, and his pantry was packed with scarce items, though Buscillo had little time to enjoy such pleasures.

In daylight, a picture window offered a view of a well-tended garden. Buscillo barely recognized the image it reflected this evening. He saw his sun-weathered face pulled tight with emotions desperate for release.

With a stretch, he could reach the lamp. He eliminated the reflection and welcomed the darkness. He sipped from his glass. Very little was understood about the intricacies of wine tasting. This wine was expensive. That was the reason for its purchase and prominent display.

Buscillo wiped his lips with the back of a hand and tasted resin. Another painful reminder had to be blocked. He needed much more time. His grief was like a sore in the mouth that won't go away until left alone and allowed to heal.

Perhaps he could offer a prayer in exchange for a moment of comfort? Who would Buscillo pray to? Frederick's religion was no help. It was as ridiculous as his administration. What was the truth? Would someone hear his prayer? Where does a fallen hero go for comfort? Who offered guidance to a vanquished champion?

He rose from the couch and left his glass on the table next to him. Endorphins would lift his spirits more than alcohol. His heart was not into it, but he put on his running shoes. At least, Buscillo received something in competition today. It was something he wanted to keep for himself and not present to the Warrior Angel. He kept his new medallion on and headed outside.

The crisp air cleared out some of his easier moved thoughts. He needed time to think. For now, a run offered a nice distraction.

It was lighter than he expected. Sunrise would be upon him soon. He had been on his couch for longer than he realized.

Several times a week, his workouts took him through these streets but never at this hour and certainly not carrying this much baggage.

"So, I lost. What's the big deal?" He asked for the thousandth time. Maybe positive affirmations would convince him that his world hadn't shattered and his entire self image wasn't left for dead on the archery range. He tried to make it sound convincing but failed in that, as well.

"It's a nice time for it."

Buscillo stumbled as he searched for the voice. Across the street, on a bench, Buscillo found the source of the raspy greeting. "Good morning." said the man, his voice gruff yet full of life.

"Good morning, sir." Buscillo offered a cursory wave and pressed on. To avoid any other early risers, he veered toward a seldom-used nature trail.

His feet struck the sand like a whisk keeping time in a blues band. He allowed the rhythm to lure him away from Peyrvi.

Ahead he could make out a human form. Buscillo heard, "Leave me alone." The pain in the man's voice snapped Buscillo out of his trance.

Buscillo suppressed his immediate irritation. *Who does this guy think he is*? Buscillo slowed his pace as he got closer.

"You want to have it out right now?" The man said. "Bring it on, my friend. Bring it on."

Buscillo stopped. It wouldn't be fair to tear into the guy without talking first. He said, "Hello there. Name's Buscillo. I was out exercising." He refrained from saying exorcising instead. He could never tell a joke. "Were you expecting someone else, perhaps?"

"Yeah, you might say that." Drace said. They stood in awkward silence.

Details were visible as dawn broke. Drace was no longer a shadow in the middle of the trail.

Buscillo said. "So, are you going to let me pass? Or do I have to pay a toll?" There was no response. He really was bad at telling a joke. "Sorry." Buscillo said. "That was my attempt at humor. You know, ease tension and all of that."

"No, there is no toll." said Drace. "But you do have to answer three riddles before I can let you by." He tried to sound serious, but his quirky smile gave him away.

Buscillo remained silent.

Drace said, "And that was my attempt at humor."

Buscillo walked a bit closer, "Yeah, I know. I was messing with you. It was pretty funny, actually. Buscillo Lane." he said and offered his hand.

Drace exaggerated his Northern Ward accent shamefully and said, "Now, wherah' are my mannahs? I'm Ace L'Adam ... Of the L'Adams of Selvine proper. That's in the Northern Ward, of course. Mighty pleased to meet 'cha." He launched into laughter. "I never could keep a straight face." he said with only a slight drawl this time. He ran his fingers though his hair, and Buscillo smiled since it was messier than before.

"Sorry for the harsh greeting." Drace said. "I'm a bit on edge. It was a rough night."

Buscillo tried to take in what he heard. Was this Drace L'Adam of Selvine? Of the many levels of distinction that existed in this joke of a society, wealth was no longer one many could claim.

Frederick's vision of utopia involved Equitable Redistribution. The program systematically took money from the wealthy and gave it to those lagging in their ability to do for themselves. Under Frederick's administration more and more lagged behind. And more and more wealthy families were destroyed.

The L'Adam family was the last dynasty. Others did not survive being redistributed.

David L'Adam, the patriarch, maintained the family's position through a family tradition, generous bribes. A host of bureaucrats in the new administration were convinced to distribute somewhere else. Drace shortened his name to Ace it would seem. Perhaps it gave him some anonymity?

Drace's family name was distinction enough. No introduction of this man was necessary.

Buscillo looked at his new companion and said, "Of course, I know you."

"A lot of people seem to know me. I usually don't know any of them. Makes me kind of self-centered, I guess." Drace turned and continued up the mountain; didn't give much thought as to why Buscillo walked along with him.

"What I mean," Buscillo continued, "is that I feel I already know you. You are a L'Adam and I know about your career. It is more than that, though. I feel like I know you. Does that make any sense?"

"Actually, you do seem like someone I've met before. Aren't you Buscillo Lane the archery champ?" he asked sarcastically.

"Oh, right."

"You know, nothing personal." Drace said. "But do you wear your medals everywhere? I know you are a sports legend and all, but isn't that a bit much?"

"What do you mean? Oh right, this thing. It's not really a medal. A friend gave this to me. It's kind of a –" They froze. The two men stared in wonder. Each reached out and touched the other's medallion.

"I knew there was something about you." Buscillo said.

Drace ran toward the mountain. "Come on, we're going to be late."

"Late for what?" Buscillo asked.

"How should I know?"

CHAPTER FOURTEEN
Sisterhood

Val squinted to make out more details about the approaching stranger. She worried about wrinkles.

"By my soul," Val said, "it's a damn sweep."

Chimney sweep had not been an occupation for centuries. The term now referred to all menial trades. Artists often wore black as a symbol of being a servant to one's art.

Val thought the black was more drama than symbolism. Her only experience with sweeps was from her job. Art students clustered in covens at the back of the theater. Black clothing made them blend into the shadows where they were less likely to get caught using fake IDs.

Val worked at the club to provide for her son. Waiting on creepy people in dark corners was bad enough. She certainly did not want to run into any sweeps outside the theater.

"Why so afraid, child?" her voice said.

"Now this too?" Val said. "Come on. I came here to get some peace."

"Of course, I want you to be at peace also. Why are you so upset about the girl in black?"

"I don't know. I don't want to be bothered, I guess."

"Dearest, your anxiety is unnecessary. You must face your fear. Meeting her is important."

"I'm not afraid of her." Val said. "I just don't want to talk to anyone right now."

"Well that's good. I'm glad this won't be a problem." Val felt the presence leave.

"You're a real smart ass, you know that." Val said. She stood to pace. Maybe the stranger would see Val and decide to leave? "By my soul, I need a drink."

Sweat formed on Val's upper lip. "So, what's a sweep doing out at this hour? Doesn't she have to return to her coffin at sunrise?" Val chuckled.

"No, we can stay out during the day if we drink human blood. Do you mind? I'm a bit low." Marina approached Val with bared teeth and arms in the air. She stopped a few feet from Val and burst out laughing.

Val looked as if she had lost blood. "I didn't think you could hear me. Please, I'm so sorry."

Marina said, "Yeah, yeah. I get it all the time." Marina stuck her hands in her pockets suddenly unsure what to do with them.

The two women stood staring at each other. Val wanted desperately to say something to break the painful silence. She could think of nothing.

"It's okay. Really." Marina said. "You were sitting in peace and some weirdo with attitude intrudes on your privacy. I would be a little upset as well. It's no big deal. Thanks for the apology though." Marina resisted the urge to sulk home, although it took some effort.

Marina's voice was as smooth as a frozen lake, and Val felt a surprising amount of strength coming from this rather odd-looking girl.

The responsibilities of beauty often weighed on Val's mind. That burden showed in her face which, despite its rounded cheeks and delicate features, often looked austere. Val tried to carry it off as an air of nobility but often feared her pretense at elegance and glamour would be revealed as a fraud. Right now, she felt awkward and out of place.

It was only on a stage Val knew her beauty was genuine. On stage was where she felt real joy. Few men who earned her laugh ever forgot the way the light on her soft brown eyes sparkled and hinted at pleasures far greater. To have made Val laugh, one was rewarded with pleasant dreams of the loveliness of her smile far into their old age. Val was not laughing now.

Marina did not want to tell her new acquaintance she recognized her; to admit she watched Val perform many times, and respected Val as both a dancer and a woman. Permission to such revealing information was rarely granted. Marina also didn't want to expose the fact she could never express herself in the way she saw on stage. It seemed to Marina, though, the dance had become old and tiresome, lately. There were still memories of subtle and exquisite grace that Marina only longed for.

Clad in military boots and a black outfit, the expression of feminine beauty was not especially obvious for anyone who saw Marina move. It was more than Val's movement Mariana admired. Val wore outfits of light flowing material and not the standard g-string the other girls preferred. The way the outfit drew attention to her perfect form by hinting at the beauty of her curves was artistry in itself. It was the gift of feminine beauty Marina longed for.

Val also dismissed the expected gyrations as pointless obscenity. Marina agreed grinding hips offered nothing in the way of aesthetics.

This was what Marina most feared. If she were to attempt any sensuous movements, wouldn't they seem tragically funny? Other dancers were abrasive in their lusty gestures, as the idea was to aggravate drunken men's sexual urges. Better to dress in loose-fitting black than to do something so raunchy. Oh, but to move as Val does. To create images of love and desire brought out by profound beauty. Balance, motion, and form were the essence of romance and fuel for blazing passions. To put so much into one's art, and to risk such consequences. A profound respect for Val was firmly in place, and Val's sarcastic remark could in no way shake that loose.

Val let her shoulders relax with a forceful and dramatic exhale. "Wow. You know. I'm not usually this edgy. This whole night has me freaked. I really didn't mean anything I was saying. Honestly."

"Hey, everything is fine, I totally understand." Marina relaxed visibly, as well. "Believe me, things have been pretty weird for me, too, lately." Marina walked to the woman and plopped down next to her. She reached up her hand to the dancing mom and said. "I'm Marina."

Val hesitated for a moment and waited for Marina's quirky smile to register. It was warm and sincere, and Val decided to place her trust in the honesty she saw in it. She accepted Marina's offered hand and sat.

"Hi, I'm Valessa. It's not any nationality, by the way. That's the first thing people ask me when I say my name. My mom just made it up." The wind at Marina's back blew her wild hair towards her face.

The effect of it framing her face Val found lovely. "You are really beautiful." Val said.

Marina smiled a thank you and said. "I used to come to a place like this with my family when I was a little girl. Last night I had a 'night full of whispers.' That's what I call them. You know, when troubling thoughts won't let you sleep? I thought a visit here might help me sort things out. How about you?"

"Yeah, I used to come here at lot when –" Val stopped talking and stared into the distance.

Marina turned to see what Val might be looking at. Seeing nothing out of the ordinary, Marina looked back and said, "Hey, where'd you go?"

"Look." said Val. "I really have to be leaving."

"Awe, come on. Was it something I said?"

"No, I'm sorry. I'm not trying to be rude or anything. It's just…"

"What is it?" Marina asked, looking again where Val stared. "Did you see something? Should I be nervous?"

"I'm sorry." said Val. "All of this is too weird for me. Strange things last night, and now this morning. I am way past my limit. I guess this is what it's like to go wacko. It's not so terrible, I guess."

"Oh no." said Marina. "You're still pretty far from 'wacko'. Right now, I would say you are a little 'loopy', maybe even slipped all the way to 'scooters'. But you're not 'wacko' yet. You want to tell me what's going on?"

"Not really." Val said.

"Look, I know weird things are happening. It's not only you, okay? Things are strange for me, and I could use someone to talk to."

Val continued to stare at nothing. The strangeness of the moment was a bit more tolerable with Marina now holding her hand. Val remained in her silence as tears formed in the corners of her eyes. Marina gently brushed the hair from Val's face.

Marina wasn't inclined to push and tolerated the awkward silence waiting to see if Val would continue. If Val chose not to respond, then the sharing of personal pain would end right here.

Val sought Marina's eyes and saw the reassurance she needed. Gradually, it became obvious to Val if there were anyone in this world that could listen to her story without judgment, it would be this sarcastic, brash, and dear young woman.

After a deep breath, Val said. "I am not sure how to say this. I am pretty sure my words aren't going to make much sense as I don't understand everything myself." There was another long pause. "I just saw something. Light on my Soul, you're going to think I am way past 'scooters' when I tell you this one."

"No, probably not,' said Marina, "I hate to burst your bubble, but you don't seem all that strange. It really doesn't matter to me if you see things or not."

"Okay." Val said. "When I was a little girl my father gave me a medal. It was a trinket really. It came from my Daddy, so it was special. It had an Ox stamped on it."

Val read Marina's expression searching for signs of dismay or, worse yet, of rejection. Seeing Marina's earnest attention, she continued. "I don't know if an Ox symbolizes anything. It had meaning to me, though. Maybe this sounds silly, but whenever I saw an Ox, I thought of my father. To me it was his way of letting me know he was thinking of me. After he died, things like that became important to me. There are no Oxen here in the desert, of course. Anyway, sometimes my imagination is pretty active. I used to pretend I could still see these Oxen. I wasn't really seeing things, of course. I mean, I knew nothing was really there. It was all pretend. It was a game I played when I was really missing my father.

"Well." Val said. "Just now, I thought I saw an Ox. But I don't think it wasn't my imagination this time. I really saw it. I don't know why. Maybe my father is looking over me? But what if it is a warning?"

"So, that's it?" Marina asked. "Oh Sweetie, I was expecting something much worse. That's not so crazy. Really."

"Well that's not totally it." Val said. "There is one more thing."

"I bet I know what it is. Is this medal a silver triangle that looks really old?"

"Yes." Val reached into her blouse and grasped the medallion. She pulled it out of the bodice, fingers wrapped tightly. She watched Marina remove something from her own shirt and hold it in her palm.

They both slowly opened their hands.

Marina said, "I bet there is one other thing that you were afraid to tell me. You sometimes hear voices, don't you?"

The tears in Val's eyes answered Marina's question. Marina leaned closer. Fearing her words would stick in her voice Marina gave Val a gentle hug.

The first peaceful moment either felt in a long time was interrupted by the sounds of people approaching.

CHAPTER FIFTEEN
Brotherhood

"We made it. Just in time." said Drace; breathing heavily. He paused at the crest of the mountain with his hands on his knees. Brilliant orange poured forth onto the horizon like yolk from a cracked egg. The sun was technically rising, but it was clearly past that exact moment considered the break of day. Drace said, "Well, at least I think we are on time."

"On time for what?" said Buscillo. He passed Drace on the way up and stood with arms crossed. "Why we are here?"

"Oh, didn't I tell you? Drace said. "I made a bet I could find an idiot and make him follow me to the top of this mountain." Drace had recovered some of his breath and walked a bit closer to Buscillo. He noticed two women sitting near his tree.

"They aren't supposed to be here, are they?" Drace nodded his head, indicating the women who now headed towards them.

CHAPTER SIXTEEN
The Four

"Now what?" Val said. The women's intimate moment was interrupted by macho banter. Val could almost make out their conversation from where she stood. To be interrupted was one thing. That the interruption came from men infuriated her.

Marina recognized the men. Why would they be here now? She wondered. *It was the champion Buscillo and that smartass Ace. If the guy has so much money, why did he always look so unkempt?* It was clear to Marina Drace was infrequently bothered by the hassle of grooming his hair.

"Nice to see you again, Ace." Marina's sarcasm turned his name into a taunt. Marina ignored their puzzled looks and thrust out her hand. "Strange to meet both of you here."

Both men accepted her handshake. Val shook their hands, as well and said. "Marina and I were in the middle of a personal conversation. Now, of course you gentlemen have every right to be here, but maybe you could keep it down a bit?"

"Well excuse me." Buscillo said. "We didn't realize this place was sold. When did you ladies buy it?" He continued to grip Val's hand. The woman had shocking red hair; utterly distracting in the way it flowed in a cascade of locks down her shoulders. Were he not a proper man he might allow his eyes to follow that hair towards her chest. He forced himself to stay focused on her soft brown eyes. He knew of her, of course. This was a woman whose beauty he had admired on stage, always from afar. And now she was right here offering her hand.

"Oh, very nice, Buscillo." Marina said. She leveled a gaze that could slice steel towards Buscillo, who dropped Val's hand and locked eyes with Marina. His dusty brown eyes did not have as chilling an effect as Marina's icy blue, but a building animosity could be read in them.

Buscillo was familiar with raw power offered as a challenge, and he bragged often that he had been with many attractive women. This was the first time, however, the attractive woman presented the challenge.

"What my friend here is trying to say." said Drace, "is we are sorry to have interrupted your private conversation."

Buscillo now fixed his eyes on Drace. "No, not really." he said.

Drace ignored him. "Nice to see you, ladies. Buscillo and I apologize for disturbing you." Drace's smile was a bit forced, but there was no mistaking the sincerity in his twinkling blue eyes. "This is interesting. We all know each other but have never met. We are meeting people we already know. Funny, huh?"

Drace's ability to brush off Marina's sarcasm indicated a long familiarity with that sort of expression as well as a level of confidence that betrayed his boyish demeanor.

It was a lot for Marina to take in. Of the three, Marina knew Drace the best, if one can call it that. They shared a stage several times at Academe award dinners. There was always someone who needed to be recognized by way of catered food. Drace, a distinguished Merchant Academe graduate, was always invited.

Academes long since adopted the practice of combining events to recognize each other. This significantly reduced the number of Frederick's speeches one endured each semester.

Marina hated these events. In every speech Frederick always mentioned her. Drace was often singled out too, come to think of it. At the requisite photo ops, Frederick would whisper to both, "All of New Hope is watching you."

Neither Drace nor Marina understood what Frederick meant. Each had some notoriety. New Hope was indeed watching them, but why would that matter to Frederick?

"So why are we all here" Marina asked.

Drace said. "As near as I can guess, Buscillo and I are supposed to be here at this time. To be honest, we are not sure why. Buscillo and I were discussing the possibilities. If we sounded a bit too spirited, it was only because this meeting is important. We thought we would be the only ones up here. We are sorry if we were rude."

"Yeah, okay." said Marina. "but we still have a right to be here." She stuck out her lower lip. She gave Buscillo another frosty glare. She finally allowed her stare to drop and looked to Val, "What do you think?"

Drace learned much in that intercepted look about the nature of bonding and trust. He allowed himself a smile, a genuine one this time. Marina, catching the smile out of the corner of her eye sensed he had not smiled very much lately.

Val did not reply to Marina's question. Rather she stood there with a deeply creased brow, eyes like dams ready to burst.

Marina walked over to Valessa and put her hand on Val's trembling shoulder. "Val, Honey, are you okay?"

"By my soul." Val said, more as a prayer than exclamation. Drace remembered what the Old Man had said about his own soul. The expression had much more meaning for him now.

Marina looked into Val's distant eyes. "What's the matter, Sweetie? You're starting to worry me. Do you see that thing again?"

Val trembled and tears flowed freely. "By my soul."

Marina wrapped her arms around her friend, but the support did not help. Val collapsed and covered her face with her hands. Marina knelt on the ground along with her.

Val continued to wail. "By my soul. By my soul."

"What's happening?" Buscillo asked.

"I was kind of hoping you knew." Marina said.

"I think I might know." said Drace. He stood with one arm across his chest. With the other arm, he held his index finger to his lips. He didn't reply for several moments.

"Well, please enlighten us." Marina said. "and try not to sound so cheesy this time."

Drace feigned a hurt look, and then like quicksilver he winked and flashed a disarming smile. "Actually..." He hesitated in such a way that distracted them and inflamed their curiosity. "It is pretty simple. Where did you get your brooch?"

"I don't understand...." Marina said. Her words faltered as she looked at the men. "Oh, Goodness."

Marina held the sobbing woman closer to her chest and caressed her hair.

"Val is crying over these medals?" Buscillo asked.

Still cradled by Marina, Val looked up at the men. Another wave of tears struck.

"We all have medallions," said Buscillo, "What's the big deal?"

"Well, here's an interesting idea, you think maybe these medallions are the reason the Four of us are here?" Drace said. He walked to the women and asked Marina, "May I please?"

Marina gave Drace a puzzled look but adjusted her position so Drace could sit facing the women. He too offered support to Val by placing his hand on her shoulder. For several moments, the three sat while Buscillo shuffled about awkwardly.

Drace looked up at Buscillo. He did not have to look up much and was reminded how short Buscillo was. Buscillo had his back to the rising sun, and Drace squinted to see his face.

114

Drace, his patience now run out, grabbed Buscillo by a wrist and pulled. The women adjusted to form a circle.

Buscillo asked, "What do you mean, 'the Four of us?' I'm not a part of this."

Val looked at him. "Then why do you have a medallion?"

Val's eyes were puffy and red. Still, Buscillo found it easy, comforting even, to look into them. "Who knows? It is probably a coincidence, right?"

Buscillo scanned each face looking for a response. They all allowed the inevitable conclusion to sink in.

Buscillo stated again, only less convincingly. "This has got to be a coincidence, right?"

"Now there is an interesting idea." said Marina. She winked at Drace. He was not the only one who could wield sarcasm. His eyes, Marina noticed, were as blue as her own. A maelstrom of emotions swirled within.

Drace said, "Nice. I was beginning to think you didn't have a sense of humor." Marina ignored him, but he detected a hint of a smile.

Buscillo was uncomfortable watching the two. It seemed a private moment meant only for them.

"Drace," he said, "the only reason I was on that nature trail was I saw some Old Man in town and changed course to avoid running into more strangers." He hoped this explanation would validate his coincidence argument.

Buscillo also noticed how similar Drace's and Marina's eyes were. Both capable of expressing subtleties that enhanced the meaning of their words. He made a note to watch their eyes carefully.

"But you're here talking to us." said Marina, "Are you saying that we're not strange? We all have these medallions. That doesn't seem strange to you?" Her eyes matched her playful tone of voice. Buscillo was surprised how quickly those eyes could change.

"What Old Man?" asked Drace.

"I don't know." Buscillo said. "Never saw him before. Nicely dressed and had an odd voice.

"It's a nice time for it." said Drace.

"Yeah, that's what he said. How'd you know that?" Buscillo asked. "How old is he? Do you know him?"

"Sort of." Drace said. "He said the same thing to me. He was the one who sent me up here."

"Why does he want you here? Do you think he was trying to get me to come here too?" A line from a nursery rhyme came to Buscillo. *The time of the Four is close at hand, Darkness unleashed to kill once again. They meet at sunrise high on a hill, The Four who are left to resist his will*" Buscillo was not sure where he heard that, or why it came to him now. It seemed to fit.

Before Drace answered Val said, "Look Buscillo, you are obviously a part of this, whatever this is. I really need some answers. Stop going on about coincidence and funny old men. Let's all figure this out."

"Actually, the Old Man is important." said Drace. "He gave me this medallion and told me to be here at sunrise. I agree this is all pretty crazy, but I know something important is happening here."

Their shadows shortened as the sun pried its way into their circle. Droplets of sweat formed on Drace's face. "In any case, I am going to do what that Old Man asks." He refrained from adding to the craziness by mentioning the Whisperer wanted him here as well.

"I understand what you mean." said Marina. "It seems obvious something big is going on here. Tears formed in her eyes.

116

She steeled herself and went on. "To be honest, I think something has been going on with me for a while now. I've been hearing voices and getting advice from imaginary friends. Plus, I can't seem to control my emotions. I feel totally out of control, you know?"

They nodded. Val squeezed Marina's hand and said. "Yeah, I feel out of control too."

Drace said, "I get where you are coming from, Buscillo. You want to believe that this is coincidence to protect your sanity, or your pride."

Buscillo stiffened at that remark but remained silent.

"We must surrender to the obvious." Drace said. "We are all here with medallions, and we are all experiencing some crazy stuff. It's okay to admit you're afraid. We are all afraid. I don't understand this. I don't understand anything in my life, really. I have no idea what it all means. And I can't even begin to understand why the four of us are in one place. I would really like to know what this is about."

"Light on our Souls, yes!" said Val. "I barely know you all. I mean, I know about you. How could I not? But we aren't very well acquainted."

"Hang on guys, I just thought of something." said Drace. "I understand that you want to do introductions, but –"

"Cut the diplomatic crap and say what you want." Marina said.

"Well –"

"But tell us about yourself first." She winked at Drace.

"Sure." Drace winked back. "You know my name. That's not important. I turned thirty years old yesterday. Instead of celebrating, I tried to kill myself. Seems pathetic when I say it out loud, but I have not told you the worst part. My truest love died a few nights ago. She was pregnant with my child. I didn't feel like celebrating my life. I didn't even feel like having a life."

He sat still, and they all allowed his private moment.

"Okay then," Drace said, "let me tell you what I figured out. Marina, your medallion has an eagle."

"Sure, more weird stuff." said Marina.

Come on. I think this is important."

"Yes, it has an eagle. So?"

Drace ignored her question and asked Val. "What's is on your ... Oops sorry. Would you like to share something about yourself?"

"I'm Valessa Nemah. Val for short. I'm a dancer and a mom. I am also lost and usually confused. You probably know all the rumors about me. None of them are true. I want you to know that. The truth is, I never defended myself because I was afraid of Frederick. I refused his advances, so he destroyed my life. We all met him. No one can deny the man is wicked. You asked what is on my medallion. It's an ox."

"Of course. It all makes sense."

"Really?" asked Buscillo.

"Yes, really. Don't you see it? Look at our medallions. You have a lion. I have a man. And the women have an eagle and an ox."

Drace faced three blank stares.

"Oh, come on. Think about it."

"Okay, I get it. Marina said. "These are the symbols for the Four Angels. The Statesman, the Warrior, the Healer, and the Artist. Where are you going with this?"

"Okay, if you guys had experiences that were anything like mine, there were probably many times when you hated your life. A lot of odd things happening, most of them challenging or unpleasant. None of it making much sense. Life was completely random and chaotic sometimes, right? But I bet each of you believed these weird events were not mere chance. They have some purpose. We are here intentionally.

They nodded.

Marina said, "Still not following you though."

Buscillo said. "I'm not sure where you are going with this either. We all had interesting lives, and you think the angels had something to do with it? That is not great news, is it? From what I can tell, being connected to the angels would not be a good thing."

"I agree with Buscillo." Val said. "The angels are not very good. I am not sure I want to go where they lead."

"Maybe the angels are not that bad." said Marina.

"They have to be bad." said Val. "Frederick pushes them down our throat every chance he gets. Nothing from that man is good."

They all looked down to the palace and saw the last of the pyre still smoldering. Already the sweeps were out to deal with the bodies.

"That place is ground zero for evil." said Val.

Drace said, "I agree, but there is something in that palace that doesn't feel evil. Something at the core. Maybe there is also something good about the angels."

Buscillo said, "I still don't know what they would want with any of us."

"I think we have to figure that one out ourselves." Marina said.

"Yes, it is some sort of riddle." said Drace. "So, what happens if we get it right?"

"More important. What happens if we get it wrong?" asked Val. "Something big is going on here. Are we up for this?"

"I am", said Buscillo.

"Me too." said Marina.

"Yeah, I got nothing else going on. I am, too." said Drace.

Destiny of Angels

CHAPTER SEVENTEEN
Letting Go

That's it. Buscillo thought. *I am.* It was so obvious. Buscillo brought his medallion before him and cleared his mind. He intensified his concentration as the others whispered questions to each other. Buscillo knew they were clever enough to figure it out and continued to focus his will.

All sensations were pushed from his mind, the sun on his neck, the warm breeze, the dryness in his throat. Just as he would with a bullseye, the medallion became his target.

Insight struck Buscillo, as quickly as a released arrow might strike its target.

"We need to put the medallions together." Buscillo said.

"Of course." said Drace. "That must be why they are shaped as triangles. They link together. Let's do it. I don't think there's any danger."

"You don't think?" asked Val. "But do you know? Do any of us know?"

No one answered.

As the Four brought their medallions together they glowed. The light emitted quickly grew in intensity.

Hearts raced as they brought their medallions closer. Each knew they were at the threshold of the unknown. Bringing together their medallions was effortless. The power such an act might invoke was unimaginable. What would happen when the power of all four medallions was gathered in one place? By that simple act would they cross the threshold?

They all thought of the simple ways in which one's destiny unfolds. From such a mundane act, was it possible to reach the extraordinary? Would reading a book bring wisdom? Did manners enhance a relationship? Could a few words spoken in prayer have reached God?

There was a common element in the relationship people had with the Divine. Some felt God was a loving paternal figure. Others feared a mighty lord who rules their destiny.

There were concepts of God as more a single cosmic force that united all. Or perhaps God was the master craftsman who engineered the universe. The common element is mortal humanity was never able to comprehend why events unfold as they do.

Why did some people seem to flourish under the watchful eyes of God while others struggled under the same eyes? Why does so much of one's life seem not to be guided by any force at all, but instead seemed merely left to blind chance?

Would bringing their medallions together be a meaningless act, or a conduit to the Divine?

Buscillo's heartbeat slammed away in his neck and threatened to choke him. Drace's throat was dry and painful. Val forced back tears. Marina's hands trembled unmercifully. No one resisted the process and brought their medallions together. It was time to see what their destinies had in store for them.

A click was heard as the pieces fit and a burst of brilliant white light radiated from the medallions and engulfed them. They withdrew their medallions, but the orb of light remained.

In the intense luminosity their bodies were barely visible. There was only washed-out color and blurred edges where arms and legs once were.

Light overcame their bodies in waves with no discernible pattern. Sometimes short staccato bursts riddled their bodies, and other times huge rushes of energy crested and then crashed into them.

The light wanted something. They were being drawn to something difficult to comprehend. How could they interact? What did they have to offer?

Who am I now?

Drace reached inward for something to present to the light. All he had to give was himself. Who was he? What was his true self? Drace had impressions of being an outcast, unappreciated, and alone after a tragic loss. Those were pathetic and, as Drace could now see, hugely inadequate notions. He thought of himself as wealthy, educated, and a merchant. Those too were sadly insufficient.

Drace had vague recollections of possessing charm, intellect, and insight. Now he saw, or rather felt, how those were definitions created by ego and not a true representation of self.

Slowly, but with disheartening consistency, all his identifying concepts faded into nothingness. Some things Drace identified with were happily released. Letting go of his discomfort around immigrants was rather refreshing. Other views were not so easy to surrender. Belief he was a righteous man was terrifying to see slip away.

Remaining perceptions of self were searched for methodically. Every aspect of his being was explored. Finding nothing else, the process ended. It felt as if the bathtub plug was pulled or the last reel of a movie came to an end. There was only Drace and the light.

Drace wished so much to reach out to his friends. He felt a strong yearning to know and understand them.

That desire had not vanished. It was who he truly was. He sought closeness with others. His true nature was one who loved and accepted people and sought connection.

Memories of Jen came to him. No wave of grief washed over him this time. Instead he felt a rush of love from the others

Drace felt warmth and gentleness. Distinct feelings came from each of his friends. Sensations of laying next to a gentle stream on a cool day came from Marina. She too had released a host of identities. She felt pure and clear. Deep wounds were purged, and this was her true essence.

Buscillo also released inaccurate concepts of self. What remained was a strength that was at once invigorating and reassuring. At Buscillo's core was power and not ego. Confidence and not arrogance.

Val too underwent a profound transformation. Drace sensed Val's dignity and pride. Her illusion of being a victim of injustice was replaced with a vision of loveliness. Fear no longer distorted Val's understanding of true beauty.

In each of them illusions, fears, and false identities were replaced by love.

CHAPTER EIGHTEEN
A White Horse

A crisp breeze carried with it an earthy pungency, indicating farms with manure-rich soil. Cultivated fields, scattered across the valley below, were separated by uneven walls of stone. A river wound its way through clusters of trees.

In the distance were a few houses, easily recognized by their reflective windows and active chimneys.

"We're in a totally different place." Buscillo said.

No one argued the obvious conclusion.

They still held hands as each struggled with one more development in this series of bizarre occurrences.

"Holy Cow." said Marina. "What in the world is that?" She pointed, with a shaking finger, to a man on a horse. If they had any thought that this transformation led towards a benevolent outcome, this sight put that notion in serious doubt.

A hulking frame sat atop a white horse. A dark, hooded robe hid his face.

The woman he escorted - and she was undeniably female - was the truly remarkable one. Her head was even with the horse's. That would make her a bit under seven feet tall Drace thought.

There was power in her, a magnificent gait that at once showed grace and strength. Her stride was purposeful yet fluid. The woman looked solid, a walking statue, and her focus was on Buscillo. The pair stopped only a few feet away. A massive sword, hanging from the saddle, glinted in the sunlight.

"I can't believe this." Buscillo said. Inside him a storm brewed. Lightning flashed in his eyes.

A dark brown tunic hung from her broad shoulders and barely reached her muscular thighs. A leather belt was cinched at her waist and crisscrossed her chest. Images of alluring femininity combined with raw power. Buscillo found her effect on him both enticing and intimidating.

She never removed her eyes from Buscillo, as she took the massive sword from the saddle. He barely adjusted to his new surroundings, but now had to prepare for this far more threatening development.

She said, "Are you worthy to wear that?" pointing to Buscillo's medallion with the cruel-looking blade.

Her voice was smooth like cat's fur. *Do not rub this one the wrong way.*

The others stared at the woman and waited for Buscillo to respond. Buscillo's features were fixed and neutral, the look of a warrior. Drace was impressed with the courage it took to remain seated while facing such power.

She said, "Come on, you silly little creature. Get off your butt and face me." This time, her voice was brassy and as soothing as a crying baby.

Buscillo said, "Hello to you, too."

He held her stare as he rose to his feet. Not a convenient thing to do. At full height he squared off with her breasts. He looked up into her intense blue eyes and cursed inwardly he had to do so.

He drew himself to full height by extending his neck and breathing deeply. She stared at him with a look that showed both contemptuous anger and mischievous curiosity. She looked at him as if he were a bug that landed on her arm.

"Little Man, you must think very highly of yourself to remain seated in my presence. Why are you so special? Is it because you wear *this*?" She flicked his medallion with her finger and forced Buscillo to take a step back. Such power was undeniable. Drace had renewed respect for his friend to face such force with no sign of concern.

There was no denying the challenge in her tone. Buscillo fought conflicting urges. He was facing a superior, and likely, supernatural force. Yet, the idea of backing down from a challenge was not one he wished to consider.

The woman gave him no time for such considerations as she turned swiftly and walked towards the Horseman. Buscillo grabbed his medallion to protect it from being struck again. As the warrior woman walked away, the medallion glowed once again.

Buscillo started towards the Horseman. Drace moved his legs and allowed him to pass and then extended a hand towards Buscillo, "Good Luck."

Buscillo did not acknowledge for several steps then stopped. He turned his head slightly and said, "Does anyone have any idea at all what is happening?"

He stood for several moments with his head down and struggled with an army of questions. What, if anything, did the transition to this place teach him? Was there a point to any of this? What was the proper way to respond to this challenge? Would it matter at all if he ever won another competition?

After some time, he offered one more look in the direction the tremendous woman traveled and then returned to the others.

Buscillo spoke in measured tones, "I have to go, don't I?" For a moment, he considered if anyone at home would miss him.

They all stared at him. The look on each face validated every feeling he was experiencing. Marina's face showed a puzzled sort of worry. Val mirrored his terror in wide, tear-filled eyes while Drace reflected tremendous curiosity. No one spoke. Buscillo looked slowly at each of them in turn.

It was not until he saw his medallion fade, he looked south in the direction the woman walked. She disappeared over the ridge without a backward glance. He expected that. She would not wait for him to respond. Once the challenge was offered, she simply moved on. Buscillo had not, however, expected his medallion would nudge him along.

"Well." Buscillo said, "if I go, I may lose. But if I stay here, I've already lost."

He gave Drace a powerful handshake.

All concern left Buscillo's face. The inner storm subsided. Now the glow of the medallion danced in his eyes. He looked content; peaceful even. It was unnerving to see how the medallion took away concern for one's own safety. Buscillo had the look of a man who accepted his destiny.

CHAPTER NINETEEN
A Red Horse

Fear hung in the air and commanded silence. Marina attempted conversation first. It was awkward, but better than the oppressive quiet.

Marina asked Drace, "Jen. That was your girlfriend's name, right?"

"Yes." He considered her question for a moment and was surprised the past tense reference did not hurt. "Why?"

"Her death was not your fault."

Drace sat in silence for some time.

"Forgive me. I didn't mean to hurt you."

"No. It's okay, really. Wounds heal. I lost her, but somehow it feels okay."

That was all they had time for. New visitors approached.

Three times in his life Drace felt overwhelming fear. He had his share of common anxieties, of course. With grace and dignity, he talked in front of a group, faced teasing bullies, asked a girl out. Three times he faced absolute terror.

Once he nearly drowned. The time he was mugged was certainly on the list. Seeing the resigned look on Jen's doctor chilled him to his core.

Often brief shocks of something perceived as terror quickly faded into persistent discomfort. Terror was not going to fade today. It was real, powerful, and walking towards him.

The second Horseman, a nightmare encased in red armor, approached, and Drace knelt before him. He wasn't sure where that impulse came from. It seemed appropriate. With head bowed, he didn't notice the small boy skipping alongside.

Drace was only aware this armored man might kill him, even as he knelt. He was not sure if he cared at this point. He was more than a little surprised that, despite his fear, he could go along with what was happening. Even so, his mind had trouble comprehending the unquestionable power of the entity who faced him.

Pungent, foul air penetrated his lungs. It assaulted him with a stench like that of rotting flesh in a sewer. He wanted to face this challenge as a man who respected life yet was willing to surrender to it to preserve his dignity. Drace took a shaky breath then turned his head upwards.

As he knelt with head held high, he saw the child.

The contrast of youthful innocence next to this embodiment of death struck Drace as profoundly ironic, almost comical. Why would these two possibly be together? He would never presume to know the thoughts of the divine, but he assumed whatever supernatural force who paired these two had a sense of humor.

Drace looked all around and, again, was aware of the beauty of this place. He was pleased to notice, too, his presence had come again. It did not come as a Voice in his head, though. This time Drace felt it penetrate his heart. It reached deep inside to find life's beat. That rhythm was found, and a song played inside Drace. The melody revitalized his failing spirit. The little boy sang along.

The women to either side offered soft words of comfort and reassurance. "Go ahead, Drace." one of them said.

Drace turned to his friends and smiled.

He said, "I will do my best." He thought of Jen and the tears shed by her bedside. Nothing could be as bad as what he already survived.

He stood and faced the Horseman. This might be an excellent time for bold words. Finding none, he looked again at the women. If Drace survived this encounter, he would look back on the sheer idiocy of turning his back on incomprehensible power.

He felt awkward, even ashamed, as he looked at the women. His song soothed him. They were all bonded now. It was a linkage that had nothing to do with looks, status, or with any of the superficial reasons they sought companionship before. They all had experiences of meaningless encounters, and shared memories of the same mistakes made.

Here was an honest offering of a genuinely human relationship he never allowed himself. He was not even sure it existed outside of his late-night imaginings. That mutual acceptance comforted the darkest corner of him, and he fully appreciated its meaning. He was, for the first time in his life, with people who honestly cared what happened to him.

"When I think of all the times I used these words inappropriately I am humbled. I say to you, Val and Marina, with my most sincere heart, I love you."

He reached his hands towards the women, pulled them to their feet and embraced each in turn. Thus, recharged Drace turned to the Horseman and the little boy.

Drace thought briefly he might be living his final moments. He wondered, in a detached way, if he left any mark. What was his legacy? His heart song suggested here was his chance to make that mark. He was not merely born into a world of fading sunsets and passing relationships. In this place, he could find a way to show triumph over the futility of life. With eyes fixed on the horizon he said, "Lead on if you please."

"Okay, great!" said the child. "Follow me."

Drace was mesmerized by the boy's energy and enthusiasm and eagerly followed. The Little One's motions were fast and endless, yet graceful and fluid. A spirit unleashed.

Repeatedly, the child turned around mid-stride to question Drace, as if walking while spinning was commonplace. Some queries were silly and appropriately childlike, while others were shockingly direct.

Drace followed along, grateful for the distraction.

"So, do you know where you are? What do you think? It's really pretty here, isn't it? I bet you never expected to be here, did you? Do you know your medallion is special? Did the Old Man tell you what it was for? He probably didn't, did he? Do you know what it means to have a medallion? Why are you so quiet? You know, you are allowed to talk, don't you?"

Drace could not answer a single question.

The child continued, "What about this guy on the Horse? Pretty scary, huh? Did you ever see anything so awful before? I bet you didn't. He is pure evil. Did you know that? One hundred percent Dark. I'm not kidding. This thing can suck out your life energy by touching you. How's that for horrible?"

The endless stream of informative dialog continued as the three of them proceeded north.

CHAPTER TWENTY
A Black Horse

Val and Marina stood close. The illusion of confidence maintained by fighting their urge to release tears. Other signs, holding hands with a fierce grip and darting eyes, revealed a deeper truth.

Like the first two, the third Horseman arrived quietly. Marina saw him first and froze. Val understood from Marina's reaction and from the strange presence she felt the next rider appeared.

It was as if a cloud passed over the sun. Indeed, as Val faced the Horseman, the only detail she was aware of was how utterly dark the man and horse appeared.

A black cloak completely covered the rider and a large part of the horse. Nothing on man or beast reflected light. The creatures, their clothing, and especially their eyes were black and lifeless.

Horse and rider approached like a jackal circling carrion. The horseman regarded Val with utter contempt and malice. She had no doubt she was the prey he craved.

Marina squeezed Val's hand even tighter. She said, "By my soul, is he here for you?"

Val's skin was pale, as her heart hoarded blood. She kissed Marina on the cheek. She felt Marina's hands prevent her from wobbling. Val, steady again, waited for the rider to approach. Despite her best efforts, Val could not face the rider with open eyes.

Something grabbed her free hand and Val let out a rock-splitting scream. She hoped it was Marina who took her other hand.

Through squinted eyes, she saw the horse was startled by her outburst. If the horse and black rider were still several paces away, who grabbed her hand? She shut her eyes again. If God did exist, wouldn't He allow her to run far from all of this?

Marina could run away with her. They could make it together. They would run until no one could find them and, somehow, they could make it. This thought Val clung to as she opened her eyes.

"By my soul!" As Val's scream left her so too did her strength. Her knees became useless, and her body fell limp. Marina managed to break her fall.

Val recognized the taste of grass as she lay face down at the feet of whomever took her hand.

Where could Val possibly find the strength to get herself out of this mess? She couldn't even stand. How could she face this terror in such a state?

A hand gently brushed her hair. Please let it be Marina's. There were many sobs before Val opened her eyes.

Her hair was stroked again. Val peeked though puffy eyes. Marina knelt next to her holding her hand.

She looked upon Marina's face. There was love and compassion there. That became the source of strength. It became her reason to keep going. Sometimes the best answer is to have no questions.

"Marina."

"You're okay, Sweetie." Marina said. "You can do this."

Val considered running again. It was not pride or character that stopped her. It was the sobering reality she had no place to go. Where could she go in a world where such creatures existed?

"This can't be happening." Val said as she stood.

"You can do this, Dearest." A man spoke. His voice was strong yet melodious. Val smiled at the peaceful tone. What a relief to hear something so gentle. No one with such a voice could hurt her. Slowly, Val opened her eyes, still ready to run, but willing to chance this encounter.

A tall man stood before her. His clothing made Val's smile even broader. He wore dirty overalls and mud-caked work boots. There was an old kerchief, slightly discolored from years of sweat, tied around his neck. Was this who she wanted to run away from? He was an ordinary farmer. He was rugged looking, but his demeanor was one of peace and dignity. His eyes sparkled.

Still, there was the menacing creature atop that dark horse not ten paces away. After a quick glace in that direction, Val felt the urge to flee once again. She focused again on the farmer.

The Farmer said, "I apologize for my escort. Please, try not to let him get to you."

"Can he hurt me?" Val asked. She absently chewed a fingernail.

"Yep." The Farmer said. "They are creatures of pure evil. Their sole purpose is to destroy life. This is a fight between good and evil. We are the good guys and, therefore, follow the rules. We must allow him here. Think of him as an observer."

"Yeah, that really helps a lot." said Marina. "Oh, don't mind him. He's only looking for a chance to eat your soul. He won't bother you. Look Mister, I really don't know what is going on here. Is there any way we can go home?"

"Marina, Dear One, you will understand everything very soon. Your escort is next. I promise all your questions will be answered soon. For now, my purpose is to work with Valessa and show her what she needs to know. Are you ready, Val?"

Val took a deep breath, smiled at Marina, and said. "Are you really one of the good guys?"

"Absolutely."

"Okay then, let's go."

The Farmer and Val walked east towards the farms in the valley. The dark horseman was close behind.

"Are you like an angel or something?" Val asked.

"That's right." he said with a wink. His smile was one Val would expect an angel to have.

CHAPTER TWENTY-ONE
A Pale Horse

Marina was alone again. Marina grew accustomed to loneliness by relying on her resolve. Her first real connection with humans showed her how much she needed the support of others. To experience this isolation, after feeling such love, destroyed that resolve.

Inconsequential thoughts begged to be followed. Somewhere back home, a young adult got a message he was granted admission to his goal academe. While somewhere else, a person felt the last of his energy slip away as he greeted death.

Why is it often at the most critical of all life's moments few people are involved? If one is fortunate, perhaps family or a close friend would be there to share the experience. Where were her friends? Why was she so often alone? That question always eluded her.

What of the other three? Certainly, this gang of misfits she found herself with would qualify as friends, if not more. Did anyone ever share such closeness? Were there people back home who had this type of connection?

Stoicism and coldness got her through most pain in her life. When it did not, caustic and self-righteous got her through the rest. None of that fit here as she faced the most significant of all her life events without family, without friends, and without any understanding of how to cope.

As she waited, she took in as much of her surroundings as fear allowed. Strange she did not see before animals existed here. A bird flitted from one branch to another in a tree that had some sort of seeds to offer. She watched for a moment to affirm it looked like any bird she would find back home and then continued her visual inventory. A rabbit made sporadic, jerky progress across the field in the valley.

It looked to be the same time of day it was in Peyrvi. The terrain as well seemed to follow a similar layout. Scattered clouds, something also found back home, cast shadows across the lush valley. It was certainly much prettier here.

Fear was felt around her like the awareness of a beast beyond the light of the campfire. It was hard to describe with detail or clarity, but it made itself known by its presence.

What to do? No response seemed adequate. Running, screaming, going numb, rage, and withdrawal all childish responses. Yet, the strength to face this situation calmly was beyond her at the moment.

Her breath came in tightened gasps. Cool, moist air filled her lungs. The tension made her shoulders ache, but she dared not shake it off. She preferred tightened muscles that could spring into action. She swallowed hard, but it was not enough to wet her throat.

"I have been alone before and have always managed to survive." she said as she had countless times before. She bowed her head and added. "This time, with your help, I hope to do better."

That sincere prayer was said with conviction, though the identity of whom she prayed to was still uncertain.

I am not truly alone now, am I? She thought. A rider would come as an escort for someone important. Someone she was chosen to meet. Obviously, someone or something out there watched over her.

Is this all my imagination? She wondered. Perhaps it is, but what of my friends? Did I imagine them too? I really care for them, so would I wish for them to face such horrors? I feel genuine love for each of them.

138

So, I can conclude I would never imagine a situation where my friends would be in danger. That is that then. I am not imagining this. That feels correct. This situation is not my imagination. What is it then?

"What is it indeed?"

It was the fourth Horseman. He was more terrifying than she ever expected. Somehow comforting was the notion he was on time. Horse and rider were pale, or rather translucent. They were in silhouette against a swirl of fog that clung to them. It was a confusion of light and shadow in the form of a man on a horse.

Their eyes glowed and lit the area around their heads. The horse's nimbus was red while blue radiated from the rider. Marina dared not blink for fear she would miss the moment of attack. Her breathing was measured to catch every sound. That level of self control surprised her, though she was unable to exert enough control to slow her racing heart.

The rider said, "Logic is humanity's greatest gift, and most tragic curse. What a strange game you play. You feign confusion to give yourself the joy of figuring things out. I think it all pathetic, of course. Though, in you it does have a certain charm."

Marina gave up her search for answers. There were none. "I didn't know you would talk so much. It seems all you horsemen can do is look intimidating and smell bad." Her face betrayed her effort to appear calm with the look of a cornered animal.

"Close actually. We only speak if doing so terrifies."

Marina coughed to catch her breath.

"Very simply put, for some, like Drace, words are comforting. For him we stayed in the background and didn't utter a sound. For you, however, insightful dialog challenges you. So, cutting right to the heart of the matter will get the best results."

"Best results? What? Is all of this planned?" Cutting words, no doubt.

"Planned, orchestrated, and coordinated in great detail. The immense power of the cosmos focused on making you as frightened as humanly possible." He glared at her. "Got it?"

"Yeah, I got it. Well, you know of course, I am just pretending to be scared. I mean, I don't want to disappoint the immense power of the cosmos after it went through such trouble."

"Oh, I see." The rider said. "That is very courteous of you. May I say that you are doing a fine job of pretending to be frightened. Well done."

"Okay, okay. You got me. I am scared out of my fredricken mind! If I had someplace to run, I'd be gone. If I could fight back, you'd be in trouble, but I just have to stand here and wait to get devoured or something."

"In other words, about all you have is sarcasm." It was incomprehensible to Marina how one with such cavalier behavior could convey such profound power. His actions were not merely staged to induce a fearful reaction. They were the behaviors of one utterly convinced of his superiority.

The rider wheeled his horse around and walked away.

Marina asked. "Hey, where are you going?"

Realization of this nature is impossible to ignore. The horseman created the greatest discomfort. He simply walked away. She stood now more vulnerable and with meager defenses stripped away.

A flurry of emotions vied for expression. Rage surfaced. "Forget you then!" Immediately after came despair. "Why me?" Then were emotions that could not be put into words. They found a hold on her. Each difficult emotion weighted her down.

After several moments of confusion, bitterness, and self-pity, her psyche was so bogged down all that remained was a pervasive numbness. Like scalding water that, after a time, only feels warm.

Rider and horse disappeared over the mountain, leaving her completely exposed. The cool breeze of before now cold and cutting. Shadows seemed longer. The sun appeared less bright. Knowledge of what happened is not the same as understanding why it happened.

Ultimately one question remained. Why? She was involved in something she only understood in human terms, yet her very presence in this place offered proof supernatural things existed.

What could it all mean? What was she supposed to get out of all of this? What of her friends? Why were they on this journey with her? She would leave the questions for Drace.

Rider and horse were gone. What about the person she was supposed to meet? Damn, more questions.

Marina sought a comfortable place to sit and wait. The lush forest towards the west offered the most comforting and beautiful area. Besides, her three friends had each gone in one of the other directions. Choosing the fourth compass point made sense.

The hill offered her an elevated view of the forest. A suitable area just inside the forest proper was selected. There was a small grove that would be suitable. It was chosen both for the cushion of grass it offered as well as its inviting location next to the river.

The walk to the forest was far longer than expected. Trees in the forest were much larger than she thought, much larger than she ever imagined a tree could grow. The woods in the Western Ward were window gardens compared to these towering oaks. She thought they were oaks anyway. She knew oaks could be enormous.

There was no real trail through the forest. The trees were large enough to be spaced a significant distance apart. There was considerable undergrowth, though, that made traveling slow going.

She questioned the wisdom of wandering away from where she encountered her Horseman. However, he did head in this direction. Maybe she was supposed to follow? Regardless of its wisdom, Marina felt this forest was calling to her.

Indeed, the further she walked, the more intrigued she became. The woods possessed a beauty she never experienced. The peacefulness seemed enhanced by the fragrant air. There were only a few animal calls to disturb the reverence of the place. It was a bit unnerving she did not recognize any of the animal sounds.

Deeper in the forest, the dim light added to the serenity. She could no longer see the mountain. She could not have come that far into the forest, a few dozen paces maybe. She felt as if she were in the heart and not at its edge. The woods swallowed her whole.

She considered marking the trail, so she could find her way back. Perhaps, if she made a pile of rocks, or broke branches in a certain direction?

This idea was abandoned as unfit behavior. One does not defile a place so tranquil by breaking things or making messes. Further, she did not mind if she stayed in this place indefinitely. Considering the life she walked away from, what did she care if she stayed forever?

Her eyes adjusted to the dimmer light. She headed towards where she expected to find the clearing. Deeper and deeper she ventured. Yet, where was her spot? From the mountain, the clearing seemed only few dozen paces from the forest edge. Certainly, she had come that far.

No grove by a river was found. Yes, what about the river? In the silence, a flowing river was heard. Very still now, she turned her head to pinpoint the direction of the running water.

There, slightly to the right of where she headed. Without a trail to follow, she had gotten a bit off track.

She walked slowly, checking periodically for the sound of flowing water. A small, furry creature scampered down a tree and stood on its hind legs in front of her.

"Oh, look at you. Aren't you adorable?"

He tilted his head and sniffed the air. It was a squirrel or chipmunk or some equivalent for this place.

"Are you looking for something? Oh, I know. You want food, don't you?" She had a piece of mint candy in her pocket for days. She offered the candy to the little ball of fur. The squirrel/chipmunk scurried to her and again sat on its hind legs to accept the treat. He unwrapped the candy and discarded the mint on the leaf-strewn ground. With the foil wrapper held in his teeth, he hurried towards his tree and chattered his thanks for the new decoration. Before Marina stood, a larger gopher/guinea pig sniffed his way towards the mint. He too sat on his hind legs to eat his rare find.

Concern she was lost in these surroundings was replaced by profound respect for the host of life gathered here. It was remarkable the animals did not show fear. What would it be like to live your existence not being afraid of everything you encountered? It was an entirely different world, hidden away beneath a canopy of luscious green leaves.

She encountered creatures of every kind. There were birds, spiders, bugs, and some lizard looking thing that idled off as she walked past. She never even considered such a place existed. Another unique animal call came and was answered from a different direction.

A bit further towards the river she found one of the massive trees had fallen and lay before her. Even on its side, it was four times Marina's height. The length of the arboreal giant extended indefinitely in either direction. Probably best to climb over the obstacle. It apparently fell some time ago as parts of it were soft and spongy. The rotted areas gave way easily and made for convenient footholds. On the other side, she brushed herself clean. Sounds from the river were louder now. Only a few more paces.

She was a good bit away from the top of the mountain but reasoned whoever might look for her should have no problem finding her here. Besides, wouldn't it be better if she were not found?

"Keep walking child, you are almost here." The words were full of life and promise. They were, to Marina, a beacon that reached through the fog to guide her safely into port.

It was a lovely voice from a lady who stood on a sandbar in the middle of the river.

"Come child, I am over here. You are much too far still." The woman motioned with her arms. She wore a shimmering dress. When she moved, the fabric flowed as an ocean wave.

"Is there some way to get to you?" Marina asked. Marina searched the broad and gently flowing river for some sort of path but found none.

"Well, of course, Dear One. Don't be tedious. Come here. I would like to talk with you." The dress's motions seemed like rippling water.

"No, I mean –" Marina stopped herself. She spoke again slowly. "What I mean, please, is there a path over the river that I might take? And could you point it out for me?"

Laughter bubbled forth. It was a sound not unlike the water gurgling over river rocks. "Yes, and yes."

"Wow, I walked right into that one. I wish Drace were here. He could handle her. Okay, woman, I am coming out there. I suppose I could walk through the water to you."

"Well, you could do that I suppose, but whatever for? The water is pretty cold you know."

"Yes, I can imagine. I don't have much choice though, do I?" She took her first step into the river and froze. Her foot met resistance when it touched the water's surface.

"Go on, Child. You are doing it."

Marina took another hesitant step. She now stood on top of the water.

CHAPTER TWENTY-TWO
The Warrior

Over the crest, Buscillo paused to take in the view. With the Horseman next to him, he wondered how long he could stand there taking it all in.

Before him were countless rows of identical white structures. The arrangement was elegant in its precision. Each building, a flat-roofed rectangle, with one door and two windows on the shorter walls. Paths from each building led to the center of the valley. In the heart of the array was a massive structure, easily six times the size of a white building.

In front of the great formation the area was open. Scores of people, all clad in the same type tunic as the warrior woman were gathered in clusters. Each group engaged in various combat exercises.

Most of the groups were occupied with hand to hand combat. Pairs or small groups of combatants fought as others looked on. Other clusters trained with swords, slings, or small blades. Of particular interest were the groups on the archery range.

Clearly this was a military training facility. These must be the Warrior Woman's comrades. An explanation for what they were training for was not presented.

None of them seemed to notice Buscillo's presence. The horseman moved and Buscillo quickly discovered he was not so inconspicuous. Archers were now trained on his position. Buscillo dashed into the valley to save himself from a hail of arrows.

Distance from his escort might be wise.

He had no better luck, however, at other locations. Even as he considered his next move, knife wielding warriors obeyed shouted commands and advanced. Buscillo ran further, searching for an escape route. Every option had its own dangers.

The Warrior Woman was not to be seen. Had she already passed through the valley and was on the other side? The futility of finding safe passage was clear. There was also the question of where to go if he found a means of escape? He had no idea where the warrior woman went.

Retreat seemed the only option. However, escape in that direction was blocked. Rather than deal with the Horseman, Buscillo faced the advancing warriors.

There was a flurry of barked commands. A formation of swordsmen cut off the route just in front. All manner of hand-to-hand combatants closed in from the sides.

Once again, it was his medallion—a thing with a life of its own—Buscillo took guidance from.

Years later, while retelling this story to friends, gathered to hear it for the millionth time, Buscillo might have time to examine the motive for what he did next. The luxury of contemplation was not available to him now. He simply trusted the medallion.

Buscillo knelt.

The medallion responded with a bright and beautiful glow. Light surrounded him as he held the medallion gingerly in both hands. It washed over his body and radiated about him.

The approaching warriors also knelt. All that existed was light. All Buscillo's fear gone.

The reason why they knelt was unclear. Buscillo had no clue about his next move. He waited for the next bizarre experience in this endless chain of frustratingly unexplainable events.

It was not a long wait. Light from the medallion washed the battlefield with its incomprehensible energy and thousands of kneeling warriors.

Buscillo was once a man who enjoyed watching competitors cower at his mere presence. Any man, though, would feel ill at ease in his situation. He understood it was to the medallion they showed their respect.

Each warrior was in total submission to the power presented by the medallion. Even though their homage was to the medallion, Buscillo found the experience profoundly humbling.

Unsure what to do, yet keenly aware that some response was expected, Buscillo raised the radiant medallion high over his head.

A resounding cheer came from the gathered warriors.

Now what? he wondered.

His answer came quickly; one more strange event in the chain. The Amazon appeared from behind one of the white structures and approached.

"Oh, isn't that adorable? The Warrior is offering his respect to his Angel."

Was it too much to ask for a break in this nightmarish journey? Some chance to allow his mind to come to terms with the weirdness. She was speaking of The Warrior Angel, Raiki. This did not seem like religious nonsense. Could she really be referring to one of the Angels?

"So, you consider yourself a Warrior? Do you believe you are worthy to associate with these champions? Oh yes, you have trophies, don't you? Then, by all means, honor the Angel Warrior."

Understanding approached slowly but did not comfort his troubled thoughts. Buscillo recalled a legend he often heard as a child.

Was he at the Battlefield in the Sky where true Warriors prepare for the final battle? The story told of a supernatural military that trained to one day stand against a demon army.

Buscillo considered the story to be no more than a myth, usually told by veterans around campfires.

What business did an athlete have among the noblest force ever assembled? The Warrior Woman was absolutely correct. He went too far with his presumption. Any of these Warriors had every right to challenge his arrogance and claim this medallion for themselves.

As he stood, a skull-crushing kick was delivered with such fierceness as to knock him several feet backwards. A last-second duck reduced the damage rendered from the Warrior Woman's blow. He found himself on his back with a throbbing centered in his forehead.

Movement was difficult, but blood running into his eyes urged him to scramble to his feet. Thus blinded, he barely saw as every Warrior in the field stood. They would surely descend upon him in a rage if she commanded, although she did not need any assistance destroying him.

"You were asked a question. Now give your answer. Next time I won't use my foot." She spoke in icy tones as she wrapped strong fingers around the hilt of her sword. "I ask again. Do you consider yourself a Warrior?"

Panic choked his words, "No, of course not." He hoped it was an answer that would not further inflame her rage. "No, I am not a Warrior. I am not here to fight anyone."

"Your ignorance infuriates me to no end, you disgraceful worm. For such an answer I should be done with you in one stroke and leave you for the maggots. To the Shadows with your false humility. You have the Warrior's medallion, yet you offer such weak and pitiful words? You disgrace this field of honor. It is out of respect for the medallion only that I give you one final chance. Accept this as fair warning, Worm. There will not be another. The question is simple. In your arrogance, you have chosen to make it far more." Her voice grew louder with each word.

Buscillo noticed considerable strain on her face as she fought to remain calm; even as the grip tightened around her sword handle. She rolled her shoulders and turned her neck slowly from side to side; like a cat waking from a nap. She prepared her muscles for another strike.

Her words were deliberate. In her voice, Buscillo heard the growl of a menacing predator. "You are obviously not an Artist, a Healer, nor a Statesman. I ask for the last time. Are you a Warrior?"

Little understanding is possible when a man wrestles with fear. The glowing medallion offered some comfort as he allowed himself some time to think. This soothing effect, plus the pulse of light at the word 'Warrior' helped Buscillo arrive at his answer. "Yes. I am."

Nothing further came from the woman for a disturbingly long time. Buscillo hoped his answer was being considered. He allowed the energy of the medallion to restore him. Harsh eyes on him kept him on edge.

"Fine. The Warrior Woman said. "You consider yourself worthy to wear this medallion. Why? Because you won lots of tournaments?" Smoldering eyes burned into Buscillo who endured the look, he hoped, without any indication of the terror he felt.

He trusted the medallion would help him respond. "No one can truly be worthy of the medallion. A worthy effort is what the medallion asks for. I shall offer the medallion the respect it is due by facing whatever challenge you present with my best effort."

It was offered as an apology, and she accepted it as such. "Well said. You may have some Statesman talent after all. Do not allow yourself to relax with one good answer." She held him firmly with her gaze, and Buscillo felt it was possible to turn a man to stone with a look.

Her movements announced Buscillo would not have time to relax. It was the unyielding look of steel that showed she was determined for him to get her point. He feared making a mistake in his response. Not wanting to push his luck with any more words, he simply bowed.

"Come." She turned towards the training area. He glanced at the medallion briefly for reassurance and fell into step behind her. Not far behind them was the Horseman.

Several thoughts and sights presented themselves as distractions. Not the least obtrusive was watching each Warrior return to one knee as the medallion passed before them. Also disturbing were the urges pulling at him as he watched her magnificent form walking in front of him.

She must be an Angel to have such a body, capable of entertaining his wildest fantasies or destroying him utterly without hesitation. That second notion was allowed, as it served to put things in proper perspective. This was not a time for fantasies. His life may end shortly. Buscillo knew fighting for a victory was madness. Still he would give all he had. He prayed whatever effort he could manage would be enough.

CHAPTER TWENTY-THREE
The Statesman

The child responded to each of Drace's answers with laughter and singing. The effects of such camaraderie were truly pleasurable. Here was an unbound soul, and Drace enjoyed running free alongside the joyful youngster.

However, there was still the Horseman. His menacing presence kept Drace's mental defenses on alert lest the rider penetrate his core, and wring from it the last of Drace's humanity. There could be no light-hearted play so close to such evil. Still the child's mirth and merriment went a long way towards making Drace feel safe.

The Little Boy's questions fit no pattern, yet Drace was able to correctly answer more and more.

When Drace answered incorrectly, the child simply redirected his line of questions until a correct answer was finally obtained. This was a method of instruction he found enjoyable.

Drace concentrated on the process and paid little attention to his surroundings. It was easier to trust the guidance of the Young One. It was no small surprise when the odd threesome came upon an entrance into the side of a mountain.

The doorway was notable for both its enormous size as well as the exacting detail carved into its surface. The pattern suggested the fine grain of wood, yet the color was unnatural. Through this monolithic door, ten people walking abreast could enter. Drace struggled to comprehend the amount of time required to carve such intricate patterns.

Its surface was full of thin pathways no human eye could follow. The color and pattern resembled a microcircuit, a ridiculous thought considering its stupendous size. What was this thing? Closer examination led Drace to the conclusion that, despite the astounding achievement it represented, the door was indeed an immense series of micro circuitry.

Millions of tiny, powerful circuits were combined into one super powerful processor. What calculations could this computer chip be capable of?

A tug at his hand returned Drace's attention to the Young One. Wide eyes were fixed on Drace with an intensity that contradicted his playful smile. The child's entire persona was an array of contradictory images. Spiked yellow hair framed his gentle face. Questions that showed depth and wisdom were asked while laughing hysterically. A rumpled shirt implied childlike carelessness, yet scuff free shoes offered proof of precise and graceful movements.

Drace's thoughts came at a far more accelerated rate. Perhaps another aspect of the medallion? It helped him interact with the macro-circuit.

This new ability was greatly appreciated. Yet, even with heightened mental capabilities, he found himself fully taxed as the onslaught of questions resumed.

The child spoke even faster now. "Do you know what to do next? What are you waiting for? Some sort of explanation for all of this probably, right?" Asked and just as quickly answered.

A momentary break in the rapid-fire inquiry offered Drace a opportunity to sort things out.

Drace considered the boy's tone, posture, eye movements and expression. This was cross referenced with assumptions about the nature of a spiritual guide. With astounding speed, Drace arrived at an answer.

The Young One expected Drace to open the door. Drace's new intellectual prowess was being tested.

154

Drace wanted to take full credit for his answer. He knew he could not. As much as he wanted to believe otherwise; Drace knew his new abilities came from his medallion.

"I am being asked how to open this door." Drace said. "My guess is this door is a gigantic processor. A computer this tremendous could hold unlimited information. The entirety of human understanding could fit inside. Whether this is a metaphor, or an actual location is irrelevant. I am at a repository of profound knowledge, seeking entrance. That is the first test. Once inside, I will be judged not only by the questions I ask, but by how I relate to the answers given. Is that about right?

"You do us all very proud."

Drace felt warmed by the pride in the Child's eyes. "So, I need to find the way in. Most likely it has to do with my medallion. That seems to be the key to a lot of things."

Drace held the medallion before him, now delightfully warm in his hands. "Well, the most universal question is 'Why?'" With that simple word, the door moved aside.

How could he find an answer so quickly? It seemed no matter what Drace said the door would have opened. That was an unsettling notion. The Child obviously wanted him inside.

How could he continue this journey alongside a supernational force who was wholly in control, yet offered no guidance? The Child wanted him to continue and did not care how frightened Drace was.

That's what's going on here. They want to terrify him and to push him past his ability to use logic and rational thought. Who was he without his clever brain? What would he rely on then?

He was not being tested on his ability to solve puzzles but on his ability to function despite tremendous terror. One positive thought brought relief as the pair headed into the mountain. At least that fredricken Horseman was staying outside.

Eric Myers

CHAPTER TWENTY-FOUR
The Healer

Val found herself on the ground again. By focusing on pleasant thoughts – chocolate and warm baths – She stood and walked a few hundred paces. Eventually terror breached those meager defenses, and she fainted yet again.

Each time the Farmer held her hand until she revived. Were it not for his loving touch, Val knew she would be lost.

No matter how much support the Farmer offered, Val could not escape the ominous presence of the Horseman. The Farmer's protection was the only thing that prevented the Horseman from ripping out her soul and tossing it aside. What would become of her son if she perished in this place?

With that thought, Val collapsed again into a trembling heap. She wanted to face the situation with dignity and courage. How could she? Revived once again, Val saw she was being carried now by the Farmer. For now, she was safe. In the Farmer's comforting arms, Val allowed sleep to come.

When Val awoke, she was in a bed. Fear clawed towards her and put her system on high alert.

Where was she? What sort of building is this? There were no structures visible from the top of the mountain. No, there was that farm with the stone fence and smoking chimney.

Farms back home never looked like this inside. Smooth walls and a polished floor were illuminated by a ceiling that radiated a soft yellow light.

Dozens of people in hooded, white cloaks sat along the walls with heads bowed, and clasped hands held close to their faces. Gentle notes, sung softly by each person, blended harmoniously. Their intricate melody filled the room with a peace felt as a presence.

"Excuse me, can you tell me where I am?" Val asked.

No singer gave any indication she was heard. Val's presence, while still a mystery for her, was apparently not so unusual for the singers. Clearly, no assistance would come from them. What were they here for then, if not to help her?

Where was the Farmer? So far, he was the only positive thing about this experience. There was no sign of the Horseman either. That, at least, was something positive.

If Val was here for treatment, then what was the affliction? Okay, that one was not difficult; hysterics, fainting, and feeling disconnected from reality. No doubt, some healing would be helpful.

The feelings of being disconnected were natural. A casual stroll this morning began a bizarre string of events that brought her to this supernatural place, which she was taught didn't exist.

She was distressed by simply being here. Was the source of her discomfort now to be the source of her healing? How could the cause now be the cure? Does a snake inject a person with the antidote for his bite? Isn't this one more thing to push her past her limits?

She got out of bed, grateful her shoes were at the foot and made her way towards the door. There was no interruption in the singing. Alone in a long stretch of hallway she was particularly vulnerable. What if the Horseman showed up to block her escape? She bolted down the hallway and burst through an exit.

Outside it was still midday. She apparently was not unconscious for long. In front of her, a lane cut across the fertile fields towards rolling hills.

It led her through a pass and towards a quaint town. It was fascinating to see signs of civilization. Along paved streets were enough dwellings to house a few thousand people.

The layout of the town was not unlike Peyrvi's. Aside from the fresh air and green fields, things looked and sounded much the same. Birds circled overhead, the wind whistled as it broke around adobe buildings, and in the distance droned crickets.

No people were around, although there were signs this place was recently inhabited.

Down a recently cleaned street was a sidewalk café with empty chairs. Plates of half eaten food were still on the tables. What could have driven the inhabitants away so quickly?

Val stood in her short skirt and tight-fitting top. Her garish attire seemed inappropriate in this serene setting. Worse still, they afforded no defense against whatever she might encounter. She considered taking off her shoes, in case she needed to run. For now, she left them on for the little protection they offered.

The streets wound past the café and homes with open doors towards the town's hub. Were she still in Peyrvi, this is where she would find Frederick's palace. There were no smoldering pyres. Rather, at the heart of this town was a wooden two-story building surrounded by a large garden. On the building's ornate bell tower was a symbol Val did not recognize.

Perhaps it was some sort of church? Before the Great Cataclysm, churches like this were attended by those who wanted to be there. Today, religious centers were replaced with civic halls and attended by those too fearful to stay home. The closest thing to prayer in New Hope was reciting the "Glory to Frederick" poem twice daily as commanded.

Glory to Frederick. All acts of worship are for him. Peace be upon us as Frederick's righteous servants. I bear witness that none has the right to be worshipped except Frederick. And I bear witness that the Angels are his slaves and messengers.

Those well positioned in Frederick's administration scorned any religion that proclaimed its followers were privileged. No one dared point out their hypocrisy.

It was true each religious group claimed some sort of privileged status by virtue of their faith. Val knew, as did everyone else, religions were a defenseless scapegoat. Whatever privilege practitioners claimed came from devotion to God, not fealty to Frederick.

The garden was exquisite, and Val yearned to linger in its beauty. A stronger curiosity pulled her towards the church, or whatever it was called. It was clean and well tended. Lit candles looked lovely through colored glass windows that depicted unfamiliar scenes.

It was odd a religious building prominently displayed images of battle. A group of warriors charged into battle with swords drawn. Another rendering, obviously done by talented craftsmen, showed an armored man on a white horse waving a banner. What sort of church was this to have such images?

The splendor of the garden called to Val again. Its beauty penetrated her defenses and rested gently on her soul. There were multitudes of colors that were at once invigorating and soothing.

A notion occurred to Val she might be in the afterworld. Was this the place beyond life? It did have an unearthly beauty that awakened her spirit. However, if this were a spiritual place, would she be filled with terror and spend most of her time fainting?

It was also unlikely hideous monsters on horseback existed in the Hereafter. Val was not an expert on religious concepts but was relatively certain a spiritual realm would be a safe place. Those creatures would never be in a location meant as a reward for meritorious behavior.

Still, what about the people here? They certainly seemed more than human. Truly the Farmer was someone who would live in a supernatural region.

It humbled Val to consider how she fainted repeatedly in his presence. Those dark creatures must also be agents of the supernatural. Did they also have uncanny abilities; could they eat her soul or burn her in eternal fire? Perhaps, but the Farmer did not fear them. That was the example she would follow. Fainting was understandable, but she resolved not to do it again.

This garden, with its astounding colors and fascinating fragrances, helped her release most of her fears.

Parts of the garden were precise with an array that guided the eye through intricate designs. Other parts were less structured and gave the impression of natural wilderness, but Val recognized the work of a talented gardener.

A winding path led her past one glorious scene after another. Val was especially drawn to patches of orange, red and yellow. Those were the same colors she followed when she first made her way up the mountain. How long ago was that? Minutes? Hours? Being transported, rendered unconscious, and gripped by fear kept her from accurately gauging the passage of time. But who could worry about such things in this place?

All was surrendered to the beauty before her. The path led her to three benches placed evenly in a circle around an enormous statue. It was a larger than life sculpture of a woman in a toga. A large ox followed her on a tether. Beside her was a goat. The cut of the marble rendered the folds of the woman's dress so subtly they looked as if they were blown by a gentle wind.

The bench closest to Val was exquisitely carved out of one block of light-brown marble with gold veins. Another one at an angle to her right was significantly darker than the first. The third, in a position to complete the triangle, was darker still. Upon that one sat the Farmer.

Val approached slowly. At about ten paces away she paused. With arms folded she asked, "Can you explain a few things for me?" Her voice strained at the end, but she managed to add, "Please?"

He replied with a soothing smile and slid to one side. Val did not move. She was scared enough where she stood.

The Farmer waited.

More out of impatience than courage, Val walked to him. Her mood was awful, pathetic really. Yet, that hardly mattered. Considering the gut-wrenching experiences piled on since her arrival, Val felt her attitude was justified. If the Farmer hoped for pleasant company, he would be disappointed. Val marched towards the bench. Again, she was graced with a gentle smile as he indicated the place next to him.

Val sat with a thud and knew that bit of theatrics would get a reaction. She fought back a laugh at herself.

CHAPTER TWENTY-FIVE
The Artist

Was this an illusion? Did different physical laws operate here? Or perhaps, the most intimidating, this was some supernatural power?

Marina stood on water; was it even possible to figure that one out? All she wanted was to make it to the other side. Time for sorting this out would come later.

With her eyes focused on the sandbar, Marina moved with as much speed as she dared.

"Way to go Marina. Good for you."

Marina was almost to the shore and needed to keep emotions in check for a bit longer. Panic still threatened to destroy Marina's progress, as well as her sanity. Her fear was so large and the destination so far. Marina was a squire against a dragon with the knight still far away.

"Holy Cow! Please get me through this. All of this!"

"Dear One, what does the water represent. Think, child, you know this one."

"No more riddles, please. Kind of busy here."

Five more paces to go. Certainly, Marina could make it now. Marina gathered a handful of thoughts and answered the woman's question, "It's about emotions, right?"

Two more steps. Did she really have to answer now? One more step to go. In the blink of an eye, the river froze and held Marina solid. She tried to break free and had to wave her arms to regain balance. Panic exploded inside. The dragon was getting angry.

"My Goodness! Please help me."

The woman stood a few feet in front of the immobile girl. The flow of her robe brought to mind a waterfall. Steel grey eyes gave Marina a look that would unnerve the most sensible of people. Marina renewed her fight against the dragon as the chill from those eyes reached for her heart.

The woman sat and her dress collected in pools around her. Clearly, she was only there to observe.

Marina asked, "Wasn't that the correct answer? The water represents my emotions, right?"

The woman smiled.

"Great, something else I must face alone. Okay, I can do this. I read a poem about how water symbolizes our emotions. The poem suggested we should let our emotions flow and walk gently on their surface or something like that. It seemed pretty silly, actually." The woman still gazed upon Marina. The ice still held strong.

"That is not it, obviously. Maybe it is not just any emotion I should allow to flow. What if it is referring only to the emotion I am feeling now? It is about fear, right? It's about not letting the dragon get too big."

Still no response.

"Come on. A little help, please? You are not making this easy you know.

Maybe I'm on the right track. This must be a lesson in how to deal with fear. That must be it. I must let fear flow while standing on the surface. Or something like that?"

Marina remained frozen, with no idea what do. Marina's emotions always seemed complicated. This situation was especially perplexing.

She knew she was on the right track. That notion developed into an idea. The idea generated inspiration. "I get it. This is all about understanding my true nature. That's it! All of it is me. The emotions, the struggle, even the fredricken dragon are all me! Oh, my Goodness, is it really that simple?"

The ice vanished, and Marina stood knee deep in water. The woman's smile broadened, and laughter bubbled forth.

Eric Myers

"Very funny." Marina said.
The woman said, "You know, sometimes water is just water."

CHAPTER TWENTY-SIX
The Choice

"I can bring them to you, My Lord. I can make them worship you. Please, Most Holy, let me give them to you." The Angel of Light said. The request was offered as he stood at the foot of the Mighty One's mountain. He was poised to take sudden flight as he waited for the Creator to send down his reply.

"They are not yours to give." There was power in that voice. The One who claims authority over all things denied the offer in unmistakable terms.

Confused, unprepared for that response the Angel of Light stepped back and said in a small, frail voice, "I thought it might please you. I thought you wanted them back."

"They are not yours to give."

The Angel's head jerked as if the Eternal King struck him. "I didn't know —" failed him. Whatever else the Angel of Light said was lost in thunderous voice of the Lawgiver.

"I want only what is theirs to give—given freely."

The Angel threw back his head and responded with a cry from the center of his heart, "Do you not want me?"

From the Angel's extended hand, two bolts of power flew. A hole in the fabric of time was torn open.

Unspoken fears were released with that burst. The Angel spoke again, methodically choosing his words, in a voice that showed confidence and mastery. "Shall I go to their world then?" The Angel challenged the True Teacher. "Shall we see if your people still give themselves to you after I have my way with them? They will worship me. I do not care if it is by force or by choice. What choice do they really have? What choice do I have?"

A host of Angels gathered to witness this exchange. Each in awe at what their Father then said.

"Angel of Light, I have given you the only choice there is. I will answer you with this, and nothing more. The Angels wanted you dead, so you would never enter the physical world. I cannot shelter you in my arms and offer you love. We are past the time for that. There is a choice you must make. You must make it freely and unconstrained. If I bind you to me now, I take away who you are."

"And if I do not want to make that choice?"

The Comforter laughed, though not harshly. "My Child." he said. "None want to make that choice. All must. Yours is the hardest, and the one that matters most. What you have from me is freedom and the right to make your own choice between Light and Dark."

"I am not here to choose, but to be chosen!"

Sheets of lightning tore across the sky. "Don't you see, Anointed One? I have no choice. If I surrender to you, I am nothing. If I extinguish the Light of your people, I can make them mine. You are the Light against the Dark. When I leave here, I will be the Dark. I know where I must go."

"If you make that choice, I will have my army of Angels stand against you."

"Then I will make an army of Demons to destroy them."

With those words thundering across the valley, the Angel of Darkness stepped through his portal into the physical world.

It would all end now. His army was at last ready and in position to strike. One heated conversation with the Almighty set into motion a scheme that took countless millennia to unfold. The first step was accomplished. He made a portal that connected the realms. The next stage was easy. He corrupted humanity and blocked their Light. Then he created another plane, a Dark underworld, and filled it with Demons.

His portal was opened again. At a precise moment, the underworld, physical realm, and spiritual realm were linked. He launched his attack. Demons crossed from the underworld to the physical plane and inhabited corrupt humanity. While the portal was still open, the army of possessed humans then followed the Four into this spiritual realm. What started, eons ago, with a few words spoken to the Most High, would finally end.

CHAPTER TWENTY-SEVEN
Intellect

Drace was always 'the smart one'. He never faced an intellectual challenge he could not master quickly. In the presence of something truly wondrous, though, he struggled for understanding.

Drace were in a long tunnel inside the mountain. It sloped downward at a slight angle. The air turned from summer-time crisp to stale and artificial. Diffused light from an unknown source clung to them like fog.

The tunnel brought the pair to the heart of the mountain. It seemed impossible this area was indoors. It felt like an outdoor setting with a leaden sky.

The Child allowed Drace a moment to take it all in.

Before them lay a path worn smooth over time. The area to either side of the path was strewn with gravel, rocks, and boulders of various sizes. The road led to the center of the cavern where it crisscrossed with others. Each path radiating from this hub led to a gigantic, square structure.

What could these monoliths be? It presented an intriguing puzzle Drace would answer later. Clusters of men and women, in utilitarian jumpsuits, worked at each of the huge structures. Near or far, everything was evenly lit.

"Hey, where does this place get its light?" Drace asked.

The Little Guy looked up at him and said, "The same place as everywhere else."

So much for that. Why were the Child's answers so cryptic?

"Please, be serious." Drace said. "What source are you referring to? Where does this light come from?"

The Child sighed. "Fine, I thought you wanted an intelligent answer. I'll give you an explanation for people who don't want to think for themselves. What are you made of?"

Drace was caught off guard by the Child's sudden abrasiveness.

"Huh? What does that have to do with anything?" After an uncomfortable silence, Drace said. "Well? Where does this light come from?"

"Look, not using your mind makes you nothing more than a talking meatball. Put in some effort, okay? What are you made of?"

Humoring the Child would be the fastest way to get an answer. "Okay, I am made of cells."

"You can do better than that."

The admonishment stung. "Umm…cells can be broken down into smaller parts. And those parts are broken down further into units of energy. So, we are made of energy?"

"Are you asking me or telling?" asked the Child.

"I'm telling. We are energy."

"Why in the world did that take so long? Your scientists figured that out centuries ago, for goodness sake. You can't comprehend an idea even a scientist understands?"

Drace knew he should answer but was puzzled by the negative implication about scientists.

"So, as energy." Drace said, "we have ways of responding to other energy. For example, eyes see light, ears pick up sound."

"Go on."

"Our bodies relate to various energies with specific receptors." Drace said.

"Close enough."

"This mountain is full of all types of energy I am able to process."

"Not too bad for a meatball." Laughter burst forth. "Just kidding. You're doing great. The Little One grabbed Drace's hand. "I have something to show you!"

Drace struggled to keep pace as they ran towards one of the large structures. As they approached, the workers at that structure faced the Child and bowed. Then, in single file, they headed for the central road. Other groups of workers followed. The Child and Drace watched a parade of several hundred workers leave the massive cavern.

The Child said, "Okay, Mr. L'Adam, all is ready. You are totally on your own from this point forward."

The Child sat on a boulder a few feet off the path. He crossed his legs. With hands resting gently in his lap, he closed his eyes.

Clearly Drace would no longer get answers from the Little Guy.

"Great, now what?" Drace said. "Would it kill someone to give me a straight answer once? First the Old Man, then the voice in the alley and now this Little Person. They are full of questions for me, but I ask one of my own and get twisted riddles."

"Hey, Little Guy!!!" Drace knew how inappropriate it was to shout. "Little Boy!" Again, no response. Drace stared for some time and let out his own exasperated sigh. "Why is everything so fredricken difficult?"

He thought better when he paced and talked out loud. "The solution to each problem is in each person." It was something the Old Man said. "The solution to every problem is inside every person. Interesting. Well, it's a place to start, anyway."

"The solution to every problem...." So now he knew where to find a solution, but what exactly was the problem?

"Begin with what you know." Drace's brow knit into deep creases, and he chewed on his upper lip. "Okay, my body can perceive energy."

"Damn, this isn't getting me anywhere. What about this building in front of me? If I can perceive so well, why can't I tell what this building is for?"

Drace walked towards the structure and examined its surface. There were no windows or doors. He could only perceive an oversized square rock circled by a smooth pathway."

"The layout of all these buildings might offer a clue." There are clusters of them spread out in the entire complex. "You know, if you looked at this place from above, it would look a lot like a circuit board."

"Wait a minute. Could it be that easy?"

He stood on a boulder and surveyed the entire area. It made sense in a way. The door, after all, was a massive computer piece. Wouldn't it follow that inside is also some sort of computer part? Like a mother board, only gigantic.

"That has to be it. This mountain is one ridiculously large computer. So, why would anyone need a computer this big?"

He approached the structure again and looked for more clues.

The wall vibrated and was warm to the touch. This entire complex was filled with an expectant buzz like an orchestra tuning for a concert. Each of these huge structures an instrument in a gigantic symphony.

Going with the colossal computer theory, these structures must be processors. Drace was awed at the enormous power even one processor must contain. He estimated there were about one hundred of these structures laid out on this 'circuit board' here in the mountain. What sort of calculations would this system be capable of? It intrigued and intimidated him to consider such possibilities.

The obvious next step was to find a way to access this system. For now, the idea of passwords and computer languages was set aside. First find a means of access, and then worry how to utilize it.

His Child guide brought him to this structure. A reasonable hypothesis was he was already at a place to access this system.

How did he do it? Was there a terminal and keyboard? Did he use telepathy? Did he plug his brain into a port and upload his thoughts? There must be some method to access this vast amount of information in an organized fashion.

"Okay, not bad so far."

Drace looked over to the Little Guy. The Child offered no response. Drace sat on his boulder in the same manner as the Child. Peaceful contemplation might help him address his situation better. In any case, it would be nice to take a break.

The idea of sitting without moving seemed to encourage several locations on his body to take advantage of this opportunity to demand serious attention.

Eventually, Drace settled into a state of peaceful relaxation. There was no rush to arrive at an answer. Besides, if Drace did access the largest computer in the universe, he really didn't know what to do then.

The only thing he understood was he was being tested. He wanted to concentrate, though he didn't understand what he was supposed to concentrate on.

"What does one ask of the largest computer in the universe?" To have access to such a fountain of knowledge and ask it for something trivial seemed highly improper.

Hello there, source of all known information. I have some questions. Where did I leave my sock two days ago?

More serious questions also seemed inappropriate. *Why am I here? Why did Jen die? Why is there suffering?* Were those answers for him to know? Did he even have a right to ask?

Drace had questions. Worthy or not, he was ready for answers. He still needed a means, though, to access this monstrous device.

"I might look like an idiot for doing this, but I can live with that." Drace said, "Are you some sort of computer?"

No answer. Drace revised his question. "Are you some sort of information storage place?"

Still no answer. It occurred to Drace to add one more detail, "I am assuming you are some sort of computer. Would you confirm that?"

"Yes." It was the Little Boy's Voice. A quick glance to the Little One showed he was deep in meditation. Still, it was the Child's voice. The sound came from every direction and carried a sense of peacefulness and serenity. This was the voice of wisdom.

"Wow. You have an impressive voice. So, ummm, Computer. I want to know a few things. Can you explain to me exactly what you are?"

"I am the energy of the universe focused on one concept."

Struggling with both laughter and a lack of comprehension Drace said, "Ahh, okay. Could you run that by me again? I am hoping to get answers here, but that went way over my head. Give me an answer that makes sense and that I can understand."

Images, sounds, feelings, words, concepts, memories and explanations flowed through him. He understood intricacies of the universe once beyond him.

Drace ran his fingers through his hair only to leave it more ruffled. Today was challenging. Until now he merely tried his best to avoid thinking about how strange everything was.

New comprehension made today's events understandable. There was great power at work here.

Drace knew what he must ask the computer. "What is my role?"

"Your role is what you make of it."

"Hey, no riddles. Please, give me a straight answer."

"Please, ask a straight question. You asked a question with many answers. I provided an answer with many options."

It was strange to hear such a human reaction. "Okay, I'll be more specific. I am here in this place because I possess a unique characteristic. Is that correct?"

"Yes."

"What is that characteristic?" He cracked his knuckles anticipating the answer.

"Your soul is in balance."

"I have a balanced soul? How can there be balance in a soul? It is interesting to learn I even have a soul. And now I learn it is in perfect balance."

"No, I did not say it was perfect, just balanced. There are Four of you who have that quality."

"Yes, the others. That makes sense. How was it we were selected? Why the four of us?"

"You have been observed and protected this whole time."

With that answer, Drace felt a shadow stretch across his mind. Drace found the idea of being watched and manipulated distressing. Even if these were benevolent entities, the notion was a frightening one.

Drace stroked his chin while he gathered his thoughts.

"That explains a few things, but now I have several other questions. Why are the Four of us here? An Old Man said something about facing my destiny or something. I really didn't get what he was talking about. Can you explain all of this in simple terms?"

Drace swore he heard a chuckle as the computer began, "Okay, let's start at the beginning."

"The beginning of what?"

"*The* beginning."

Drace scratched his head and said, "Oh, that beginning. Okay."

"I will try to be simple, but you must accept what I say without question. Agreed?"

"I've heard that before. Okay, I agree."

"Your physical world was created through God's will. God then created humanity. Each person is filled with God's Light. You have a physical form. This means in your physical world you cast a Shadow. God created humanity, but humans create Shadows. A full soul has more of God's Light to fill the Shadow. Those with God's Light in their soul do not live in darkness."

Drace followed so far and the voice continued, "A partial soul cannot shine enough Light to eliminate the Shadow. They must face the Darkness."

Without God's Light, the partial souls believe the Darkness is real. They believe pain and suffering comes from outside them. They believe it comes from God. They spend their lives looking for security, and they commit horrible acts to fight their fears. This further diminishes their soul and makes the Shadow stronger. Those on earth have become so dark they have changed form. They have become demonic. It is a horrible life. It will be difficult for them to find God."

"Yeah, that's sounds about right. So, humans have become demonic and we Four are the only ones who can see it. That doesn't explain why we are here though."

"You are here to overcome all of the fears facing humanity. You must deny Darkness the chance to fully manifest."

"Your explanations are straightforward, as you said. Are you firm on that "no question" rule? Cause I got a lot of them."

"Very firm."

"That's what I thought. Please, continue."

"If every human lives in Darkness, they would never find God. If even one person understands Shadows are not real, then humanity can be saved."

"The others on your world are buried under the illusion theirs is an evil place. They believe it is through the hands of others they suffer. You Four are the last who understand pain is created by one's lack of understanding. Recent events put that in great danger. Each of you allowed the illusion of pain to dominate your thinking. You were brought to this place so you might see reality once again.

"So, what is your part in this? Who are you?" Drace asked.

"Drace, that is a question. Listen with an open heart. I will explain everything in detail. I was created by Light, as you. I am an Agent of God. I am an Angel. Only Four Angels remain who have not had their abilities diminished."

"What are you talking about? How can Angels be diminished?" Drace could not resist asking.

"Angels have Free Will as humans. Unlike humans they do not live in the physical world. Thus, they cast no Shadow. Angels were given a destiny. We are here to help humans find their own Light. We do that by sharing love. The more love we share, the more humanity is filled with Light. The Light of Humanity, which is the Light of God, nourishes Angels.

When people get stuck in Shadow, their Light diminishes. As their Light fades, so does the power of their Angel. There are multitudes of Angels, but they are now weaker aspects of themselves. Humanity grew ever darker as more and more people were consumed by Shadow. One by one, the host of Angels weakened. Only Four Angels with their full power remain."

"What happens to a weakened Angel?"

"Once again." The Angel continued, "I must remind you of the no question rule. It is a reasonable restriction I am asking you to follow."

"Reasonable?" asked Drace. "You expect me to be reasonable? You sure don't know me very well."

"The four Angels are destined to guide you Four. You represent hope for humanity. Should Darkness take over, all would be lost. People would not be able to escape their Shadow prison."

Drace avoided serious responsibility at every major point in his life. In childhood, he avoided fights and taunts from bullies, and was perceived a wimp. At the Academe, Drace was far from serious about his education, and relied on wit and charm to get his diploma. Today, he shouldered his first heavy burden and felt the task was beyond him.

"You must have the wrong guy. In what way do you think I can represent humanity? I'm not even good at representing myself. I've been saying this ever since I met that Old Man. I am not the guy you want for this job."

"No, you truly are not. You are quick to judge anything that frightens you and quite a bit seems to do that. You have a narrow grasp of fundamental life truths. Your education may be broad but has no depth. Many times in your life you have taken the easy way out and avoided anything meaningful. Your charm and wit can quickly annoy as they are your only good qualities.

"Hey! Way to kick a guy when he's down. Is all this mean crap supposed to make me want to help you? I should walk right out of here." He did make a show of standing up but waited for a reply.

"Are you saying I am incorrect?"

"Well, you are right. But you focused on all the bad stuff. There are good things, as well. If you think I am so awful, then why do you want to work with me?"

"For all the reasons I have explained."

"My soul is in balance."

"It is more than that. You blend altruistic intentions with selfish desires. You mix personal goals with generous giving. In you is both Light and Dark. You are the perfect one to face this challenge. God fills your soul with Light. But you have Free Will. You must accept His gift. It cannot be forced. Since are neither all Light nor all Darkness, yours is the ultimate choice. You can choose God despite your Darkness. In doing so, you become an example for others. They can learn from you how to make their own decision and find their Light. You can help them find God."

"I get it, but I still have lots of questions."

"For those questions, you must find your own answers."

Drace fidgeted in the silence. Apparently, the interaction with the Angel was over for now.

Drace turned his attention to the Child. "Little One, I can answer your question now. I see the world through my eyes, and the information is processed with my mind."

No reply.

"Everything that appears to me is a product of my mind." Drace said.

The Little One looked up. He pointed around him with a slow wave of his hand. "Is all of this from your mind?"

"Yes. I see everything in my mind."

"You are talking about self nature, are you not?"

Drace relaxed, trying to capture the insight to find the words he needed. "Yes, that's right. I am talking about self nature. Wisdom beyond my own nature is not possible. It is like Light. There is wisdom in the Light. But to understand, I need a mind. Like water needs a bucket, Wisdom needs a mind. Without my mind, I cannot have Wisdom."

The boy smiled and closed his eyes to allow Drace to be alone for some time with his discovery.

Drace accepted the pause gratefully. Several things fell in line in rapid succession.

Drace continued, "My mind is a small container of God's Light. God is all there is. God is limitless. God is Light. Thus, Light is all there is, and Light is limitless. God created everything inside my mind. Everything outside my mind is God. Therefore, it is incorrect to say Darkness exists outside my mind. If I perceive Darkness, it cannot be from God. Thus, Darkness is an illusion."

With a radiant face, the Little One said, "Excellent. So, let me ask you. Why do people believe the illusion of Darkness?"

"They are told lies. They see their Shadow and feel fear. They are told their fear is real. They are told it was God who made them afraid. The people turn away from God. Their Light grows weaker, and their fears grow stronger."

"If God is all that exists, and God is everything inside a person's mind, then why do people believe the lies?"

"Because humans have a Shadow. Lies can hide in the Shadow and take hold of one's mind. A lie cannot exist in the Light of God."

Those last words filled Drace with warmth and love. His medallion glowed as a small sun over his heart.

"Why would someone whisper lies to people?" asked the Child.

"Angels have Free Will. One Angel attempts to make himself an equal with God. That Angel is the one who Whispers. He calls himself "The One with Light." That is one of his lies. The Light in us draws us toward God. Those who only see Darkness will not seek God. They will think the Whisperer is God."

"So then, what is your role in this?" The Little One asked.

This was where the learning process was leading all along. Here was the answer Drace sought.

Drace began carefully yet purposefully. "I have the Light of God that can shine in people's Darkness. I must spread that Light as God wills. If I do not, the illusion of Darkness will be made real through Free Will. It is why God made me. I cannot allow people to suffer if I have the ability to help."

"See. Taking responsibility is not so hard." The Little One smiled in a peculiar way, as if watching a child take its first steps. "How do you share your Light?"

"Through love." As Drace looked into the Little One's eye, he saw wisdom and experience that went far beyond the Child's youthful face. Here was an ancient entity in the guise of a child.

"So, Mr. Responsibility, what now?" The Child asked.

"Well –" Drace paused to consider and realized he had no idea. "I guess I am going to face a challenge of some sort and learn how to overcome my Darkness."

"What sort of challenge?"

Drace carefully considered his answer. "I am to face something that is an illusion. But it will be terrifying. If I can hold onto my Light, I will emerge victorious. If I believe the lie, I will be defeated."

"You make it sound simple. Don't let the simplicity fool you. The fear you will face will be more horrible than you can imagine. Only with Light in your soul can you banish fear."

Drace rose to his feet and waited with his hands clasped in front of him. The child responded to the implied invitation and rose to face him.

Drace began purposefully, "My name is Drace L'Adam. Recently I faced great pain and tried to run. I see now why that was wrong. However, the pain of losing my Jen is still here." He gestured towards his heart. "The desire to run has only grown stronger since this ordeal began. I will not run anymore."

"Well, Drace L'Adam. My name is Troy."

"Troy, as in the Angel of Fortune Troy?"

"Something like that. Angel of Wisdom is more accurate. Do you feel yours is a worthy cause?"

"Yes, the world can be painful, and I must fight the Darkness."

"Isn't that a rather pessimistic view of your life?"

"I would say that I am a realist."

"Okay. You can say that you are a realist if you want. A realist with a distorted view of reality though."

Drace backed away from the statement and said, "I offer what I can to end people's pain. And my own."

Troy smiled and said, "No, you Ninnie! You don't do this to avoid pain. That makes you weak. You don't do this to help others. You would lose your identity. You do this because that is how God made you."

Drace smiled he understood.

"Good for you." The boy walked towards the entrance.

Drace followed. He still had one unanswered question. How can a benevolent God be responsible for creating pain? Doesn't that imply God has some cruel ideas of life?

It was a question that deviously eluded the most gifted intellects, yet Drace knew his fate and perhaps the fate of many others depended on him coming to terms with an answer.

It started to unravel. Each thread wrapped around his mental spool loosened as one idea discarded led to another idea tossed aside, as well.

A God who created everything in his mind also created his pain and suffering. It may be pain and suffering are not of the Light. Pain and suffering may not be of God. But it is still pain and suffering. Illusion or not, it hurt, and God allowed it.

Doesn't that mean the presence of pain and suffering in a person's life is attributable to God and not to that person's lack of knowledge? Regardless of Drace's education, hard work, honest actions, and sincere intentions, it seemed his lot in life was determined. He could do nothing to reach beyond his fate.

It seemed then God did not care about one man's struggle to find meaning in the death of a loved one. God does not miss one life taken far too early. If that was true, isn't God an uncaring tyrant?

Drace cared his Jen was gone. He was upset by how cruelly she was taken away. It may be pain is an illusion in the abstract. But this was his life in the moment. He still did not understand why he had pain. Calling it all an illusion was not a convincing answer.

"Is there meaning in any of this?"

"Would you explain that please?" The Little One was several paces in front of him and had no intention of stopping. He spoke over his shoulder as he continued towards the entrance.

Drace said, "If humans do not suffer for things they value then what point does life have? The love of my life died a horrible and painful death. I want to know why. All you can say is it is all an illusion?

None of this makes any sense. You tell me my pain is not from God; that it is a Whisper. So, what am I supposed to do with the pain? Ignore it? Pretend I don't have it? My pain is here." He thumped his heart. "Pain is what makes me human. Take it away, and you take everything I am with it. I understand God did not make pain. I understand I feel this way by choice. That is because I WANT to! I want to feel the pain of having lost someone I love."

Troy slowed but didn't stop. He asked one final question as he headed up the tunnel. "Drace, if you are feeling this by choice, then what does that say about God controlling your destiny?" He started up the tunnel and didn't wait for an answer.

It came to Drace in a flood of emotions. "I decided my life. I decided to love someone. I decided to be with her as she was dying. I decided to mourn her loss. I decided to take my own life after she was gone. Me. These decisions all belonged to me.

God is not a part of my suffering. His Light is real; the Shadow is not. God is always my real identity. He is there at all the events in our lives. We are the ones who give those events meaning."

Drace shouted with the fury of a hurricane unleashed. "That is fine. But I want more!" After months of hospital vigils, a tragic loss of a loved one, passions extinguished at her funeral, his decision to end it with a suicide, meeting true friends, freakish encounters with supernatural entities, and being forced to comprehend the incomprehensible, he was finished.

The fury of the storm was set free. Drace screamed again with all the energy of his being. His spirit sought freedom from this emotional prison. Emotions burst forth and flew unhindered. "God, I want more!" It was more than freedom from his pain. It was his life's purpose finding expression. "God, I want more!" To this cry was added his affirmation life did indeed have more to offer. More friends, more love, more meaning, more purpose.

"God, I want more!" It resonated from every surface in the chamber. The appeal to God reverberated through the entire mountain. "God, I want more!" Drace released more than heartfelt desire. The unbound energy created vibrations on every surface it touched. The walls trembled, and the floor vibrated. Drace felt unsteady on his feet as the ground responded to the surge of energy that pulsed from him.

The reverberations were doing damage. Drace stopped shouting, but the rumbling continued. The mountain itself was adding to the energy already released. The entire complex responded to his expression of wanting more from God.

Drace's cries sought their way towards God. The mountain was in the way. Cracks appearing in the ceiling were deafeningly loud. Drace had little time to respond. The place was coming down. The time to get out was now. To emphasize that point, a house sized boulder crashed to the floor several paces from him. More boulders were on their way.

The mountain would be down in moments. Drace wanted more, but first he wanted out. With as much speed as he could find in his spindly legs, he headed for the entrance. The very heart of the mountain, though, was fractured. Everything was coming down now.

Drace hoped to make it up the tunnel. That was not going to happen. The remaining structure collapsed. He dove under a triangle formed by two enormous boulders. In a place that could barely accommodate his body, he wondered how long his air would last.

The mountain was down.

Eric Myers

CHAPTER TWENTY-EIGHT
Power vs Force

They passed though the valley at a pace that left Buscillo winded. He began this day with a long run. He should be exhausted. Perhaps crossing to this Realm rejuvenated him. That answer was good enough for now. Buscillo's thoughts were needed elsewhere now.

Buscillo faced the most challenging competition of his life. Losing an archery tournament was put into perspective and reinforced with a blow to the head. In the big picture, what did losing matter?

His identity as an archery champion made losing a tournament significant. Buscillo was upset about not getting one more trophy. Was he really that petty?

Buscillo played a sport well. It did not make him a hero. He was certainly not a warrior. Doesn't the Amazon woman have every right to destroy him for his arrogance?

Could he lose his life in this place? Was this reality or an elaborate dream? He touched the knot on his head and felt the blood. It seemed very real.

The Warrior possessed a power of a totally different nature and was not dependent on a medallion. Buscillo could only speculate where the Warrior took him. He stayed alert and hoped for the best.

Quicker than expected for such a large person, the Warrior attacked. Her sword came down in a monstrously long arc.

Buscillo ducked to his right only to meet her boot; precisely timed to strike his nose. The impact drove him backwards and to the ground, again. He had no time to break his fall. Lying there, he pushed his nose into place with one hand and squeezed his medallion with the other.

As he regained his feet, for the second time today, the medallion restored him. Intense pain reduced to an aching thud.

Even with this source of revitalization, his situation remained virtually hopeless. She could break him in one blow and wonder if it was worth her effort. None of his experience in competition prepared him for a contest of this kind.

It was not merely the fact she was armed with a hideous sword. Her body too was a deadly weapon. How many times would his medallion heal him? And what about a sword wound? A bloody nose was one thing, but a gash across the chest?

Buscillo needed a way to fight back. There must be some offense he could use to put up the respectable fight he promised.

Those thoughts were chased away by a ferocious battle cry. With both hands, the Warrior swung the tremendous sword in an awkward overhead slice. The speed of the blade gave no time for criticism. Buscillo crouched first, to avoid the sword, and then lunged upwards into her midsection as she was upon him.

The Warrior twisted her body. Buscillo's fist glanced off her body, and he staggered to regain his balance. She adjusted her sword strike and slammed the hilt into the small of his back.

The woman stared at him lying in the dirt.

It was no use. The Warrior's clumsy moves, in no way, indicated incompetence. They were purposely crude to taunt him. Healing energy would address his lower back but, without a doubt, there was no way he could win this battle.

Forget about a noble fight. This competition was deadly. Buscillo was alive only until she tired of embarrassing him. His back was repaired enough to move. He pulled himself to his knees and said, "I surrender."

"What? After only two hits?" The Amazon thrust the tip of her sword into the ground and rested her hands on its hilt. In a calm voice, she asked, "Tell me, please. Why do you stop?"

Buscillo took comfort in how soothing her voice sounded. "You win." He fought to catch his breath. "You're playing with me. Can't fight back."

The lioness pounced and grabbed her prey by his head. Buscillo's ears seared with pain as she lifted him off the ground. Hatred twisted the beauty from her face. "Little man, this is not a game you choose to play or not! It is something you choose to win or not. Give me a reason to not kill you for being so pathetic."

Nothing else existed at that moment for Buscillo. Only the calm one felt in the eye of a hurricane. The storm was about to strike again. She dropped him and raised a knee to deliver a devastating blow to his midsection.

Buscillo fought the urge to vomit. He wanted to cry, to scream, to beg for mercy. Rage and fury burst forth instead. He was not so enraged to forget his fear. Nor would his fury make him any more formidable. He simply did not want to face his death passively. Anger provided enough resolve to face his destiny on his feet.

Buscillo stood as tall as his pain would allow. The pair locked eyes and circled one another.

Time to reassess. The Warrior had size, speed, power, and skill, plus a true weapon of war. He had none of these. Yet, there was the medallion. It healed him, but could he use it for offense?

Buscillo ducked and the sword sliced through where his neck had just been. He managed to cross his arms and block the knee aimed at his face. In that instant, he sprang up and thrust out his hands. His counterattack was clumsy and unpracticed, but he managed to land another glancing blow to her midsection. His follow through knocked her off balance.

She did not fall, merely cart-wheeled away from Buscillo. She kicked him in the head as she did. Again, he needed the medallion to address a serious injury. He fell to his knees and said, "Please, I surrender. This cannot continue."

Buscillo saw a look that might be confused for pity flash across her face, but it was a face of stone who addressed him, "You are a reptile, alive only as an act of charity. Why do you attempt to become a better reptile? So you can be more versed at slithering? You must become like a bird and leave the ground behind completely. I demand an answer in exchange for sparing your life. Why do you surrender?"

"What is the point? There is no way to put up any sort of fight. I promised a worthy fight. I cannot fulfill that promise."

The Amazon turned, walked a few steps and stood with her back to him. Perhaps there was enough time to stand. Surrender was bad enough, but to do so on his knees, was worse.

Her next attack was upon him. She arched backward and launched herself towards him with unimaginably powerful legs. Fists came at him like missiles. They struck him squarely in the face and drove him to the ground.

Enormous hands pinned his head as she remained in a handstand. The entire weight of her pressed into his head as she held her position. Fingers restricted Buscillo's breathing. His world turned grey. Facial bones cracked, though it hardly mattered. He would die in a few moments.

The Warrior granted momentary relief and returned to her feet but not before first tweaking his nose as she stood.

Buscillo feared his last image would be of her standing there, watching him die.

"You know the question, little man. I want to know why you give up so easily. I will give you another undeserved chance to answer."

Buscillo recovered. Even though the medallion mended his nose and his skull, he was still unable to speak clearly. The Warrior expected an answer. What could his response possibly be? Buscillo needed to end this now.

Speech returned, but Buscillo had nothing to say. This contest was so far off balance as to be tragic. He would die here, and nothing he did could prevent it. He may die for giving the wrong answer. But he can at least make the attempt.

Buscillo stood. He had no weapons. But he had his mind. The medallion restored his body. Could it also assist his mind?

"Medallion. I gave you my body to heal and to restore. Please guide my thoughts. Guide me and use me as you will. Let this be a contest between the Medallion and the Warrior. Use me as your weapon."

"There it is. Do you think you are good enough?" said the Warrior. "Hear these words, worm. *In my eye the prize, in my mind the goal ... but destroy my pride for the Victory.*"

She assumed a fighting stance with her sword held over her head. The blade angled down, so the tip was before her face. Buscillo moved into position. Or rather, was moved into position, as he considered her words. Did she misquote that famous line from the Angel of Wrath? Understanding came in a flash. She did not misquote at all. Here was wisdom.

Buscillo stood with legs slightly apart and arms relaxed and took in his surroundings. It was a truly beautiful land. From this hilltop he saw fields of lush grass. The sky was blue with shocks of white clouds. In the distance a river sparked. A cool breeze replaced the smell of blood with the scent of flowers.

Buscillo watched The Warrior thrust the sword at his heart. As the blade approached, he clapped his hands together to catch the tip. There was a burst of light where the medallion pressed against the sword. Power met power in a shower of sparks.

It amused him to see frustration flicker across her face.

Her expression was fierce again as she countered with her knee. A protruding blade on her kneepad was long enough to reach his heart if she connected.

A backward bend avoided the thrust. Buscillo pulled her towards him as he rolled onto his back. With feet placed on her exposed midsection, Buscillo flipped her neatly over him. The ground shook as the Amazon landed squarely on her back. If Buscillo were quick enough, and he had no doubt he could be, he could pin her now. The move might humble her, and he would love to see her face then.

His movements were not his to control, though. Buscillo kicked forward, pushed off with his hands, and landed on his feet.

She did the same. He wanted to face her in a contest, not humiliate her. The Warrior's face was twisted in rage and her movements were no longer clumsy. A swift blow descended upon Buscillo with enough power to rend him in two. He stepped aside and the arc missed his body. As swift as the first, the return swing sought his neck again.

Medallion met sword and deflected the critical blow. Sparks flew from where the two implements of power connected. The blade was by his head, and he saw the Warrior tightened her muscles to bring the weapon closer.

That knife on her knees sought his heart again. With no place to move, offense was the only option. He twisted and struck the Warrior with an elbow. It was enough to move his neck out of the sword path, but that boot knife still ripped across his stomach.

He would deal with that wound later. He had to time his next maneuver precisely. Her right knee was still raised, and Buscillo dove underneath her leg. A perfect blow to the back of her knee collapsed the leg she stood on.

She came down but was able to drag her sword across his shoulder as she did. He had a few moments to get on his feet and ready himself for the next attack.

Fury burned in her eyes as she stood. With sword at the ready it was her turn to assess the situation. Beads of sweat glistened in the light of the setting sun. There was a nimbus of light around her flushed face. He wondered if she ever exerted herself this much. She was exhausted but there were still multiple ways she could kill him.

He wanted to press the attack but was held back by the will of the medallion. They stood with eyes locked as she searched for a way past the medallion. What weakness could she find? Where was he vulnerable?

Seconds passed then minutes. Calmness found him as he waited.

Every one of her attacks would be met with an equal force. Minutes ticked by, and she offered no signs of backing down.

His medallion was not urging him to press the attack. Following the guidance of the medallion kept him alive. If the medallion didn't want to press an attack, that was fine with him.

It was a stalemate. She would destroy him if given the opportunity yet could not because of his medallion. He wanted to retaliate in kind but again was denied by the medallion. *Now what?*

He looked briefly at the medallion, hoping for some indication of his next move. During that quick glance, the warrior tried to advance. They locked eyes again, and she reigned herself in. Muscles in her arms twitched, and her eyes narrowed a bit more. Here was balance. Two equal forces prevented by each other from any action.

How do you turn balance into victory? How could he press forward and resolve this situation?

Buscillo was perplexed. He was in this stalemate for reasons he could not understand. Was the warrior meant to be destroyed? Was he supposed to press on to victory? What was to be gained if he won?

Buscillo remembered the Warrior wanted to destroy him because he answered, "I have nothing to gain."

Okay, there was some ego there he admitted. He chose not to fight because he could not win.

Was that the answer? Was it all about ego? Was there a way to proceed in this match without ego? Ideas came slowly at first. To fight from ego is to use force to get what one desires. It is not a victory. Someone gains and someone loses. Nothing is not won; merely taken. Those conflicts create imbalance.

True Warriors prevents imbalance by being the power that opposes force, they are the true champions. Warriors are a counter to wicked intentions and selfish desires.

Very slowly, but with intention, Buscillo went to one knee and said, "I do not surrender; I merely yield for the moment. You did not take anything from me, nor do I claim something of yours. The medallion is not mine to claim. It is a symbol for all. The power you displayed is an expression of the phenomenal power of God. The medallion comes from the same source. I accept this medallion as I accept my responsibility to see that power will always resist force. I accept it because I am a warrior. Whenever an evil force seeks to take, I will resist."

"Very well, Warrior. Listen to me." The Warrior Woman approached with joy on her face.

Buscillo waited in a relaxed pose, trying to conceal his mounting tension.

Sweat dripped into her eyes, but she did not wipe her brow. A cloud that hoped to block today's last light hung at the horizon. A gentle breeze cooled him. He allowed a smile to rest on his face.

The woman offered one of her own in exchange. "I am Raiki, the Warrior Angel. With God's guidance, I created this medallion. It is with great honor I offer this benediction." The Warrior Woman raised her sword and touched the medallion with its tip.

Buscillo examined the medallion, and its glow increased. The medallion recognized him.

The Warrior Angel said, "With this medallion you have the ability to understand power, and its proper application."

Buscillo's hands trembled, and he swallowed hard to find his voice. "I cannot imagine how such a thing was created, but holding it proves God exists. I am humbled to have such a blessing."

"You are now recognized as a true Warrior. Remember the words of the *One True Book*. "Your titles mean nothing yet wear them with pride."

He replied. "Thank you is not enough, but those are the only words I have. With all that I am, I thank you."

CHAPTER TWENTY-NINE
Surrender

"What in the world?" Emotions built up inside Marina like water against a dam. Venting her emotions might relieve the pressure; likely instead they would break through and flood her mind. Not putting feelings into words was a path to insanity. However, not getting her emotions under control would also lead to madness.

A glimmer of intuition pushed Marina forward. She followed a hunch and stepped the last few feet towards the island. She paused a moment to marvel at how the sunlight sparkled on the sandy beach. Golden grains glittered in the sunlight. Such a beautiful scene offered her mind a pleasant distraction, but reality struck back. Numbed and confused, she simply whispered, "Now what?"

"Well done, Child. There is one final step for you. I wasn't sure how far you would come. This is very impressive."

The woman lounged on a large rock. Her shimmering blue gown beautifully offset against the glistening sand. Her legs stretched to soak in the cool water. One arm was extended behind her for support. The other held back waves of auburn hair against the breeze. It spilled down her back and reached the sand.

A warm smile came with her supportive words, "I am proud of you, Marina. You handled that marvelously." Her gown shifted to green as she moved.

Marina, feeling a bit older than a few minutes ago, said, "Thanks. But what did I do?"

A radiant smile shone forth as a breeze tousled the woman's hair again. The woman sat up, and her gown flashed turquoise. "I understand your confusion, Dear One. But didn't you figure out how to walk on water? That's what I am referring to, of course."

The breeze carried the words to Marina like a craft on the water. With it came a floral scent Marina decided to identify later.

Marina hoped to maintain the emotional floodgates and said, "Well, I guess it is not as hard as it looks."

That one felt awkward to say. Nothing made sense, and Marina needed answers. "Did I really walk on water? Or is it some sort of strange effect of being in this place? Could I always walk on water and never tried? I don't think I really did this. Maybe you did it and said it was me to boost my confidence?" She was unsure if she could handle the answers.

"Do you feel confident, Dear One?" the Woman asked.

"No, not at all."

"Doesn't that suggest something to you?"

"No, as a matter of fact. That doesn't tell me anything at all." The pressure at the gates broke through.

"You know what I think." Marina said. "I think somehow I died on that hill. I must have led a pretty messed up life, and I was sent here as punishment. You look beautiful and have a nice smile, but really you are some evil bitch who wants to screw with me. No, I don't feel confident at all. But, if you think you can mess with me so easily, you have got a lot to learn about Marina Scerpio."

"Oh Child, you were doing so well."

"Oh, screw you, freak. If you want me to do well then why do you speak riddles? Is it fun for you to make me just guess what's going on?"

The Woman did not answer. She brushed hair from her face again as her gown turned royal blue with streaks of purple."

Marian let out a scream. That full expression of raw emotions drained her of energy, and she fell to her knees.

On all fours in a few inches of water, Marina did not care she was wet and muddy. The scream turned into sobbing that shook her entire body.

The water around Marina thickened. Why would water change like this? In a few more moments, the water was solid, and Marina was stuck.

"What in the world?"

"This is your second lesson, Child."

"I don't understand." Marina said.

"Yes, you do, Dear One. The answer is not elusive. It is right in front of you."

Wave upon wave of difficult emotions washed over Marina. "What is going on? Is it because I am getting upset? Is that it? If I calm down will this turn back to water?"

If there were a reply, Marina did not hear it. The water was as hard as glass. Marina searched through the pool of emotions for something logical. Finding nothing, she resigned herself to the despair that flowed over her.

"Why did you do that?"Marina asked.

"Dear Child, you were so close there for a moment."

"Fear only allowed a few choked off phrases at a time. "I don't like this! Why is this happening?"

It took time, minutes or perhaps much longer, for Marina to come to grips with her situation. Breath came in shudders as she worked through her situation. The water, or rather crystal, around her wrists hurt with even the slightest movement.

From here it was difficult to look up, but Marina turned her head enough to see the woman. Auburn trestles were set off nicely against the woman's now lavender robe.

Marina returned her attention to the crystal trap she fell into. What did she know about the problem so far? The water and her emotions somehow were connected.

The water responded to her. No, not responded; reacted. It sensed what Marina felt. Would the water release her if she felt a different way?

Yet how could she feel anything but terror? Marina was alone in a world full of threats with no clue how to deal with them. Rules were obviously different here unless Marina could always walk on water and never knew it. That seemed unlikely.

What is more, a woman who called her 'Dear One', refused to help. Why did the woman refer to her as 'Dear One' the way her *voice* did?

Her mind quickly followed an idea. "Hey Lady, why do you call me Dear One?"

"Because that is who you are." The Lady offered a smile that could melt ice but said nothing else.

"That's it? That's your answer?" Marina stared at the lady with a glare as unyielding as the water.

So many ideas swirled around, too many to hold onto. One of them might turn out to be the solution but sorting them seemed impossible. Better for now to let them all go and find some calm in this chaos.

Marina took a deep breath, closed her eyes, and sobbed. She gave into the tears as grief washed over her and then faded away.

Ideas and questions still battered her mind like a storm. At least, Marina did feel a little better. She took a deep breath and another emotion showed itself, anger. Marina's body stiffened.

She let out another fierce scream followed by a string of curses jumbled together in a primal chant. Primitive rage spewed forth in guttural tones with an ancient beat. Her body shook as she took up the chant with full vigor. Marina rocked as she repeated the curses over and over.

Intensity diminished with the constant repeating, so Marina allowed full sentences to come forth. "Why am I here?

What do you want from me? What is this place? Am I being punished? I hate it here. I hate whatever brought me here. Why am I stuck? Why won't anyone help me?"

Many questions, but no answers. Marina went back to screams and curses. Somehow that seemed to bring out her anger from much deeper. Without words she could express rage from her core.

She gasped for breath after a particularly gratifying scream and choked on a bit of her own saliva. Her eyes watered as she coughed her throat clear.

Eventually, that too subsided. Marina took another deep breath as fear flooded in.

She wished someone could hold her as she shook and trembled, as if naked in a snowstorm. Many times, Marina experienced expressions of fear such as a shaky voice, shudders up her spine, quivering hands, or weak knees. All those signs were now present, but with an intensity that overwhelmed her.

Was it possible to feel this level of fear and not suffer horrible consequences? Would her heart stop beating because it pounded so hard? Would she bite off her tongue as her teeth chattered? Would such nausea make her vomit? Would she suffocate because she could not catch her breath? No beneficial outcome seemed possible. Marina would likely die here and now. So many varieties of terror wanted to consume Marina's troubled soul.

In a land full of many legitimate threats, would it be her emotions that would do the most damage? Marina would not die from the solidified water, nor from horrible beasts on horseback. She would die from overwhelming emotions. Marina welcomed death.

Mercifully, the fear subsided. Marina breathed deeply. She wanted to recover her breath, and her dignity. She felt humiliated to be at the mercy of such powerful emotions.

Marina waited a few moments for the next crippling emotion to strike. Nothing happened. Afraid to hope, Marina wondered if the process were complete. It seemed unlikely to be done so soon. Hard to say how long she dealt with grief, anger and fear. It hadn't seemed more than twenty or thirty minutes. Is that all it took to transform her psyche and come to terms with her situation? Hardly. She took more deep breaths and waited.

Something was wrong. How could there be nothing? Realization slowly came to her. That was the emotion. Nothing.

This too she expressed. Perhaps to move on? Perhaps not. Marina didn't really care. Someone else could figure out her situation. It no longer seemed crucial to her. However, there was no one else. There were only a few people in her life who would believe her story and fewer still who would care.

Only her three new friends would be concerned about her now. She pushed through the numbness a bit and considered their current situation. What happened to her new friends? What about Buscillo and that terrifying woman? Where did Val go? Was Drace safe?

Why should a group of strangers have such a purpose? What power brought them together?

Her hands moved in the water. Something happened. Apathy faded, love rose to the surface and drove away painful emotions.

Love brought the Four of them together. Marina cared, not for herself, but for her friends. She cared a great deal, in fact. Marina thought of the love the Four shared. She recalled how wonderful love felt. Love became her life raft, something to cling to as she fought for understanding. Her medallion glowed.

"I want them to be okay. Their love means something to me. My life means something because I love others."

Love emerged. Other emotions cleared, and only love remained. Marina put it all together.

"The water was not connected to my emotions. The water was my emotion. When I was overwhelmed my thoughts seized and the water became solid. When I was above doubt and fear, I walked on the surface. When emotions flow through me water flowed. All that remains is love. I understand now. This is really me. I am love." Marina's medallion created a nimbus of light around her head.

"Nicely done, Dear One. Nicely done, indeed. I was concerned you would stay with apathy a lot longer. It was brilliant how you turned to your friends to help you out of that. I am proud of you." Her robe was sky blue, a clear sky after a storm. The woman moved to where Marina still squatted.

It was inappropriate to be on all fours now. Marina stood quickly.

"Who are you?" Marina asked.

"I am Teya. You call me an Angel. I am this and many other things to you."

Insight caressed Marina. "I know who you are. Holy Cow, it is a pleasure to meet you."

The woman gave Marina a smile that turned quickly into laughter. It was laughter unlike any Marina heard before. It was high spirited and without a trace of malice.

Teya said, "Dear One, you passed this test in an impressive manner. Such effort and ability doesn't go unnoticed."

She gently touched Marina's medallion and said, "I quote from The *One True Book. People watch where they are going. It is better to focus on the person doing the watching.*"

Marina also touched her medallion, gingerly placing her fingers next to Teya's. In that tender touch, Marina understood how her gift would be utilized.

First, her medallion guided her to self-awareness. Now, it called to her as a lost lover, and Marina longed to hold it.

As if crafted from pure thought, it weighed nothing in her hands. Yet it felt solid and real. The coolness Marina first felt was gone. The medallion was warm and vibrant. Marina could not take her eyes off it as she said, "I know why this was given to me. It's because I have something to say, right?

Yes, Dear One. You have something to say. And you have something to give.

"But why did you enhance it just now?"

"Dear One, you have been enhanced. Never again will expressing love be an issue for you. You are truly an Artist. Art is more than crafting with a medium. Art is about expressing love. As an Artist you rise above your pain. You then share your art with others so they can rise about their pain."

"In the spirit of true love, I express my gratitude. I will dedicate the rest of my life to sharing love."

"I know, Dear One. I know."

CHAPTER THIRTY
Forgiveness

"I have a few things to do, care to come along?" The Farmer asked.

Val followed, curious to learn what chores someone who lived in this mystical place might have.

They entered a large shed next to the garden. Inside were tools and supplies, precisely organized on clean tables and shelves. Towards the back was a greenhouse filled with plants and seedlings. Val was intrigued by the warm light that emanated from the plants. Even in a mundane work shed, things were mystical.

The Farmer pulled a large cart outside and returned to the shelves to gather supplies. The cart was loaded with fertilizer, jugs of water and a few hand tools.

The Farmer said, "That is about it. You ready?"

She let her question about the plants go for now and followed the Farmer to the garden. They stood for a moment in peaceful silence.

Val sat on her bench and watched the Farmer work. He slowly raised his hands waist high. He gently turned at the hips as if scanning the ground with his palms.

In front of a bed of purple flowers the Farmer paused.

Satisfied with what he felt, he returned to the cart and tossed a handful of fertilizer into a jug. It was mixed by swirling the water in a circle then poured on the purple plants. The empty jug was returned to the cart, and the process of "reading" the garden continued. For some, he gave a bit of water. For others, he created a special mixture of fertilizer or other stuff from the bags.

Val knew the Farmer was absolutely accurate in his assessment and prescriptions. Each plant was as healthy as she had ever seen. The entire garden was without weeds, dried leaves, or sickly branches.

Val envied the Farmer's ability to sense exactly what was needed. Wouldn't it be a nice if she could give Delvid exactly what he needed, at the right time, in the right amount? She thought.

Delvid was a human and not a plant. It was difficult to tell what a person needed. "Still." she said to herself, "Too bad it doesn't work that way on people."

"Are you sure about that?" asked the Farmer.

Val was embarrassed she interrupted the Farmer's work.

"You wish it were this way with people. How do you know it is not?" His face was gentle and soft. Val looked deeply into his eyes and was grateful for what she saw there. In those gentle brown eyes, she saw the wisdom from years of practical experience.

This man could not only explain things logically but could make everything seem sensible. All her life she wondered why life was so complex and confusing. Finally, she would find desperately needed answers.

"Can you explain that to me?

"Sure." said the Farmer. He offered a smile that guaranteed the truth of his answer, as he sat next to her.

"Val, do you know anything about being a mother?" He asked.

"Wow, that's direct." Val said. "I know being a mother takes a lot of dedication and patience."

"Good for you. What else can you say about it?"

More than direct, his questions struck at the heart of her concerns.

"Being a mother means anticipating your child's needs and providing for them as best you can."

"Yes, in many ways that is true." He was not totally agreeing with her, but she loved how he accepted her answer while suggesting there was more. It was a pleasant way to be taught. She wanted to remember that technique for future use.

"Being a Mom for me means I plan ahead in order to provide for him." She hoped she worded her answer correctly.

"Nicely put", he said with a wink. That comforted her. "Does your son like all the things you do for him?"

"Certainly not."

"Yet you do them anyway. Why?"

"For his own good. It's like his education. He dislikes school, but I make him go for his own good."

"How do you know his education is imperative?"

The answer seemed obvious. Everyone knows that education is vital.

"Education is important because... ahhhh. In life a person must have an education so that they can... ummm. You know what I mean, right? Education is required if a person is to get anywhere." She hoped he would accept her answer and move on.

"I see." He was patronizing her, but she was eager for him to continue. "So, you make your son go to a place that he doesn't want, so he can get to an undefined place in life. Am I getting this right?"

It wasn't that bad, was it? "Are you suggesting education is not important?"

"Not at all. I wanted to show you how essential it is to have clarity. It is the key to everything. You wanted me to explain how you can do for people what I did for this garden."

Truth be told, she never got much out of school. It was full of painful reminders of how slow she was. Getting an education was one of those necessary evils in society. Everyone needed math, reading, writing and so on. However, she considered the entire process inherently cruel and inhuman.

"I sensed what these plant life forms needed and gave it to them. Why can't we do the same for human life forms?"

"How can you know what a plant or any life form needs?"

"That's the easy part. They tell you. With plants, you must listen carefully. They are rather shy communicators. People are very loud. You usually have no doubts about what a person wants."

"What if what they want is not something you want to give? What if they want to hurt you? What if they want to do something that is harmful for them? Then what do you do?"

"If that is what you hear, then you are not listening very well."

The Farmer looked at Val with his tender eyes and could tell comprehension was still far away.

"Val, you must understand a very simple truth." He stood. "We are done here. Come with me, and I'll show you what I mean."

He resumed talking as they returned to the shed. "People are no more complicated than any other living thing. Now, it is true some folks do not think very well for themselves. They think about themselves, of course, but that is not the same thing. They waste a lot of energy deciding how to spend their time. This only complicates things. Without such mental chaos, things are pretty simple."

The Farmer put away the cart and headed back through town towards the hospital.

The town had come to life. Streets were full of worried-looking people, all in a great hurry.

The church was holding a service. The priest, or whatever he was called, stood at the wrought iron gate and shook hands as the congregation bustled in.

Out of upstairs windows people called to folks passing by. Intersections were crowded with people engaged in heated exchanges.

210

"Where did all these people come from?"

"From God."

"No, that's not what I mean." She stopped herself. What did she mean? Why did she not see anyone before? Where were they, and why did they go in such a hurry? No matter what question she asked it seemed foolish.

At the hospital all the beds were full. A dozen or so people scurried about, focused on tending to the patients. Several more hooded singers lined the far wall.

The Farmer said, "Something happened."

His comment was understated to the point of absurdity. Val allowed the scene to wash over her. Something happened indeed. Each bed in this once peaceful place displayed the worst form of suffering Val could imagine.

Once, in childhood, she visited a sick uncle at the hospital. While there, Val clung to her mother's leg, fearful of the sights and sounds. She vividly remembered the boy in the bed next to her uncle, severely burned. He barely looked human.

It was the ward for terminal cases. It was unlikely the small child made it through that night. Perhaps it was for the best. They boy must have been in excruciating pain.

Val recalled the terror and sadness she saw in the child's eyes.

Until this moment, that was the worst Val ever witnessed.

One person, their face no longer recognizable, had suffered a severe blow to the head. The object that inflicted the wound must have been made of wood. There were grotesquely long splinters protruding from the crushed skull.

Attendants cleaned them while one person held a tiny device that bathed the head in a golden light. The worry on his face told Val all was far from under control.

Every hideous wound Val saw seemed worse than the last. More wounded arrived every few minutes. Four more came on stretchers, and two others were carried.

One woman had a gash through her shoulder into her torso. Her arm hung from a few strands of sinewy flesh. Attendants tried to detach the rest of the arm and close the wound before blood loss ended her life.

At another bed, a stench caused Val to gag. An attendant noticed Val's reaction and brought over a towel moist with astringent to mask the odor.

The towel helped but the air was still fetid. Curiosity held her in place. Val had to know what created such a stench.

The wound penetrated his gut. The eviscerated area reeked of rotted flesh. Whatever caused the wound wanted to inflict more than injury. It sought to contaminate and utterly destroy. This was no accident. Whatever hurt this man was intended to kill cruelly.

There could be no doubt. These were combat casualties. The enemy was unknown. By the nature of these wounds something about the enemy's character was clear. The attackers were hateful and wanted to inflict as much pain and suffering as possible. Val felt a passionate hatred for this enemy and what they stood for.

"You! Come help me." A man pointed directly at her. "Come on, Come on. This man doesn't have time to waste. Can you insert an IV? He demanded.

Val hastened to answer as quickly. This was life or death. "No, I can't." She felt inadequate and ashamed. She quickly offered, "Is there something else I can do?"

"Are you a surgeon?" He asked but didn't wait for her answer. "Okay, stand here and use this." He thrust a large plastic bottle into her hands. "Wherever I point, I want you to squirt this stuff. Got it?"

The task was easy to grasp. She was to go behind and disinfect as the man was operated on.

Val knew next to nothing about medicine but understood this procedure was centuries old. How desperate they must be to fall back on such primitive techniques. This patient could not wait for them to set up proper equipment.

She watched in shock as the attendant cut with a laser scalpel. At least his tools were not out of date. As she squirted the antiseptic, another attendant tied a mask over her face. Another hung a gown in front of her tied in the back. She was grateful to have her slutty outfit covered.

The odor overwhelmed her.

The first cut was made, and the sight appalled her. The swollen abdomen could no longer contain contents that slopped over his hands. Globs of sticky matter splattered onto the floor.

The area steamed as warm flesh was exposed to cool air. Nothing looked like it belonged in a living being. Slimy masses of tissue oozed and pulsated with the patient's breathing.

She squeezed furiously to wash the matter away only to be shocked yet again at how pervasive the infection was. Those guys better start singing harder. Unless a miracle occurred, this man faced a painful death.

The bottle was soon emptied. Someone thrust a full one into her hand. She resumed her work in earnest. Somewhere the infection had to end. Large pieces of gruesome flesh were cut away by the knife. No attempt was made to finely separate healthy tissue from infected. It was all a mess of disintegrated organs and pus-filled discharge.

Each time a bottle emptied, a new one was at the ready. Pools of fluid collected at their feet. An attendant was there with a wide broom to push the refuse towards a central drain.

Bottle after bottle was used to clean the wound. Val struggled to understand how the man was still alive after much of his insides were flushed away. It seemed futile, but she wanted to give her best effort anyway.

Handfuls of innards were sliced away, and the surgeon began to reassemble what remained. It was difficult to sew such fragile pieces. Val was amazed at the surgeon's skill and precision. His fingers were flying, and Val saw the insides of the poor man begin to resemble something human. Val said a quick prayer for the man. Attendants now assisted the surgeon. Some had new needles with sutures, while others reached in with devices that held organs in place.

The final stitch was tied off. Val lost count of the number, well into the hundreds. Rolls of wide bandages were wrapped tightly around the man's waist. He would sleep for several hours.

Most of the attendants left to work with other patients. A few remained to check IVs and adjust bandages.

Val wondered if she would be here long enough to see if the man recovered. Only a few hours ago she fainted in terror. Now she hoped she could stay a bit longer.

Was it only hours? Time seemed distorted. Her fatigue suggested she had assisted with the operation for days, not hours. Most likely it was approaching sundown.

Val wanted to ask the Farmer more questions. At the top of her list was what sort of monster would inflict such horrible wounds?

Val located the Farmer bringing in another patient. Val caught his eye and he motioned with his head for her to come to him. Whoever they were bringing in was enormous. He, Val knew it was he, was clad in all black. A shiver violently took hold at her shoulders and finished at her heels. "It can't be!" she gasped.

She froze in place at the horrific notion. "Why would they bring that monster here?" Surely, they were not thinking of...and they cannot expect her to... Her thoughts halted as if run into a wall. Again, she wanted to collapse. Pride, if nothing else, held her up. She dared not move her legs lest those fragile supports give way.

Two attendants at either arm helped her towards the monster. She resisted only as much as the strength in her legs would allow. After a few jerky steps, she found herself looking at the hulking figure. She forced down an urge to vomit. Her arms tightly wrapped around her were her only armor. She scanned the corners of the room concerned there were other horrors lurking in the shadows. The beast of a man was the only one of his kind in the room. One was certainly enough. He was an overdeveloped mass of hateful ideas.

Neither fury nor lethal intent was evident in his eyes. Far more frightening was the look of disinterest. In those eyes, Val saw no concern, no remorse for the evil he obviously committed. Black eyes fixed on Val. A wicked smile announced his belief in his superiority over those foolish enough to stand before him.

The brute must be in severe pain. The only indication of his suffering, though, was the manner he clutched the object that caused his grave wound. Gloved fingers, too weak to be effective, tried to remove a metal object protruding from his chest.

The black fiend looked at the people working on him. His eyes returned to Val's. In her entire existence, no one ever looked at her with an expression that utterly drained her confidence. She might never look anyone in the eyes again for fear such a debilitating look would meet her.

The creature tried again in vain to get at the square metal plate that caused him such torment. Being too weak was one limitation. The main reason was the glowing hot plate in his chest scorched his fingers. The beast let out a wail. The sound was wholly unnatural, and the very air shimmered around her. The pain in that voice echoed in her mind.

Attendants seemed unfazed by the cries of anguish, but Val felt her knees go even weaker. There was another attempt by her stomach to empty its contents. Adding to the grotesque scene was the smell of burned flesh that emanated from the smoldering wound. Again, the foul creature pried at the object; only to bury the plate deeper into his chest.

Staff now surrounded the bed. Some placed extra supports under the metal gurney to hold the tremendous weight. The Farmer stood at the foot and was obviously in charge. At his signal, the attendants grabbed hold of the demon.

It seemed an unnecessary show of force. When two attendants, at the beast's right arm, were sent flying, Val understood the necessity of their numbers. This thing was powerful beyond comprehension. The two displaced attendants were tended to as four others replaced them. Ten were positioned to hold down their charge and treatment began.

Val stood in stunned silence as she struggled with the question of why. Why should any effort at all be wasted in putting such evil back on its feet? Why not let him die a painful death? The more painful the better.

A female attendant handed a device to Val. Words were seldom used here. Everyone was well trained and automatically understood what needed doing. Val remembered how the Farmer went about his work at the garden. Maybe these healers sensed what was needed?

Val did not sense what the attendant wanted, though. Words were needed. If they expected Val to help, they must provide a lot explanation and encouragement.

Again, the female pushed something towards Val. It was a mask of some type, connected by a finger thick hose to a machine rolled next to the bed. The female did not offer any words. She placed the mask in Val's hands and went to her next duty.

Val watched as the ten attendants struggled to hold down the ferociously strong man, or thing, or whatever it was.

Val understood what she must do. She moved into position and held the mask firmly to the face of the creature. She turned her head away from the vile odors.

The man breathed the gas delivered through the mask. Nothing happened. There was a sickening sweet smell from the gas the man was forced to inhale.

Val was not sure what the gas was supposed to do. Whatever its purpose, it was not up to the task. Still, she held firm with the rest. Muscles in the demon's body slowly relaxed. For good measure, she held the mask in place a bit longer. No one asked her to stop.

The attendants released their hold and went about the next order of business. Several wielded sharp instruments, while others used wicked looking blades the length of their arm. With both precise cuts and aggressive sawing, the spiked leather clothing came off. An attendant ran a blade up the length of the man's pant leg and revealed muscled thighs covered in hair.

The creature was a bit less fearsome wearing only a metal codpiece. She removed the mask and looked closely at the creature. The face was vaguely human. The structure, though, was distorted and hideous as if bludgeoned by a mallet. Lines were worn deep into tough skin. By their pattern it was obvious a smile never touched his features.

The size of the brute was unbound by physics or reason. Attendants prepped the man for surgery. Val loathed the idea of doing anything to help this thing. No matter how human it might appear, this was a thing of pure evil and not worth saving. Were it not for the Farmer watching, she would have left the beast to die. Who was she kidding? She would have run and never look back.

It helped that the demon was now unconscious and under her control. She still held the mask. How long would it take to kill the thing if she returned the mask to his face? These people only helped others out of habit. It was their job to treat everyone who came here. Val knew this monster was unworthy of their care. There would be no need to explain. *All I would have to do is bring the mask back and –*

"You really want to, don't you?" The Farmer asked.

Val offered the Farmer the first idea that popped into her head. "It would be a peaceful way for him to go." She did not defend her murderous thoughts. She merely suggested it might be for the best.

"Indeed, it would be." His eyes met hers and held her there. Val blinked at the intensity of his stare. He looked right through her and examined her soul. She shivered and hoped for enough courage to survive his withering looks. He maintained his fix on her and repeated. "You really want to, yes?"

"Yes." Val said, and exhaled, as the weight of her answer sat squarely on her shoulders. The contents of her stomach crawled up the back of her throat. Did she want to do this? She knew nothing of what a demon was except that it was evil.

Wasn't that enough? Don't you destroy evil? Do it quickly. No questions. No hesitation. Do it and be done. Isn't that how it is handled?

She shifted her weight and felt the discomfort of having been on her feet so long. Her discomfort? That was embarrassing. What about these others brought in? Wouldn't they prefer to have weary legs? She was tired and sore but owed it to those patients to endure her minor discomforts and press on for their sake. That was why she wanted this thing destroyed after all. For their sake.

To punctuate her point, she said, "What of these people?" Indicating the beds filled with incomprehensible suffering. "This thing did this to them didn't he?"

"Yes. He was one of attackers."

How could he be so certain? The Farmer was right, of course. Val felt it too. What else, but a demon, had the strength and the hatred to create such injuries? This thing must be destroyed.

Val put her conviction to words. "Then I want to finish this. This thing deserves to die."

The Farmer said nothing. He took a step back and made a quick nod with his head. The attendants also took a few steps back. All eyes were on Val.

It would be easy. Hold the mask in place long enough to do the job, plus maybe a few minutes more for good measure. That was all.

"You created a lot of suffering today." Val held the mask ready to place over his mouth and nose. This felt empty to her. She wanted this evil man to be destroyed but was unsure if that was the right decision.

Val's face twisted with dread and anticipation. She felt compelled to do something horrendous.

The Farmer placed his hand on Val's shoulders. She was unsure why. Did the Farmer wish her to continue and was offering support? Or did he want her to take full stock of her actions?

She was in no hurry to finish the gruesome deed and put a few more thoughts to words. "If this stops him from destroying again, it will be worth it." No one offered a counter to her argument.

Was killing ever justified? How could Val decide that? That was a question for scholars or theologians. Such esoteric musings she had no taste for. This was a despicable act. Val dropped the mask and took several steps back.

The Farmer was there, and strong hands kept Val from falling backward. He helped her to a chair quickly brought forward by an attendant. With her head buried in her hands, Val sobbed. The Farmer offered her the best kindness possible. He knelt next to the chair and hugged her.

Breathing came in fitful gasps and words were hard to form.

"You're okay, child."

In due course, she recovered enough to lower her hands. "I can't do it. I cannot make myself do the same sort of evil. I cannot kill in such a cold manner. That would destroy anything human in me. I know it is weak to back down in the face of evil, but I can't do it."

Val thought she would have been all too happy to eliminate a threat of unconscionable magnitude. Why should she feel remorse from ridding the world of something utterly vile?

She knew the answer, and it was difficult to accept. To eliminate this creature in such a manner was itself evil. Doing wrong to do right simply didn't add up.

Instead, she overcame her base nature. That took far greater strength and courage. It was, she hoped, an act of righteousness. Never did she consider herself to be a morally strong person. To sell her body, or rather rent it out by the dance took little courage. It took a great deal of will, to be sure, but was certainly no courageous thing.

This was a step in the right direction, at least. Changing everything in her life would take still more courage. Val danced for tips presented to her in outright crude ways. She was not enrolled to become a healer at an Academe and even lacked the discipline to take on that dream one class at a time.

How could Val expect her son to show any of the discipline she lacked herself? Perhaps that was why she did not enforce a proper way of life for Delvid. To do so would make her a hypocrite.

Val accepted The Farmer's support gratefully but could not look him in the eye. She did not want to see his condemnation for her having such vile thoughts. She wanted to hide in a closet until everyone left.

A quick glance at the room revealed no one focused on her. Many patients still needed immediate attention. Thankfully, no new ones came in after the demon. There was no telling how many would become fatalities. The one with the severed arm may make it. Likely not to survive the night, was the one with most of his insides removed.

The hooded figures, showing impressive endurance, still filled the room with harmonious tones. Strange idea that. Maybe music does enhance healing. Who knows in a place like this? That was a thought to consider later.

Medical techniques here were a bit primitive. Then again, who was she to judge? At least none of them wanted to kill one of their patients. The singing may or may not be effective, but lethal doses of anesthesia were certainly not prescribed.

Several attendants worked with the demon again. Without a doubt, they were intent on saving his life. Good or bad would be determined by others at a later venue. Sometime in the future, perhaps when Val sorted through her box of memories, she may have occasion to look back at this moment. When that moment came Val wanted to have something other than homicidal urges to recall.

Val took a deep breath and looked for a useful task she could claim as her own. On cue, one of the attendants handed her another bottle of antiseptic wash. With renewed purpose, she took to the bottle as a firefighter takes to a hose.

Her resolve got her as far as the table. Foul air assailed her nose again and her strength drained. Why would a wound to the chest, the center of life itself, create a scent that conjured images of death and decay? In this creature especially, the task of overcoming the putrid smell was an onerous one. Val squeezed the bottle at the beast hoping to reduce the emitted gases visible as a greenish fog.

Still to deal with were his eyes. They remained half opened as he lay in a stupor. Val recoiled from the hatred she saw in them. Hatred did not have a single target but meant for the entire world.

Val looked onto his eyes and held that gaze. She felt his glare like a force, and it tore into her confidence, into her will to live. The eyes were dark shiny orbs without whites, like the eyes of a statue. They had no detail other than the reflection from the lights.

Even without pupils, Val could tell he stared directly at her. He never blinked. His purpose in life was clear. He was a creature of evil designed to bring out the deepest and most hidden fears of a person.

To know he existed, and not horrible nightmare was difficult enough. The thought such a thing lived gave Val troubled thoughts she worried he could read. Val was in the same room with a living shadow; a thing created to terrorize and destroy. Here she stood trying her best to keep it alive.

Val considered aiming the fluid directly at those eyes to get them to close. It was a foolish notion and she refocused on her task. Why doesn't he blink? It was getting to her. Val wanted to scream, "What do you want?" She needed to hear from the Farmer all was well and she was fine. Where was he now?

Val scanned the room and found the Farmer standing over the woman with the nearly severed arm. He made a valiant effort to reattach large sections of muscle tissue to the shoulder. It looked hopeless.

A raspy breath from the monster returned her attention to her own crisis and to those horrible eyes.

"Please, stop staring at me."

It was more than unnerving. It was exposure to death and destruction Val never even imagined. The lady with the shoulder, in fact, all these victims were likely struck down by this thing before her. And now he stared with a look that communicated he wanted to do the same to Val.

Her knees wobbled as a signal her legs would give out again. She grabbed the bed behind her and steadied herself.

With head lowered, to ward off dizziness, she noticed her medallion.

Several times she wondered about this thing. It came to mean a great deal to her in a short time.

Thought came slowly. The reason for having this medallion was unknown, yet Val knew it was meant to be hers. After all, the medallion came from her father.

He could not have known; however, it was a powerful device that gave her access to another world. Who knew what other powers it had?

That was it. What other powers did it have? Val envied Drace's ability to arrive at a conclusion before most people even understood the problem. She wished he were here.

This medallion was hers. That was clear. It felt like hers. They discovered it had an extraordinary power to transport them here. What else could it do? That was the conclusion she needed Drace for. He figured out their purpose while Val still trembled on the ground. She could do better than that. Wouldn't it be great to tell Drace she had figured it out by herself?

How could such a thing help her though? Drace's ability to jump ahead was foreign, even magical to her. Val dealt with what was right in front of her and slowly worked forward.

What was this made from? Who made it? Why did they make it? When was it made, and how? Does it require instructions from the user? Does it obey commands, or operate on its own? Were there consequences for using the medallion?

Gathering information like this was an effective way to decide. She still wished she had Drace's talent of making assumptions and then taking an intuitive leap. His way seemed faster in situations like these.

Still, she was not limited on her own. Val would find out her own answers in her own way. What is wrong with being logical and practical? Was she in any hurry to be anywhere? Val could take all the time she needed and arrive at the same conclusion as Drace.

Does this thing respond to commands? There is an obvious way to find out. "Medallion, give me strength."

Golden light shone forth from the medallion. It calmed her nerves and revived her spirit. Val knew with certainty fear would not take her legs from underneath again.

"Medallion, show me the best way to use you."

Insight came in a flash. Everything was about clarity. Val understood the path to all wisdom began with clean and clear thoughts.

It was simple, yet its beauty brought tears. God formed the universe with precision and perfection. From the orbits of the planets to the bonding of the atoms; life was about precision and perfection.

God worked in marvelous ways. Humans, on the other hand, were far from clear in their intent, in their purpose, in their clarity. Wisdom was achieved by examining God's perfection. God brings clarity.

Clarity of purpose, clarity of intent, and clarity of vision led to the outcome God intended. The golden glow of the medallion grew. Understanding rested in her very soul.

Val had raw notions of clarity when she danced. In her performances there was intent behind each movement to express beauty. The beauty of her dance, though, was nothing compared to the magnificent harmony that was the universe. It was all a fabulous dance where each movement was coordinated, every activity orchestrated, and each person a piece of a masterfully created whole.

There was clarity to observe in God's precisely calculated movement. Life flowed with intent. Through clarity, perfection can be reached. It was not in a small way she her perception changed.

Art showed us clarity. Art was a path to understanding the divine.

Clearer too were the ways in which precision was not being followed. The beds along the far wall were nearly precise in their spacing. Someone with obvious intent placed each bed a measured distance from the wall and from each other. Their form was noted for its attempt at perfection.

Far more noticeable was the one bed askew. During the bustle, a bed was knocked out of alignment. That the bed was a few finger widths from its proper center was noticeable perhaps to only Val.

There was harmony in the movements of the attendants. Their ability to function as one was understood. They received instructions from a single source.

They responded to that voice and to each other in a way that was natural and harmonious. Each of their movements were orchestrated within the symphony. Their intent was to restore clarity to that which was no longer precise. Service to others was about restoring clarity to individuals, to families, to groups, and to nations.

Her role in the universe was clear. Val was here to serve the needs of others by bringing clarity. The entire universe was precise and perfect. She was here to restore anything misaligned.

This demon before her existed as an essential aspect of the universe. To vilify and hate an entity that was a part of the whole was not appropriate. Still, within the entity the lack of clarity and understanding was apparent. Val's purpose was to restore understanding.

Val's hands glowed golden yellow and radiated warmth. They were placed on the demon's chest on either side of the metal object. The man gasped and shuddered. Val renewed her focus on restoring clarity to help him adjust to the process.

At times, his muscles twitched chaotically. At others, they were silent, as if the man were dead. Val kept her golden light flowing.

He took in a deep breath, but this one gentle and even. The exhale was slow and measured. His breathing fell into a soft rhythm as his chest took in more and more light.

The chest wound was still a critical issue. The bleeding stopped, but the object still protruded from the sternum.

Several attendants came to offer Val their support. One reached for the metal plate and pulled slowly but firmly. One added fluid to IV lines and monitored equipment. One more flushed antiseptic wash on the wound. While yet another placed a comforting hand on the beast's forehead.

The metal came out and the wound sealed itself. A few moments later, the demon's breathing was erratic. A new level of harmony had to be reestablished once the object was freed.

Val renewed her focus and continued to pour forth golden light into the man's chest.

Her own breathing was shallow and barely perceptible. One by one, the attendants left the man to hurry to other duties. Last to leave was the one at the equipment. One monitor indicated the man's heart rate was near zero. Val tried to restore the man to his natural precision, but the monitor did not register any change. The man was still going to die.

How could it be? How could the natural order be death? What was Val here for if not to heal? Was she to be the one to end his life after all? Why?

226

It ended without any ceremony. The monitor beeped its warning for a moment before an attendant shut off the power. Val took a few steps back, stared at her hands, and wondered about all she learned.

There was order and purpose to the universe. It was a central truth she held with utter certainty. Where was the order in this? Death played a role in maintaining harmony. Still, this was beyond her grasp. In what way had death restored the purpose of things here?

"Because Darkness cannot exist in the Light." The Farmer stood behind her. Val was aware of his presence and was grateful he had not interfered. Now she appreciated his guidance.

He leaned against a bed and folded his arms casually in front of him. His relaxed manner, while discussing such things, indicated he possessed profound wisdom. Despite her tremendous new insights, Val understood she was still a student before the master.

Val sat on the bed and crossed her legs. That the position was one a child took when being taught was not lost on her. She laughed, stretched her legs, and leaned back on one hand. The Farmer noticed the joke and smiled along with Val. It was doubtful there was much he did not notice. Val was in awe at the magnitude of this man's power and humbled by the relaxed way he wielded it.

He searched her face for a moment before beginning. Val knew he saw triumph in her newfound knowledge, and pain from the burdens that came with such insight.

He said, "My name is Therosi. Do you know who I am?"

She nodded. Was he saying he was one of the Angels? Therosi, the Pleasure Seeker? He was nothing like what she was taught. That was comforting. Therosi was gentle and loving and not a self-centered hedonist.

"Light is the source of everything." Therosi said.

"You mean like energy?" Val asked. "Are you saying energy is everywhere in the universe?"

"No. I mean Light." And in the manner he spoke Val heard the capital 'L'.

"Light is the source of everything. It has energy, yes. But it also has purpose, intent, design, and meaning. Light is more than energy. It is the force that created everything.

She knew this with a comprehension beyond words but marveled at how his words enhanced her understanding.

"Light also has direction. In ways both big and small we know where Light comes from and where it is going. Light comes from God. When something blocks God's Light, a Shadow is created."

Therosi took a step closer and placed a hand on Val's shoulder. "Light has purpose. Shadow seeks to hide purpose. Light has meaning. Shadow only exists because of the Light. Light has vision. Shadow can only cause blindness. It is quite simple, Val. That was an entity created by Darkness. You filled it with Light. It could no longer exist once you did."

"Then I killed it. By my soul, I killed something, and all my life all I ever wanted was to be a healer."

"No, you did not kill. You removed a block and allowed the Light to flow. That is all. Through your willingness to serve, you allowed Light to remain and Darkness vanished. You are, indeed, a Healer."

His confirmation eased her mind. But something in her could not accept what he said. Expressing her doubts might help solve her crisis.

"What you are saying then is Light is real and Shadow is an illusion?"

"There is truth in that, yes."

"Then how can an Illusion cause real damage? That lady has a torn arm. Isn't that real? There is a man missing most of his insides. That is as real is it gets, isn't it? How can something not real cause so much damage?" She approached the heart of her dilemma.

"Val, a Shadow is not created by Light. The source of a Shadow is not God; rather it is created when a part of God is hidden. It is an Illusion to think Shadow has form, substance, or dimension. But if only physical senses are used, a person can fall for the illusion and create fear. Fear stops the flow of Light and creates Darkness. People in Darkness are not able to accept the Light of God. As people get Darker, their physical form gets denser. When that happens Darkness can, indeed, cause dreadfully real damage.

"The only intent of Darkness is to create more Darkness. It needs to create fear, so Light cannot flow. It needs us to believe the Illusion of Shadow. Darkness can only serve itself. It cares only for its own survival. It seeks to disrupt God's plans. It is separate from anything truthful. Its damage is real. However, thinking of it as real is an illusion. Valessa Brown, what do you want to do now?"

"I want to serve God."

The Farmer smiled and said, "You have been given a tremendous gift, but there is still much for you to learn."

"Before I start this learning." said Val, "I want to put a few things in order back home. I will return as soon as possible."

With that Val went to find her friends.

CHAPTER THIRTY-ONE
Reality

"Get off! I want the whole Fredricken world to get off me!" Drace screamed, as if expecting the pile of rocks to move on their own. They had the nerve to resist. *Time to assess my situation.*

Here in this fortunate shelter was life. Drace was alive and, as best as he could tell, uninjured. Other than cramped legs and a few bruises, he was essentially intact.

Drace was able to move a bit from side to side in his stone shelter. In every direction were several hundred yards of massive rock. All was not lost, however. The darkness was not total. Cracks in the rocks above allowed light to shine through. His path to freedom would be straight up. Considering the tremendous weight of the boulders that pinned him, going up would still be extremely difficult.

Only yesterday Drace tried to end his life. He desperately wanted change. His life was given over to whatever fate was in store for him. By drinking the concoction, he took a step over the edge and plunged into an unknown world. Fate can be a challenge.

Drace sought change in his life, but this was not the sort of change he expected. This change involved fear resting squarely on his shoulders. With this type of change, Drace faced the possibility of death for himself and for those he loved. A change of this nature presented a lethal puzzle without a ready solution. This change was terrifying.

Drace adjusted his position and froze as a rock slid overhead. He could be crushed at any moment. How could he find a way out of here? Normally, his mercuric mind rapidly sorted through dozens of creative options. No solution presented itself. His mind was numb.

Fear was the only thing that drove him forward. It pushed him to find an answer and energized his spirit. Drace smelled fresh air. The surface was not far. Already his intellect assimilated information.

"Okay, I can smell the fresh air and see a bit of light. Now what?"

There must be a way out of this mess. Like it or not, he was being tested. Powers much stronger than Drace expected him to overcome these deadly circumstances. He could get himself killed in a variety of ways. In doing so, he would let many people down. "If that happened, I would just die." His attempt at humor fell flat. Still, if he made light of his situation, it might help him deal with the problem at hand.

People counted on him. Foolish on their part, perhaps, but people depended on him none-the-less.

"Why me?" Drace remembered the Old Man's admonishment about whining. The Whisperer, too, reprimanded him for not being confident.

Confidence was not something Drace had now. He was buried beneath a pile of boulders with little idea how to get out.

He wished the Old Man were here to help in some way. Even if it were only advice, it would be more than he had now.

It would also be nice if his friends could help. "Did any of you guys happen to bring a shovel? A really big one?" That was a little funny.

The Old Man said Drace could never get rid of him. A promise as solid as his granite prison. "I can't get rid of him?"

A puzzle piece was placed on the table, and its edges examined. Other pieces with similar edges would fit with this one. The Old Man was a solid fixture in Drace's life. That was the first piece. Others must fit in somehow with this primary one.

The Old Guy sent him on this weird mission. The Angels knew why all Four were here. The Whisperer, too, played a part in this. This entire scenario was planned. There were even rules to follow. These puzzle pieces fit together somehow.

Drace was on the other side of a wall and heard his neighbors throwing a wild party he was not invited to. These all fit together.

The suicide attempt hastened this event because it brought Drace's soul closer into balance. What of this?

Angels protected Drace and his family. While growing up, people in his life helped him develop his intellectual gifts. An Old Man with tremendous power gave him a medallion that would further enhance his abilities.

To fully develop his gifts, Drace was transported to this spiritual boot camp. The goal here for him, and likely all four of them, was to learn to utilize their gifts.

This horrific situation was Drace's final exam. The Little Boy said the challenge would be facing an incomprehensible fear. Drace knew success was a matter of overcoming fear to see truth, not illusion.

That was the final piece to the puzzle. Fear would be overcome by using what he had learned to see the truth of his situation.

One lesson learned was he must use his intellect for more than questions. Gathering information was not the path to Wisdom. Wisdom is a matter of accepting concepts, not compiling facts. Sometimes you must go with what life presented and not over-analyze. That was a point the Old Man stressed. In childhood, Drace's Voice often told him he thought too much.

What was he over-thinking? What concept must he accept?

Again, Drace wanted to cry out, "God, I want more." But he feared another dramatic reaction to his words.

"But I do want more."

How could wanting more cause destruction at this level?

Drace sought Wisdom. Expressing such desire brought down a mountain full of knowledge. Wisdom destroyed knowledge. That was it. Drace's desire for understanding destroyed the facts. It was through his declaration of wanting more all of this happened.

It started to make sense. His neighbors invited him to the party.

A lack of purpose drove him to suicide. The willingness to accept the medallion and begin this journey came from his desire for purpose. His openness and vulnerability to his friends came from that same desire.

In his first lesson, Drace learned Wisdom exists. The next lesson showed him Wisdom was a process of surrendering the mundane and reaching beyond.

He expressed his desire to reach beyond and destroyed the mountain. It was all connected. Pieces fit together.

The Little Boy hinted Drace's explanation of the mountain was marginally accurate. Was there a different way to understand a mountain of knowledge? Was there a different way to understand the Little Boy?

My perception of the mountain was incorrect. Drace decided what the mountain was by looking at the facts. Wisdom, though, not knowledge, was what Drace sought.

"It's not actually a mountain, is it?" Drace said.

A boulder cracked.

"Just as the Little Boy is more than a child, this place is more than a collection of facts."

Another boulder crumbled.

"This is a mountain of knowledge, but I must surrender my own understanding to obtain Wisdom. I must let go of my understanding of the mountain."

Reaching beyond him brought down the mountain. Reaching for more would bring it the rest of the way down. If he changed his perception, he would change his situation. The puzzle pieces were locked together.

There was another resonating crack, and the sound of boulders sliding over one another.

Here is Wisdom. What other way could Drace conceive of an immense storage unit of knowledge? Wisdom struck him with the force of a falling boulder.

"God does not need a storage unit. God does not ask for me to understand Him. He wants me to accept Him."

Boulders became rocks. Rocks were reduced to stones. He was free.

He reached for and finally obtained Wisdom.

His reality was based on how he perceived facts. Life changed by first accepting it can be different.

Around him were facts the size of pebbles and ideas no larger than a rock. None of them were bigger than what he could hold in his hand.

Troy stood at the edge of the debris field among a throng of angels. They walked towards Drace.

The bounce in Troy's step was replaced with a determined gait. He was focused on an important task.

Troy stood before Drace with a grim look. Had Drace failed after all?

"Just kidding." said Troy. The Child's somber expression was chased away with peals of laughter.

Drace laughed with him. "I get it now. We create our reality based on our perceptions. We can never perceive all that God perceives. Wisdom comes from surrendering our own understanding to God's greater understanding."

"Well done, Drace. You found the Truth. I am immensely proud of you. I want to give you something you've earned. There is a fancy ceremony with pretty words to go along with this. We both know frilly is not your style. Here." The only ceremony was a wink from Troy. He touched Drace's medallion.

"You suffered a painful process. You now see Truth and not Illusion. I grant you the ability to help others find Truth. You are now a Statesman."

The final rays of the setting sun created the perfect setting for Drace's ceremony. This long day was over. A new day would dawn soon.

Drace's friends approached. No sight could be more welcome or bring more joy.

Troy said, "Well, Drace, your lessons are over. I will leave you to your friends." Troy and the group of angels headed down the far side of the hill and left Drace to his reunion.

CHAPTER THIRTY-TWO
Fateful News

Buscillo was the first to say something. "We started to worry about you, Drace. I was afraid you were dead."

Drace replied, "No, I am not a ghost." He patted his body and said, "Yep, still flesh and bone."

Buscillo smiled, "Glad to hear it. It's nice to see you again." Buscillo offered a handshake that was warm and comforting. "

"Oh, what's with this handshake stuff?" Val said. She wrapped her arms around Drace.

Buscillo took a step back and said. "Well he's covered in bruises. I didn't want to hurt him."

"I can take care of that." Val placed her hands over Drace's heart. The feelings that flowed into Drace, not unlike the feeling from the Old Man, filled him with wonderfully soothing energy. His bruises vanished. She then ran her fingers through Drace's hair and put it in perfect order.

Drace noticed Val wore a surgical gown with blood on it. He wanted to ask. No doubt there was a long story there. He also wanted to know how Val got this new ability. But first he wanted to show how happy he was to see everyone.

Drace went to Marina and lifted her off the ground with an immense hug.

Between giggles, Marina said. "I can't tell you how good that feels. Wait, yes I can."

She too placed a hand on Drace's heart. Through that connection, Drace felt it all. Feelings once fiercely guarded by Marina were now shared freely.

In that embrace were ideas of love and tenderness, a baby held at its mother's breast, a father helping his child master a bicycle, and chocolate cookies baked for a loved one. Marina shared all she had inside. Wiping a tear from his eye, Drace said. "Thank you."

Marina winked and messed up Drace's hair.

Buscillo turned to Drace and said, "A hug from one of you guys could never harm me. In that embrace, Drace felt the strength of a mighty oak.

Drace stepped back to take them all in. After a long look, at each in turn, Drace shared his own experiences.

Drace now had a hard edge. His childlike playfulness remained, but eyes that danced with laughter were set in a face with a firm jaw. Those eyes looked at them differently.

To show his experiences did not change him completely, Drace shook like a dog drying off. A cloud of dust formed around him. With a wave of his hand, the particles disappeared. He stood before them utterly clean.

"Hey, nice trick." said Marina. "Do you work parties?" Laughter erupted among them.

They had stories to share and new gifts to explore. The desire to be known was the driving force in past relationships. Now, the desire to know was what mattered most. Here, communication was not waiting for one's turn to speak. Each person sought to listen to what the others had to share.

Time for sharing would have to wait. Val was the first to notice. Each stood silently and watched as the Four Angels crested the hill. The last of the sun's light cast the four in silhouette.

"Now what? Can't we just go home?" Drace spoke for all of them.

"What do you think they want?" Buscillo said.

They waited in silence. Drace gathered whatever reserves he could find.

Marina let the terror of the new encounter wash over. What was so momentous all Four Angels would come? The implications gripped Marina by the throat like a butcher grabs a calf and drags it to the chopping block.

Val had no intention of letting her legs fail her. She resisted the urge to pace.

The Four Angels were upon them. Troy stepped to one side. He locked his fingers together before him. With a bowed head, he waited.

Raiki took a position next to the Child. She too bowed her head as the remaining two advanced.

Teya approached next. Her gown displayed an array of somber colors. She too lowered her head in prayer and waited. Therosi then came along side the others. He did not bow his head, rather stood with his palms turned upwards.

The Farmer spoke, "Dear, friends. We come to you now for a far different reason than before. We cannot compel this of you, but we ask with sincere hope you will honor our request."

Drace did not like where this was going. This was a buildup to something crucial. Though, what could be bigger than what they already experienced?

"Val, you witnessed an event that has never occurred in the living history of this Universe. While its occurrence was considered a possibility, not one of us thought it could ever come to pass. Throughout time evil has taken many names, but always the same face. You know the enemy as Frederick. Our enemy is indeed wicked, but what happened today is an evil far greater than any of us could have imagined."

Therosi lowered his hands and bowed his head. Teya continued the oratory, "We took a tremendous risk bringing the Four of you here. To transfer you across the dimension meant a door had to be opened. Our enemy understood this. That is why he forced our hand. The enemy gave us no choice. That door had to be opened. Doing so made us all vulnerable to —"

"Attack." Raiki said.

The Warrior addressed them with her hands set defiantly on muscular hips. With her chest thrust forward, Raiki made it obvious the egregious offense would not be tolerated.

"Our enemy took advantage of an opportunity and did something completely unexpected. Demons crossed over. They killed, and they will pay."

Troy took his turn to address the Four. The Child skipped away only minutes ago. His radiant smile now twisted into a grimace.

"Time for a proper response will come soon. Our enemy will see the consequences for what happened today. Each of you has been trained and enhanced. You will all play a vital role in the upcoming confrontation. That time is not now. At this time, we grieve for those fallen and mourn possibilities lost. It is our desire you help us honor what they stood for."

Four Angels joined hands. Drace resisted smiling, though the sight of the Little One on the tips of his toes holding the hand of Raiki was amusing.

The Little One winked to acknowledge Drace's observation but maintained his somber expression.

They spoke in unison. "Will you please join us for their funeral?"

They left so the four mortals could consider the request.

Buscillo looked at his friends, who nodded their assent. He said, "We should not linger in this place." His tone reinforced what they all thought. Here was where evil went unchecked.

They hurried to catch up and fell in step alongside their Angel guides. In silence, the retinue headed for town.

CHAPTER THIRTY-THREE
The Wake

Four pairs walked in silence. Buscillo, Drace, Marina, and Val were no longer strangers in the Realm. They were no longer afraid of their guides. They were, however, terrified of what lay before them.

Therosi and Val walked close together. She wished she could ask Therosi some questions. "Who was the funeral for? Which patients did not make it?"

Buscillo walked in step with Raiki at the head of the group. What did Therosi mean, "This has never occurred in the living history of the universe." Never occurred?

Never was an overused word that dramatically conveyed a sense of rarity. When Therosi used that term, it was not hyperbole. It was a somber word that conveyed the direness of the situation. Why did Therosi call it a living history? Is the universe alive? Buscillo's thoughts darkened as they continued towards town.

Marina felt tremendous sympathy for Buscillo. Of the Four Angels, Buscillo's was by far the most intimidating. Raiki was a well-defined form full of purpose and menace. Marina had no idea how Buscillo faced down such a formidable power. No doubt Buscillo's medallion helped, but Marina still held Buscillo in much higher regard. Buscillo was not as tall as the average man, but to Marina he had grown much larger today.

Marina considered the words, "Now we grieve for those fallen and mourn possibilities lost. It is our desire you help us honor what they stood for."

Those words echoed in Marina's heart. *We mourn possibilities lost.* In a single sentence, the weight of their tragedy crashed down upon them. 'Possibilities lost." It spoke of something infinite reduced to something that no longer existed. It suggested something precious was destroyed, and could not be replaced, words full of anguish and foreboding.

What happened was not expected; it caused irreplaceable damage and altered the course of their future. All was conveyed in one sentence. Marina felt alone and wished to reach out and hold hands with her friends. Teya took Marina's hand into her own. The gesture comforted Marina greatly.

The twisted logic this place offered disturbed Drace from the very beginning. So many things here were offered as common sense. When looked at closely, though, they didn't make any sense at all.

Drace and the others were selected for their unique abilities yet had to be trained. If they were given these extraordinary abilities, why weren't they also taught how to use them? And what about these Angels? If Angels were here, then why did they need Drace and his friends? Drace was sure Raiki could take on an entire army herself. What use would a bunch of misfits from Peyrvi be?

All this was presented as it were a part of everyday life. Though, everything was ridiculously out of the ordinary. Drace found it comforting to let his mind wander and not dwell on how absurd this all was.

This funeral also presented an unanswerable question. A funeral in the physical world was to send loved ones into the afterlife. What kind of funeral would you have for those already in a supernatural world?

Sometimes the best answer is not to have any questions. Drace would let things happen and see how it unfolded. He did not need any other mountain-sized lesson to remember that.

Once again Drace's curiosity was stronger than his reason. Troy walked next to him wearing a grave expression. Drace missed the Child's twirls and banter. The formal mood seemed acceptable on Therosi, Raiki and Teya. On the Child, it stood out like a blood stain on a snowdrift. Drace knew Troy was as old as the universe. Still, it felt like a knife to his heart to see a child suffer.

The hardest part of all was the fact this Realm became vulnerable because of Drace and his friends. They were responsible. That thought twisted the knife deeper.

Troy looked up with a gaze so penetrating Drace's steps faltered. They both stopped and with his eyes locked on Drace's, Troy said, "You did not do this. No human could ever cause this much pain. The events of today were eons in the making. Frederick began his Whispers when the world was formed.

The sun set along with Drace's heart. The most fascinating, yet troublesome day came to an end. Drace wanted to go home. He wanted his warm bed. He wanted to forget about this strange day and fall into a dreamless sleep. With Troy's explanation came the understanding this experience was far from over.

A simple life was all Drace ever wanted. His greatest desire was to have a place where he and Jen could enjoy his modest income and spend their days watching sunsets and walking their dogs. Was that too much to ask?

His father's ambition was to amass enough wealth to influence the government. Drace's goals did not seem like much in comparison. His father accomplished his goals and more. Why were Drace's simple dreams so elusive?

In his cozy apartment, full of bookshelves and antiques, Drace retreated from the struggle his life had become. Drace desired such refuge again, a reprieve from the demands of an odd Old Man and a quirky Young Boy. Instead, he faced yet another encounter with the bizarre and illogical.

Troy took Drace's hand. Another twist of the knife, but Drace doubted Val could heal this wound.

The hand was tiny and delicate. For Drace, it was a connection to something that made sense. Power and tenderness come together.

In a world full of unexpected wickedness and random disasters, the hand of a youngster offered much needed love and compassion.

The pavilion in the center of the town was crowded, which created a new mystery for Drace. There were far more people here than could fit in this small town. An intuitive leap landed on the conclusion this town was not the only inhabited place in this Realm. Drace estimated six or seven times this town's population were gathered. Perhaps they arrived from a handful of other towns this size. Maybe they are from one good sized city?

Was this Realm a parallel to New Hope? The notion intrigued him, but there were not enough facts to arrive at a conclusion. The idea seemed plausible. This town seemed to match Peyrvi. Was that enough to conclude the entire Realm had a matching component on New Hope?

He allowed himself a few assumptions to come up with a working theory. There were similarities in geography and demographics. Could this Realm be populated with millions, as in New Hope?

In New Hope, a population of 14.4 million was considered a failure of government. In the days before The Cataclysm, people feared overcrowding. Fourteen and a half million survivors were a heartbreaking when one considered that for each one alive, over one thousand perished.

Entire civilizations were wiped out by horrific weapons that vaporized millions at a time.

Frederick came to power at this time. People were frustrated, lost and in anguish. They no longer felt any connection to their country. Still though, they were unwilling -

244

even after seeing the consequences of not accepting personal responsibility - to make the changes they needed to rebuild.

Those who survived The Cataclysm yearned for an end to their pain in whatever manner it came. Frederick organized them into a community. The disaffected and disenfranchised from across the country were lured to follow Frederick with his promises of greatness again. Frederick promises were ludicrous. The people were too hurt, angry, and afraid to see the lies. They surrendered all rights to Frederick.

They did not know - no one could have known - their liberator would turn his promise into a bitter lie that festered in their souls.

Less than fourteen and a half million remaining was an indictment of the evils of humanity. Here in this Realm there appeared to be even fewer.

Here in the town square were perhaps ten thousand. They crowded the streets and made walking a challenge. It was crowded, but each individual respected personal space. The four pairs moved slowly but effectively towards the center of activity.

Raiki led, with the entourage pressed close behind. The crowd noticed her, it was hard not to, and gave way with a gentle bow of their head. In this manner, the group reached the center and the shock that awaited them.

Val was the first to see the bodies. "By my soul."

Raiki looked back at her and said, "Indeed."

The others saw the bodies too as claws of fear scratched at their heart like talons of a crazed bird of prey. There was row upon grizzly row. Torches placed at interval through the courtyard barely lit the area. Smoke from incense hung in the air. Drace was grateful many details were not visible in the low light. The manner of death tore at their understanding of what it meant to be human. Only a soulless creature could have wrought this horrific scene.

Bodies without heads were the most common; the neck apparently a favorite target for the monsters who fell upon these victims. Missing too were arms, legs, sections of torso. A wholly intact body was not to be seen.

Buscillo scanned the area and took in each of the fallen. He understood the nature of the attack. Large weapons were used to hack through as many victims as possible. The vast numbers, perhaps as many as a thousand, suggested the enemy moved quickly. This was not a well coordinated attack, but more like a hasty maneuver intended to do the most harm in a short period. Only a corrupt soul could execute such brutality. Buscillo had no doubt who were to be held accountable for this scene.

"This was done by Demons." he announced flatly. It was said as an indictment and meant to be accepted as fact.

No one replied. They stood and watched in silence.

"There were several of them." said the Farmer.

The mass of people continued towards the display of bodies. It was a reviewing line. As people filed by, they stopped to lay flowers or to touch a face and say a prayer. A little girl laid flowers on a female torso and fell into a sobbing wreck. The next person in line gently lifted the child and cradled her in their arms.

After the procession, the crowd gathered to await the rest of the ceremony. The courtyard long since filled. People now found places on roofs, porches, and balconies.

"We will leave you now." said Therosi. He bowed deeply then gave Val a tender kiss on her cheek.

"You will know what to do." Troy said to Drace. He too bowed deeply then gave Drace a strong handshake.

Teya offered a graceful courtesy that looked like a waterfall then kissed Marina on the forehead. "Trust your heart, Dear One."

Marina understood what Teya meant. Marina wanted to offer comfort to the people gathered here. Teya encouraged that sentiment. Not trusting her own voice Marina only nodded.

"Buscillo." Raiki said, in a voice that echoed off the buildings. "I pushed you hard." She walked a few steps closer to him and lowered her voice.

"You were in my sights as a target. No one has ever survived that. You earned your victory with the help of your medallion, but do not ever think it was your medallion alone. You earned the title of Warrior because of your spirit, your strength, and your passion for excellence. Those gifts are yours forever. I remind you of them as we conduct this ceremony. These fallen individuals also had a fierce spirit, the strength of a noble heart, and reverence for all things in life."

Then to all she said. "I ask that you remember them this way." Raiki drew her divinely crafted sword from its sheath. Its point drove into the ground as she went to one knee. The Warrior bent her head to touch hands folded over the hilt. She said in a voice barely above a whisper, "When you arrived you were as children, innocent yet ignorant. Your suffering has brought you enlightenment."

The Warrior stood, gave the sword back to Buscillo and stepped towards the other angels. The Four Angels spoke in unison, "It is time to send them home." They headed towards a platform in the middle of the courtyard.

CHAPTER THIRTY-FOUR
Eulogy

Drace, Val, Marina, and Buscillo were as perplexed about their responsibilities for this ceremony as they were with the notion one was needed in the first place.

Apparently, a great deal was expected of them.

Raiki and the three Angels stood on the platform. She opened the service with a benediction, "Purpose may escape us, meaning might elude us, yet wisdom is always at hand. All who serve find fulfillment, as those we mourn today found theirs. We mourn selfishly, wanting to keep those we love from moving on. Our selfishness too is part of a greater design. For it is out of our love we want them to remain. Let us now use that love to send them Home."

A more informal memorial ensued. A striking woman—as much for the flowers in her hair as her beauty—spoke softly.

The woman stood and with arms outstretched said, "Yas Tosinati earned her place among us as a philosopher, a poet and as a woman who added humor to our lives the way the winds from the south add warmth. I will miss the kindness in her touch and the way her words floated to others as if carried by a gentle breeze. Laughter from Yas tickled the hairs on your arms. Her embrace lighted upon your heart as a bird. Hers was the Way of the Light."

An older woman stood next though, in this Realm, age was only a matter of appearance. Her eulogy began, "Thoman Forg, a man created from the purest of Light, lived with fire in his heart. His inferno ignited those touched. He inflamed passions and fueled dreams. His heart was like the sun that shared Light and warmth with the universe. His was the Way of the Light."

Some mourners simply stood and held palms toward the sky. Others stood next to their loved one and said, "He gathers the Light to Him."

An aged man rose, and the crowd fell silent.

He scanned the crowd slowly then said, "As far back as the days of throngs and multitudes, I have known many with a magnificent Light that surged through them. Few, however, filled my soul with life's nectar as Sistral Myore. Sistral was one of the first to reside here, and one of the finest. Her presence washed away fear. Her touch was as refreshing as the first rain of spring. Her smiled washed others with love. Gone is her laughter that cascaded over us. But forever will remain the love that filled our hearts."

Marina was in tears as he spoke. All were silent for several heavy moments. A child came forward. A precious little boy, no more than three or four, walked towards the body of a fallen woman.

He placed a rose on the woman's chest. He spread his arms and said. "She was my Mommy. Everyone loved her. I loved her the most. She is gone. But I will always love her."

Val grabbed Marina and buried a sob into her shoulder. Marina clutched Val firmly and whispered soothing words.

Buscillo looked away to avoid showing emotions. He could not contain his tears, though. He fell to one knee and buried his face in his hands. Everyone respected his privacy. Drace placed a hand on Buscillo's shoulder and said, "God, please grant us peace."

"Is everyone holding up okay?" Drace asked. It felt forced and awkward. Words, no matter how inadequate, were all Drace had to offer.

Val placed her hand on top of Drace's. Buscillo reached up to place his hand over Val's. Marina added hers, as well. Connected so, they waited to play their role in the service.

A small group of mourners stood and walked to the deceased. They wrapped a body in a shawl and then carried that fallen person to an awaiting train of wagons.

The corpse was laid tenderly on the wagon bed and sprinkled with flower petals. Only after the first of the body was resting in the wagon bed did the next group proceed.

It was late evening now. The procession to the final resting place would occur at dawn.

Drace felt a need to be among the grief stricken and walked towards the crowd. The other three followed.

Mourners fell to either side to create a pathway as Drace approached three young women sitting on a curb.

The first to notice him jumped up and said. "Get up. It's Drace."

Drace was taken aback. "That is not necessary. You have no idea how unnecessary that is. Please sit down."

He sat next to them and said, "Hi, I'm Drace. I'm not from around here."

The three girls could not contain their laughter. Drace smiled along with them.

"Everyone here seems to know who we are." Drace said. "But we are kind of confused by all of this. Can you explain a few things?"

The one who stood said, "It will all be clear soon, Drace."

"See, that's what I'm talking about. Everyone we talk to speaks in riddles. No one has given us a straight answer since we arrived. We follow along and hope for the best."

"Seems you've learned a lot already." she said. "We understand how you must feel, though. I am Yarni, and these are my sisters Laerni and Thelka. It is an honor to meet you Mr. L'Adam."

Drace was unable to respond. Her words confirmed what he believed from the beginning of this odd journey, all four of them were being guided, coerced, and manipulated.

"This is all fascinating." said Drace. "Can you explain what is going on here in a less cryptic way?"

The girls stared at Drace like cats on a sill with birds outside the window. Their eyes found Drace's, and he looked back with the same intensity. He could ask them to go into battle, and they would charge forth without hesitation.

"We are waiting for the procession to begin." said Laerni. At the proper time, we will take our fallen to the Site of First Light and return them to their Source."

Drace saw eyes lightly wrapped in tears. *Site of First Light*. Drace loved the image it created, although he did not understand what it meant. He knew it would be a perfect location to say their goodbyes.

"What will we do once we are there? At this Site of First Light, I mean."

The girls whispered to each other, though not softly enough. "I don't think he knows. You tell him."

"Tell me what? What's going on ladies?"

Thelka stood and led Drace away by his arm. "Walk with me. We have much to discuss."

As they walked Thelka said, "We are all Angels. Rather we were once Angels."

"Were? I sort of understand, but could you explain that, please?"

"It is simple really. Angels are pure Light. Our purpose is to assist those who cast a Shadow. We share our Light with people so that they can find their way to God."

"Makes sense so far."

She winked at him and said, "I knew you would catch on quickly. Those who have Light in their soul can find their way to God. Those with Darkness need our assistance. The Darker their soul, the more we must pour into them. Until recently, Angels could handle such as task."

"Something changed that?"

"Something indeed. The Whisperer corrupted every soul on the planet. All but the souls of you Four, that is."

"I get it now. It happened when Frederick destroyed families." Drace said. "People born without with only a few people to genuinely love them do not have much light to begin with."

"Then Frederick took away religion, she said, "People never learned how to build up their Light."

"And without Light they have little understanding of how to find God. There is no chance of overcoming Darkness without that understanding."

"Precisely. God offered instructions for people through The *One True Book*. With those teachings, people could find their Light. God wants to gather the Light to Him. If Light is gathered in heaven, God's Angels are powerful. Dark souls have no Light to offer God. Without that Light, Angels become weak. This was Frederick's plan. Weakened Angels would be vulnerable to attack."

Drace froze. "Did you say Frederick? As in The Pontix? Frederick is the Whisperer?"

"Yes. Throughout time, evil had many names, but was always the same being. Angels were not concerned about an attack at first. Frederick's Demons could not reach heaven. People with Dark souls are easy targets. Frederick used his Demons to attack the people. Each Dark soul became a host to a Demons brought from Hell. An army of Demons was created in the physical world. Frederick finally had the means to launch an attack. If the gate to heaven were ever opened, Frederick's army could pass through."

"That gate was opened when the Four of us passed though. That means we are responsible for all of this."

"We had to open the gate. We needed to offer you Four the chance to develop your Light to its fullest. We knew opening the gate meant Frederick's army could travel here. It was a risk we took willingly. You Four are the only ones with Light in your souls who exist on Earth in physical form."

"You knew the attack would come!"

"We knew Frederick would try something. We were willing to take the risk. Each of those fallen made that sacrifice so you Four could come to this Realm."

Drace was overwhelmed. From the beginning, he thought he was the wrong person for this mission. Whether he was the right person or not, he knew he must sacrifice everything to save humanity.

Thelka continued, "Angels were created to Love God. To absolutely Love God, we must have a choice. Angels were given free will. One Angel did not choose to Love God. He sought glory and honor for himself. God cast that Angel from here and offered him a promise. Should Frederick succeed in turning everyone from God, then God will allow those humans to worship Frederick. If, however, one person freely chooses to sacrifice all to God, then Frederick would be destroyed."

"Pretty high stakes" Drace said.

"Indeed. Frederick accepted the challenge. From that moment, Frederick was intent on denying God by darkening every soul on the planet. It was done with Whispers that preyed on people's fears. Events have been manipulated towards Frederick's final plan. Frederick hid *The One True Book*. Souls were corrupted. Demons took control of those souls. Now an army of Demons attacked weakened Angels. There is no *Book*, no religion, no Angels to give their Light. The only hope for humanity now is you Four."

"I still wonder if you have the right guy. Okay then, what do we have to do?"

"Come with me. I have much more to tell you."

Eric Myers

CHAPTER THIRTY-FIVE
Release

Cold winds brushed clouds over the silver canvas of the night sky. Val concentrated on walking and did not allow herself to feel the chill that made her exposed legs ache.

It was the same moon, she thought. A small wonder that. Was this place really all that different from where she came from?

Buscillo stopped and Val nearly ran into him from behind. He steadied her with a comforting arm around her shoulders. It was the warm embrace of a family member given in troubled times. It felt delightful.

Where they were was special. The Realm, as Buscillo now called it, was a place where beings of unimaginable savagery and unfathomable grace existed. Here were sources of Light far beyond what was found in their mundane lives. And here too existed forces of destruction that eliminated hundreds of these life forms as one might swat at flies at a picnic.

The brutal method in which these Light beings died was horrible enough. That this damage was inflicted in such an offhanded manner terrified Val and chilled her far more than the cool breeze. This cold went to the marrow of her soul.

The long processional stopped in the center of a valley.

"They call this place the Site of First Light." said Buscillo. This is the cradle of the Universe. Here is where it all began."

Two young boys walking close to Val held up their palms and sent beams of light into the night sky. Quickly other beams were added. Incredible rays of light of every color shot out from more Angels in the procession.

The air shimmered in the waves around them, and Val felt giddy in the middle of so much energy.

Raiki stood before them. She bowed her head slightly before speaking. "It is time for them to return."

Buscillo pulled Val and Marina close to him, and hand in hand they followed Raiki to the head of the line. Buscillo looked for Drace but still could not find him. Since Drace wandered off with that girl, no one saw him. As they walked, more and more palms sent up. Each mourner contributed their unique hue.

At the front of the line Troy, Teya, and Therosi stood abreast facing the mourners. Raiki took her place alongside them. Buscillo and the girls stood before the Four angels and bowed their heads.

"It is time." Buscillo said softly to the girls.

"Time for what?" asked Val.

"Just follow my lead."

Buscillo took off his medallion and held it before him. The girls quickly followed.

They gave Buscillo a look that expressed both fear and excitement.

"One of the mourners filled me in a bit on what we need to do." said Buscillo. "I am not sure I get this completely, but we are going to be the ones to send them home."

"Home? What do you mean home?"

"Yeah, that's the part I don't get. I kinda' thought they were home." said Buscillo.

"It will come to us." said Val.

"Actually, we already know what to do." It was Drace.

"Nice of you to join us." Marina said. "I think you would be late for your own funeral." She winked at Drace.

"Just like the first time we all met."

They placed their medallions together and, as before, the four triangles clicked to form a glowing plate. Mourner's now directed their palms towards them, adding their Light to the glow.

Their Four Angels, too, sent their light energy. Drace noticed something a bit different about the Light coming from the Angels. Troy sent forth green, a lovely pure green like leaves in summer. Raiki sent forth the fiery red of a forge. Teya added her majestic blue topaz, and Therosi contributed a vibrant yellow.

All the Light left their hosts as living entities, creatures lost and looking for the home they found in the medallions.

"It is time." said Drace.

Drace turned the metal square they held, and a brilliant beam of white light, too bright to see through, emanated from the medallions they held. Intuitively, the Four caught on to the purpose of the shaft. A fallen loved one lying on a wagon was the first to become a target of that beam of light.

The golden energy hit the body squarely, and its effect was immediate and profound. The beam broke apart what was once solid and scattered the energy in a shower of sparks. The sparks shot skyward, streaking towards the stars. They returned the body to God.

"We sent this one home."

Understanding was instant, and they were overcome with profound joy. Tears blurred Marina's vision as the next form lying on the wagon received its release.

One by one energy was trained on a loved one, and one by one that individual went through a transformation as beautiful as it was simple.

"It is so amazing." said Val.

Drace remembered his experience deep under the mountain. One's physical form is more an idea of perception rather than a concept of reality. The conversion of energy is an easy notion to grasp, but he never realized how beautiful it actually was.

Buscillo assumed the lead and moved their medallions as the others added their loving attention. He picked up the pace somewhat, perhaps concerned all the loved ones would not get the release they sought before the ceremony concluded, and the mourners could no longer send their energy. He had no idea how long everyone would focus but considered it proper to move the process along.

One after the next, release after release, each was returned to their source, the center of the universe.

Buscillo had no reason to fear the mourners would not maintain their energy. They all held firm, and the entire process was over in a few hours. The sun began to rise, but still the mourners sent their full energy to the few remaining loved ones.

And then it was over.

Just as profound as the process of release was the aftermath. Without any further ceremony, those who just sent their loved ones back to their source simply lowered their hands and walked toward the town. Many of them held hands. Some walked arm in arm.

As they slowly drifted away, they began to sing. It was a lighthearted melody in a tongue Drace did not recognize, but language was not necessary to comprehend the song's meaning. It was a love song for those departed. It invoked memories of laughter shared with good friends and tender moments appreciated by one's self. It was a song of hope and of appreciation for all the wonders life offers. But it carried too, a note of sadness as the voices would rise in beautiful harmony and then fall silent for some time as a single voice carried the melody. Just as in life there are moment of joyful harmony and poignant solitude.

The ceremony was over, but the golden shaft of light still flowed as the Four guides continued to focus their light on the medallions.

The next step came quickly, too quickly for Drace, who could not ask questions. Despite all he learned about trusting his intuition and letting go of his constant desire to seek answers, he still hoped to know why they needed such elaborate lessons.

He wanted to talk things over at length with his friends. He wanted to question each of the four Angel guides. He wanted to simply sit and rest.

There would be no rest.

They saw the armies. A mass of black figures grabbed a distant hill like a claw and crawled their way towards the valley.

Demons—far more than any could imagine—swarmed towards them. From their shouts and speed, their intent was obvious. They sought to finish the job started yesterday and eliminate the last of the Angels.

"What is that?" asked Val.

"Most Holy God, not now!" said the Farmer. "More Demons. An entire army of them."

"That can't be right." said Drace. "How can an army get here?"

"The gate." said Raiki. "We opened the gate so you Four could come here. That gave Frederick an opportunity."

"Yeah, you already explained that. But how did so many get here?"

"This must have been his plan all along. Frederick knew we would have a funeral here in this valley. The first attack was simply to bring us all here, so he could have a strategic advantage. In this valley we have no place to run."

"That still doesn't explain how so many Demons got here."

"It doesn't matter how they got here, Drace." said Buscillo. "We better do something fast."

"Indeed." said Raiki.

I agree." said Drace. "We have to do something. Any ideas?"

"I am not going to simply stand here and watch. We have to organize an attack."

Drace approached Troy and asked. "How could you not have known this? Haven't you been expecting an attack from Frederick from the very beginning?"

"You're right." Troy faced Drace squarely. "We owe you an apology. We placed burdens on you we knew you were not prepared for and you met the challenge. We have no excuse for not being prepared ourselves. Sometimes, with our eyes always on God, we do not notice the attacks all around us until too late."

The Child Angel did not wait for a reply. Turning toward Buscillo, he said, "My thanks to you for keeping faith. I agree with you. All is not lost. We must do what we can to recover and address the situation." Then Troy sat down crossed-legged and closed his eyes to try to think of some way to salvage their battle plans.

Drace sat next to him looking deflated yet determined.

Fatigued, Val and Marina leaned on each other for support.

Buscillo spoke, but Raiki interrupted in a voice loud enough for all to hear. "No more apologies. We do not take the accomplishments of you Four lightly. What you did was nothing short of miraculous and truly showed the Hand of God. But hear me. We do not take Frederick and his demons lightly either. Without God we cannot expect victory." Once again, she thrust her sword into the ground, knelt before it then lowered her forehead to the hilt. "Almighty God, may our hearts be pure, our thoughts aligned, our purpose clear, and our courage unwavering."

She looked toward the sky and spread her arms as if baring her heart. "We are yours to command. The Enemy leads an army against us. We shall meet them in battle. Not for ourselves but for you, Lord."

She stood and lifted her sword above her head. "My friends, hear me. This is our burden to bear which, in the end, will require more strength than we have. We will experience fear that can overcome us. Chaos will undo every plan and strategy. All that is logical will be threatened. All we have is our faith in God. But God is all we need."

"Amen" said the Farmer. "We have prepared for this moment since creation. The only thing we knew for certain was the Father of Lies would not be predictable. Now here we are. We are presented with a few simple facts. The army of our enemy is one hundred times our number, and we face the possibility of heavy losses. That is but one of our problems. The other is the terrain. A battle with massive armies forced into a central plain will favor whichever force is larger. No doubt the Enemy wanted it that way."

"My idea is to meet him in the valley then we will retreat east, luring Frederick after us toward that hill." The Farmer pointed to the hill where Drace and his companions first arrived. "We can create defensive positions and hold the higher ground. That is the only place to take on an army this size."

"It will not be as simple as that." Troy spoke. "If we are on the run like that, we will not have time to dig in and put together any sort of defense. We must send some of our forces there right away to dig in and build some fortifications."

"That gives us even fewer numbers to meet the Demons head on." said Teya. "Will we have any of our army left to make the retreat?" She paused for a moment as they considered that.

"We will hold long enough." said Raiki. "We must trust what forces sent forth will be strong enough.

Her expression of faith touched Drace. He swallowed a sudden lump in his throat before he spoke. "There is a way we can do it. It's going to be hell, but it is possible."

For a moment he faltered. Hell was a mild word for what they would have to endure.

"How?" Raiki was watching him steadily.

"I absolutely guarantee Frederick will follow us out of the valley. It is the Four of us he most wants. We will go to the hilltop and wait for him. He will come for us."

"Indeed." said Raiki. The other angels nodded. "Then we must go to face Frederick in the valley before his forces can block our retreat to the hilltop. All right then. We have about a hundred horses. Unhitch them from the wagons. Mounted Warriors will take the Vanguard and meet the Demons in the center. Teya and Troy will lead forces from either side. If we flank the Demons and spread out Frederick's forces a bit, we have a chance of holding the line. A small regiment will escort the Four to the hilltop and create fortified positions. Let's go Warriors." They quickly made for the horses to form a mounted attack force.

Teya and Troy organized the Angels who would take the flanking positions. Several hundred led by Troy were assigned to create weapons. They swarmed over the wagons as bees on a honeycomb. Every piece of the wagon could be converted into a sword, club, lance or even a bow. Several Angels distributed the weapons to the angels as they formed into fighting units.

The Farmer pulled together a small number of angels from each of the four groups. With the Four humans in the center of a squad, they headed out.

Drace had a sword thrust into his hand. The two women chose daggers and whips as lighter and easier to manage. A small Angel Child stood before Buscillo, wearing a smile that lit up his face. From him Buscillo accepted a bow and several large quivers of arrows.

The bow was exquisite. It weighed nothing and felt perfectly natural in Buscillo's hand. A horsehair bowstring was at the ideal tension. The details were immaculate. The handgrip and sight precisely fit his hand. Buscillo's name was carved into the upper limb of the bow. The lower limb displayed Buscillo's lion symbol.

"You made this with your hands in a matter of minutes?" Buscillo asked.

"Yes, I did. It was my honor to make this for you."

"Amazing. Where I am from, a bow like this would have taken a master craftsman months to complete."

Buscillo bowed deeply and said. "I am the one being honored. Thank you for this."

The Child smiled and said, "You're welcome." Then he scurried off to receive his next task from Troy.

Troy was acutely aware the main thing the army lacked was a means of communication. Without such a system, they would be even more vulnerable than they already were. He organized a network of riders to shuttle from place to place in battle. And he devised a simple set of codes using banners so some messages could be communicated visually. He was not happy with the crude system. The fate of humanity was at stake. But it would have to suffice. He would have faith in his tactical skills.

"You've got to buy us the time we need." The Farmer said to Raiki. "Go with God."

Teya said, "There's something I want to say to you Four before you leave. My friends, the time has come, and war is upon us. Hear me. You must know we all believe in you. We are all dedicated to the service of our God. We battle the Enemy and pit our strength against him for the sake of all humanity. These are my words but each of us here believe you have within you the power to prevail. Do not fear. The spirit of fear is not of God. Be of strong heart and pure mind. Let your faith never waiver as you are God's child."

Teya held her arms high. Her hair shone about her like a diamond. "This peril is great, the gravest danger of all time. Again, I say to you, do not fear. The coming battle is our greatest challenge. It is also our greatest opportunity to serve God. A God who made us in his image. A God who made us to love and serve him. In His service, we see His wonder and magnificence. We are all His children. Victory is our birthright. Glory is our destiny."

She began to sing. Soon all the angels stood with their arms towards the sky and joined their voices with hers. They sang of war and of peace. Their voices swelled in beautiful harmonies as they gave full expression of their love for God. As they sang, they glowed. All around them was a glorious light. In that state of ecstatic adoration for their Lord, as all their passion and love were released, so too were their wings. The sight of thousands of gleaming pairs of wings shining all around brought the Four to their knees and filled them with hope.

"No evil can stand before such wonder and not cower." thought Drace.

The army of demons advance to meet the winged angels. Like a tide, they flooded into the valley, washing away hope. What Drace saw was staggering, a sight worse than he could imagine.

Marina grieved for the Angels and what they now must face, but there would be more grief to come and more darkness in the valley. Her place was on the hill with her friends, the healers, and a contingent of warriors assigned as guards. They would deal with a great deal of wounded very soon.

Val stood beside her and clasped her hand. Drace and Buscillo joined them. Together they watched as one group of warriors marched to the right and another to the left. The strategy was simple. Spread out the horde with a mounted charge up the center and have the flanks attack from either side. The Warrior Woman advanced the mounted vanguard. Even at a distance Marina saw her imposing form atop a magnificent horse. A nimbus of red light emanated from her unfurled wings as she unsheathed her sword.

The sun was at its zenith now. From her vantage Marina watched the Demon army take position on the opposing hill. She saw an angel blowing into a large, curved horn, signaling the start of the battle

The Four, with their contingent of escorts ascended the hill.

The Angel leading the charge from the left was the first Marina saw die. The angel thundered toward the first line of Demons led by the Red Horsemen who escorted Troy to meet Drace. The forces met with a crash loud enough to be felt. Momentum and a massive sword sliced through both Horseman and his flaming red horse. Before the Angel could make his return swing his mount was attacked by several Demons wielding hideous spiked clubs. As the horse fell, dying, the Angel's side was exposed and a Demon sprang forth, a cruel-looking knife in hand, and drove the blade deep into his heart.

Marina did not have time to react, or even think about the death. She and her friends still had to make it up that hill. Angels were dying everywhere, bloody, and maimed. Already the line on the left began to crumble. Demons shrieked as their bodies were added to the mass of slain Angels now covering the ground.

Fighting for room to swing her sword the Warrior Woman urged her mount forward. She cut a swath through the Demons with a fury that drove her onward. Her sword dripped blood as it cut repeatedly. Wherever her sword struck Demons fell, dead before the hit the ground, only to be replaced with more Demons.

The passing of time was indeterminable, and the Angel line was not pressing forward, only standing their ground. Mounted Angels began to fall back to avoid swarms of Demons who could kill from below.

The Four reached the top of the hill and looked over the battlefield. With the entire surreal scene played out before her, Marina was forced to acknowledge, no matter how hard she tried to avoid the thought, the sheer brute force of overwhelming numbers would defeat them.

The Warrior Angel's mount trampled a club-wielding Demon, even as her sword severed the arm of another.

Raiki felt a slash across her leg, ignored it, and killed the attacker with a mighty blow of her fist.

A rider from the right flank closed in on her position.

"The left is already being driven back. How are they doing on your side?" Raiki shouted.

"Our line is also breaking. It cannot hold."

A quick glance confirmed the report. The Horseman on a pale horse led the mass of Demons that chewed through the Angel line.

"Fall back!" Raiki wielded her horse around. "Pull back and reform the lines. We have to give the others a chance to make it up that hill." She mowed down Demons as a scythe through shafts of wheat as the remaining Angels withdrew.

Marina saw the retreat. "This is horrible. They are losing."

"It is worse." Buscillo said. "Look over there." He pointed to the right.

"Dear God, no!"

"Indeed."

Demon reinforcements flooded into the far side of the valley. The Angels, already in retreat, yielded the rest of the valley to the horde. They too took up defensive positions at the top of the hill.

"That's not the worst of it." said Drace, his voice barely above a whisper. An unnatural silence fell upon them. Drace was acutely aware of his breathing, the warmth of the sun on his face, the sweat on his brow. He reached desperately for a peace inside him that would be his strength. It was there, but feeble and distant.

"Frederick." Drace said. It came as a snarl.

"The Whisperer himself leads the reinforcements." Buscillo said.

The others nodded but said nothing more.

It was Frederick who spoke. "Greetings to you four." His voice assaulted their minds. "It pleases me greatly you are here to witness my most glorious triumph. See how ravished my friends are today? I promised they would dine on Angel flesh tonight." He laughed and a roar erupted from his army below.

The Four made no reply. In grim silence they stared at the man who mocked them.

Frederick laughed again. "Tell me, mighty warriors of God, is there but one of you who feels your victory is certain? Search your hearts for the truth. The outcome today is all but finished. You have lost. It is time to accept your defeat. Surrender while you still can."

Drace saw Buscillo, teeth clenched, draw his bow.

"No." said Drace. "He is right. We cannot defeat him alone."

Frederick's slimy laughter spewed forth again. "But who will help you? God? I have a message for your Lord." The voice changed; it became colder, full of hatred. "This ends now, Old Man. You could not stop me before. You will not stop me now."

A wave of revulsion threatened to knock Drace unconscious. "This is not God's battle. It is our own. Buscillo, you cannot face Frederick alone." But together we can defeat him."

"I agree." said Buscillo. "We will probably all get killed. But we must try at least. How can we not face him, Drace? How can we claim to have Light in our hearts and not stand up to this challenge?"

The Demon army drove the Angels even further up the hill. The Angels formed tight clusters and stood back-to-back to better deal with the onslaught. Even so, Drace could see this strategy was a desperate play at best. They would not last long.

They were hopelessly outnumbered but managed to slow the advance.

Drace saw the tattered remnants of those Angel already destroyed. A few hundred remained standing but would soon join their comrades.

They all saw the horses were completely exhausted. Only their fear of the Demons kept them up and running. Just next to them were the units led by the Farmer and Teya. Those warriors were in no better condition. None of them lacked injuries. Dirt clung to them and clotted their wounds, making the cuts and gashes more pronounced. Drace had to tear his aching gaze from them to stab at a Demon who lunged and nearly reached Marina with its blade.

Many of the Demons halted their advance to rend and eat the bodies of the fallen Angels.

Buscillo bellowed like a madman at the scene, shooting at every Demon within range. The pause in the attack, though, allowed time to tighten the defensive line around the Four. For now, the Demons were still held back.

The horde of Demons pressing in on the Four would eventually break through. The Warrior Woman shouted orders to organize a counterattack.

A Demon hurled a blade at Drace, who barely saved himself by swatting away the blade with his sword.

"Do something!" he shouted to Troy. "We're being slaughtered!"

Troy shouted to the Farmer and Teya, then ran through the line to stand next to the Warrior Woman.

"On my signal!" Troy yelled over the clamor. "Move on my signal!" The Angels dismounted and allowed the horses to flee. They all moved to form a single line.

When Troy saw last Angel had taken position, he nodded to Raiki. The Warrior Woman swung her sword and struck the ground of in front of the line with all her might. Instantly, a shimmering wall of force sprang up between Angels and Demons. All the Angels set themselves firmly and added their energy to the wall. When the first Demon charged the wall, it burst into brilliant white flame, and was hurled back.

Raiki shouted to all the Angels, "Pray for strength! We cannot hold this indefinitely!" The Angels needed no urging.

Several gravely wounded warriors reached the top of the hill and collapsed. Val and Marina tried to give aid. Marina tore robes into strips for tourniquets and bandages. Val laid her hands on those who seemed the most critical and praying for more light to flow from her into.

Drace and Buscillo stood guard. Already the Demons were preparing to defeat the wall. They sent several thousand Demons to either side looking for the ends. The rest—easily five thousand—retreated a short distance and re-formed themselves into a huge, single wedge.

Drace knew at this rate it would only be a matter of time until the sheer numbers of the enemy prevailed. A smaller army only had a chance it the largor army was poorly led, cowardly, or lacked motivation.

Raiki said the army of Frederick should not be taken lightly. They were all fighting for the ultimate prize, the fate of humanity. Driven by a single-minded hatred, Frederick and his Demons had that prize within their grasp.

Frederick was here at this moment after eons of subtle manipulations. By persistent exploitation of humanity's fears and insecurities, the Whisperer nudged the course of history.

There was nothing nuanced or understated about his approach now. With brutal efficiency Frederick fought to bring the last of his designs to fruition. Drace and his friends were Frederick's target. Anything in the way of that goal was to be destroyed. Only Four people remained to stop him from achieving his ultimate victory. What could four people do to stop something millions have tried to stop and failed?

When those reinforcements arrived, the Demons would prevail. Like ships in a harbor the Angels would be swept under a wave of evil. The battle was in its final stage.

The wailing and screaming from the valley rang in Marina's head. Her arms were crossed, tight against her chest. Her medallion now hung cold and lifeless around her neck. Her blue eyes, usually flaunting an expression of mischievous humor, were sunken and hallow.

For all the sights and sounds surrounding the hill, Marina found herself focusing on the silence within. Going inward was a way to escape the death surrounding her. But there was another source of the silence. In the middle of so much evil Marina sought to concentrate on the good she carried inside her.

The evil unleashed here today was enough to fray the fabric between worlds. Whatever nefarious region that existed beyond her physical world felt close enough to reach out and touch.

She thought the last of her emotions were spent, used up by the experiences she went through, but as she watched the legions of Angels fall dead from the enemy's blades, more emotions flooded through her. It was hatred, loathing, sorrow she found deep inside.

The long savage history between these two supernatural forces was about to have the scales unbalanced. She would find her way through the overwhelming emotions and find the peace on the other side. The deaths of this day deserved that much from her—after all, it was her journey here that allowed this to happen. In the valley below, the bodies of Angel warriors made a carpet of death. Limbs jutted upward here and there.

"They're here." said an Angel. A wave of Demons made their way around the wall of force.

Drace watched the hated Frederick walk around the shield wall and approach. Drace held his sword hilt tighter, and he fought to control the fury swelling within him. Frederick destroyed the world Drace knew and nearly wiped out this realm. Every impulse in Drace urged him to run forward and slash Frederick's head from his shoulders.

Yet honor demanded Frederick should at least be heard. After that I will kill him, thought Drace.

Frederick approached the Angel Warrior and offered a bow. "Your warriors fought well." he said.

"Your compliment offends me." replied Raiki. "Talk—then return to your Demons and prepare to die."

"Indeed, I will speak. I have waited a long time to say this. You cannot win. You can, however, see the remainder of your Angel army slaughtered. I can prevent that. I can tell my Demons you have agreed to let this be about the Four."

"The Four have to go to you willingly, you know that." said Raiki. "You cannot use extortion."

"At least this way no more Angels will die." Frederick faced the Four. "Are you really prepared to send Angels to their death to defend you? You can end this right now. You have the chance to save the Angels."

"That would mean you live?" said Drace. "Nothing can ever really end that way."

"Indeed. Do you have an alternative to suggest?"

Silence.

"I thought as much. I offer the only reasonable option, Drace. So, do I have your word?"

"You have my promise not a single Angel will rise against you." said Drace.

"I will not be bound by this promise." said Raiki. "He is a snake, pure evil, and must be destroyed."

"This is our decision to make, Raiki. I know I speak for all Four. We were brought here for one thing—to make this single choice." Drace said. "Are those Demons really so different than us? Didn't we also believe Frederick's lies? Haven't we also damaged our souls with the life we created? Whatever we do to these Demons we are doing to ourselves. We will offer peace and make a promise. As long as they follow this simple agreement the peace will remain."

Turning to Frederick the Warrior Angel said, "Very well, Frederick. Have your Demons surrender their weapons."

Frederick bowed and said, "A very noble decision, Drace."

Frederick returned to the Demons. There was a great deal of discord when Frederick told them they were to be disarmed. Drace saw a Demon with a gash across his face urging others to refuse the order.

These were truly evil creatures, who did not give up a chance to destroy easily. Yet here was their leader, praising their actions, and offering them victory. It was too good an offer to refuse.

Angel soldiers moved in among the Demons, removing knives, spears, and swords. Finally, even their hard leather uniforms were unbuckled, and all was laid at the center of the valley in a huge pile. Stripped of their armor the Demons were no longer as terrifying, merely a group of confused faces, awaiting their fate.

Frederick returned to stand alongside Raiki. The Angel Warrior called out an order, and the Angels surrounding the Demons leveled their swords. Realization hit the Demons then. There was to be no release after all? Now they were disarmed were they to be slaughtered?

Then Raiki stepped forward. "Creatures of Evil" she said coldly. "I am the Warrior Angel, Raiki, and I serve God. My entire purpose is to stand against you in every way possible. Since creation, many Angels sacrificed all they had towards your defeat. Your leader does not care how many of you die. To serve his own selfish interests he is willing to have you all slaughtered."

Raiki gazed at the defiant faces of the Demons. "Now hear me. I would rejoice to see your flesh shredded, your throats gashed, your blood spilled. I would welcome your screams. Instead, it has been decided you are to be given an opportunity to live in peace."

Drace saw the shock on the Demon's faces. "You heard correctly." Raiki continued, rage straining her voice. "I will tell you why you are offered this peace. God wants you to live, and to come to Him of your own choice. Worship Him and live in peace. Make no mistake, I want you to die. The Angles want you to die. But your God wants you to live."

A silence fell, and Drace shouted to his friends. "Get him!" The Four jumped on Frederick. Drace and Buscillo pinned his arms behind him and Marina and Val held knives to his throat.

"I had your promise!" screamed Frederick.

"Yes, you did, and it will be honored." said Drace. "No Angel will lay a hand on you."

Laughter came from Troy. "You are the Father of Lies, Frederick. How did you not see this one coming?"

Seeing this, the Demons released an explosion of hatred. Even without their weapons their rage and fury made them formidable opponents. The Demons attacked. Again, Angels were slashed, gutted, and left in a heap.

The Four dropped Frederick. When he stood Drace asked him, "Now what? They rejected peace. What can we possibly do now?"

"Nothing. You can do nothing at all."

"It is done." Drace said.

A flash of wisdom, like a ray breaking through the clouds, shone on Drace. In that moment—a well of peace on a field of chaos—Drace possessed true wisdom.

"Buscillo." Drace asked "Will you stand with me. Be the power to resist their force?"

Buscillo bowed his head slightly and moved to stand closer to Drace.

"Marina." Drace turned to face her. "Help us release our fear. Stand with us and show us how to forgive."

Then to Val, Drace said. "We must serve with humble hearts. Join with us so our purpose is clear, and our focus is on God only."

"What do you think you are doing?" asked Frederick.

"Enough, Frederick." said Drace. "Stand over there behind me."

The Four formed a close circle. As before each of them removed their medallion and held it before them. The medallions glowed once again. Each of them surrendered their control over the medallion and allowed the light in the center to build. With arms spread they turned their heads towards the sky and said in unison, "God, into your hands we give our light."

In a world where people follow selfish goals and believe in all variety of fears what happened next would seem extraordinary. In truth it was the only normal thing to ever happen to the Four. The Four merged into one being. They walked down the hill, through the horde and stood at the center of the valley.

A wall of flame burst forth from them. The fire rushed out of the valley, pushing debris and dead bodies before it. It blasted outwards with enough force those standing were tumbled like a child's hands knocking away toy blocks. The intensity of the flames caught them all off guard. The entire valley had become a lake of fire.

For each Demon their destruction was absolute. Flesh rotted from their bodies. Eyes melted in their sockets. No physical body remained. What was once a Demon was now a black ball of energy.

Those dark masses flew out of the fire intent on their target. That energy struck Fredrick squarely. Dark matter clung to him. Black masses completely covered Frederick and the grew ever larger. Earth began to collapse under the weight of the dark ball. A fissure, then a chasm formed as each ball of Demon energy added its own weight. Further and further down the dark ball went until nothing remained but a very deep hole.

The speed and power of the wave of fire cleared the valley in seconds, and when the Angels looked, there were no demons. The entire area was devoid of any plant life and the surface glazed over as smooth as glass.

"The Four. They arc gone," said Troy. "They were destroyed in the ball of flame. There's nothing left down there."

"No," said Teya, "Everything is down there."

The Farmer smiled and said, "In the end they chose God over all else. They are victorious"
"Victorious, indeed." said Raiki.